Mining Justice

Monarchy of America: Book 3

Thomas Gondolfi

TANSTAAFL 🐻 PRESS

TANSTAAFL Press
891 PH 10
Castle Rock, WA 98611

Visit us at www.TANSTAAFLPress.com

Mining Justice

First printing—TANSTAAFL Press
Copyright © 2022 by Thomas Gondolfi
Cover art: Kristin Bryant at www.kristindesigns.com

Printed in the USA
ISBN: 978-1-938124-73-0

Book layout by Hydra House Books

Monarchy
of America

with Duchies defined

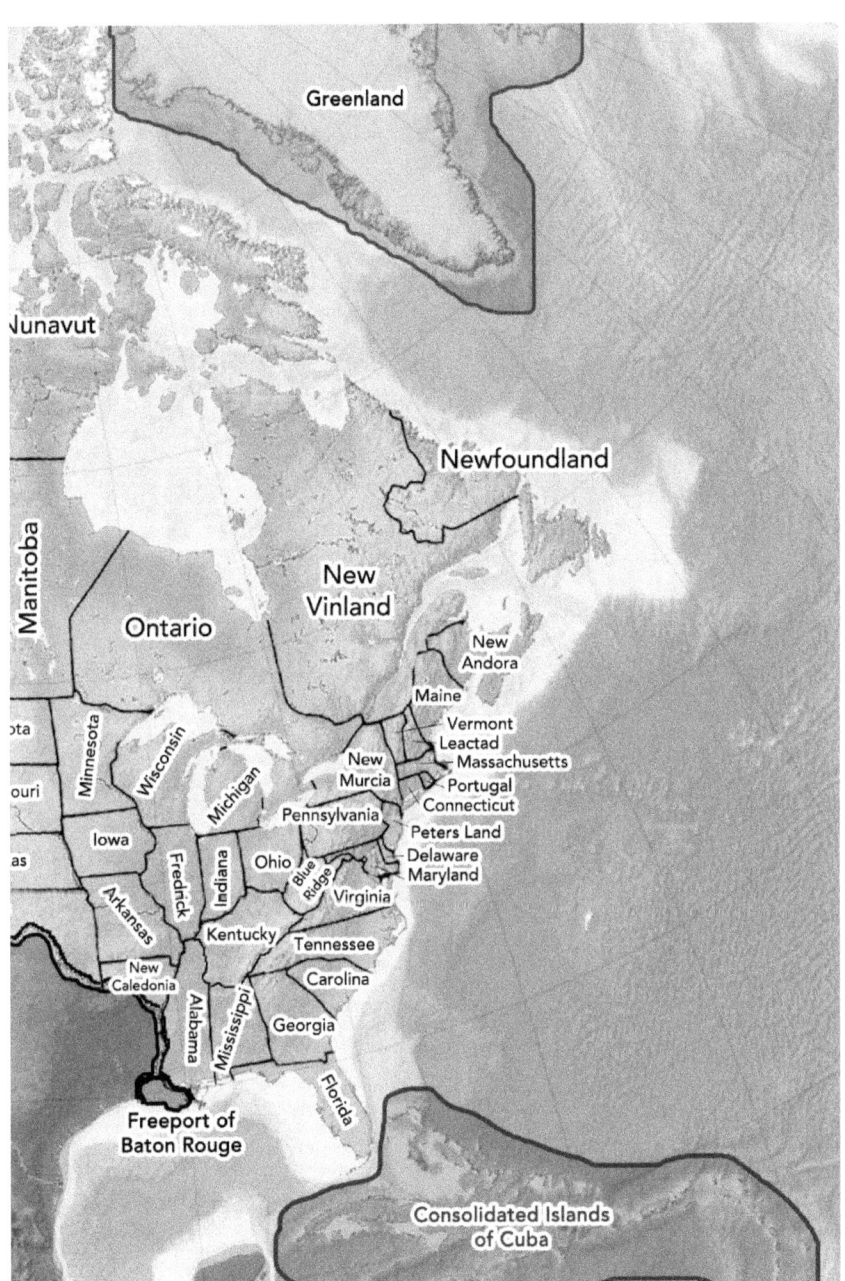

1—Saturday, November 17, 1888

The bell summons me to fight the most horrific beast, this time in an upper-class neighborhood of Boston—Chester Square. Fear eats at my middle. As a professional hellfighter and with the title of Mistress Earth Witch, I've faced fearsome demons. My team, the *Dos Campanas*, or Two Bells, have faced down dozens of hellspawn. I personally have sent a reigning prince back to hell when he tried to eat my soul. But my palms are sweaty and my belly is threatening to lose its lunch into the adjacent rose bushes. What possessed me to come and confront this monster?

The beautiful green door with a gilt knocker opens, and I'm face-to-face with my worst nightmare. Doesn't the Bible say something about bearding a lion in its own den?

"Good morning, Mother," I say. "Ozias finally see sense and run off?"

My mother is an elegant woman and one of the most desirable catches in the monarchy. She is also my personal boogeyman. Absently, I finger the disfiguring scars at my neck. As proctor to my practical witching exam, my mother, bless her, allowed me as an inexperienced teenager to summon a demonic royalty of hell. That beast burned forty percent of my body before she sent him back. It is just the most visible scar from her lack of maternal compassion.

"Ah, daughter. I see you got my cable. Even the most dedicated butlers get a day off. I believe Ozias mentioned something about seeing the bullfight at the arena. Please, come in."

"Thank you," I say perfunctorily as I step in out of the late fall wind. "Why did you want to see me?"

"Good to see you too, Stella. You are looking well."

"And isn't that *The Blind Guitarist* by Goya? That wasn't here last time. You must be doing well yourself." Our conversation doesn't mesh. I'm trying to riposte the emotions that her presence wells up within me.

"I do what I can," she replies, holding her arms out to emphasize the new designer gown she is wearing and its matching silk shawl.

I'm still quite sick to my stomach, so I decide to press the point. "You didn't bring me here to show off your new pretties, Mother."

"Oh, come now, daughter. Can't we have a little civility between us? I know what you think of me. I try to abide by your wishes to stay out of your life, especially that old derelict factory you insist on living in with all of the vermin you chose to live with." She refers to the fact that I have taken an unused portion of my home and dedicated it to the homeless girls in Boston.

I put my hands on my hips, feeling the iron corset underneath my skirts. I don't mean the iron of my corset but rather a corset made of iron. Even with my would-be-assassin, Heinrick Meier, and his employer and my ex-boss, Mark Carlton, sentenced harshly, there are others who might do me harm.

They were members of *Non Patiatur Phythonissam*, or the NPP, which hates all witches. Translated from Latin, the name means "Suffer not a witch," a bastardization of Exodus 22:18—"Thou shalt not suffer a witch to live." They are all nasty customers, which is why I tolerate the weight around my middle, as it will turn away bullets, and most often a knife.

It will protect me physically, but the armor, won't deflect the arrows of misfortune that have recently pierced my heart. I've lost my precious husband, Aaron, to the Irish War of Independence, and now Adrianna Helms is lost to me because of God. That the Church ripped Viscountess Helms from my life still tears at my emotions. Love is painful.

At least I could properly mourn Aaron's loss. But the viscountess I see in town from time to time. She is like a recurring ghost that shreds off any scab I developed since the last time I saw her. Almost worse, I get weekly tea invitations from her. There is no way I can possibly bear her radiant presence knowing it is forbidden to me. Instead, I find myself absentmindedly remembering her delicate wrist and fingers, her curvy frame, her flashing green eyes, and the pale skin of her ankles. Even after six months of our enforced separation, my tears still leak down my face when I fail to corral the emotions that still bubble in my heart.

This is not the time to have water dripping down my cheeks. "Now, Mother—"

"Don't 'Now, Mother' me, young woman. It's disgraceful for someone of your stature to be running a flophouse."

"The Brick Factory is not a flophouse. I have eight boarders and a cook. All of them are above reproach."

"But that doesn't count all of those street urchins you let sleep under your roof."

I scowl. "And doing good for those less fortunate isn't worthy?"

She crosses her arms and gives me that Mom-is-right face. "Take care of yourself first, daughter, then donate to a charity. You are living like the lower classes. Remember, I only have your best interests at heart, my love."

Sure you do, madre. She is much more interested in my lack of societal stature impacting her own social standing. Damn her to hell, anyway. I close my eyes and take a deep breath and count. *Uno. Dos. Tres. Cuatro. Cinco. Seis. Siete. Ocho. Nueve. Diez.* I let it out. "Mother, you brought me here for a reason other than to argue about my living arrangements."

"This is true, daughter. If you will come with me to the parlor," she says, unnecessarily pointing the way.

I've come this far, I think. *What are a few more steps?*

My mother's parlor could have paid for my entire home, even as expensive as the Brick Factory has been for me to purchase and renovate. Her walls are decorated in Cadiz-imported burnout velvet wallpaper bearing repeats of the Crusader's cross. The furniture was designed and crafted by the famous artisan Robert J. Horner. Lead crystal chandeliers have been rewired for Edison's new electric lights. I'd hazard a guess that nothing in the room cost less than ten dollars, except for what her guest is wearing.

There's a woman sitting in front of the tea service. She is worn beyond her years. My first conjecture, because of callouses on her hands and crow's-feet around her eyes, puts her in her forties. But seeing her smooth lips and shiny hair, I revise my estimate down to her late twenties with a hard life.

I hazard another speculation that the simple sheath dress, in calico print, is her best dress. There is a very skillful patch over her right knee. I'd not have noticed if the light hadn't caught the slightly shinier thread. The woman perches at the edge of Mother's opulent chenille couch as if her very presence might sully it. I wonder why my social-climber mother would allow someone of this woman's lesser station into her home.

As I enter the room, I can feel my skin crawl, but not in a bad way that you might want to run from. It's rather something more akin to what I feel through my untrained talent as a white witch whenever I enter a church.

"Mrs. Ochoa, my daughter," my mother begins formally, "please meet Luciana Riley."

The woman, with just the hint of cinnamon in her brown hair, stands. She's skinny as a rail, and her dress hangs on her as if she's lost a hundred weight. With my robust figure, I'd have made four of her, maybe six. Not that I'm fat, but let's just say the artist Rubens would have enjoyed my shape. The hand she extends in greeting shakes with tremors.

"A pleasure, Mrs. Ochoa."

"And you, Miss Riley."

"Mrs. Riley is married," my mother says, correcting me.

"My apology. Mrs. Riley."

The woman frowns but nods in absolution of my *faux pas*.

"Coffee, daughter?" my mother asks.

"Yes, thank you," I say, sitting in an armchair across from Mrs. Riley. Dark circles like you might get in a week without sleeping are the only things holding up her eyes. The intelligence behind them is obvious. Mrs. Riley inspects my person as much as I'm investigating hers. I do wonder when my dearest mother will get to the point. But, as always with Josephine Romero, Senior Mistress Witch and social climber extraordinaire, proprieties must come first. Only after she has served me with a cup from her second-best china set does she get to the point.

"Mrs. Riley has sought out my expertise as an earth witch because her husband, and potentially two hundred of his colleagues, have been trapped in a mining cave-in. She would like me to go down and rescue the lot of them."

"The Centralia, Pennsylvania, cave-in?" I ask. "The one I've read about in the paper?"

"Yes, Mrs. Ochoa," the guest says. The single tear I see in Mrs. Riley's eye and the rest of her physical demeanor are indicative of someone who is numb and hasn't any more grief to give. She nods while muscles at her neck tighten into vertical bands to her chest.

"I'm sorry to hear that, Mrs. Riley. But if you don't mind an indelicate question, why do you think your husband isn't dead?"

The woman takes a deep breath. "As I told your mother, I have very weak white talents. I've never been trained, so I won't say that I am a witch. But when I'm near the mine, I can feel his presence and that of at least some of his coworkers."

That explains the hairs rising on my arms when I came into the room. Witchcraft can sense like witchcraft. "Well, that is something, at least," I say. "What is the mining company doing? Or maybe the rest of the miners?"

"Oh, the miners are digging but without great coordination. The Coal Syndicate claims they are doing everything in its power."

The mention of the company raises hackles on my neck. I still believe that the owner, Bruce Jasperson, was behind the release of excessive numbers of demons earlier this year. I believe he did it to discredit the demon power industry. But I've never been able to get evidence of it. He remains an elusive splinter under my skin that I can't seem to rid myself of.

"That will be the day," I mutter over my coffee cup.

"I have to agree with you, Mrs. Ochoa," Mother's guest says. "If Adam had any choice of profession, I'd have encouraged him to leave the coal mines long ago. The company doesn't care about him or any of the rest of them. He's a replaceable commodity."

I want to say that everyone has choices, but intruding on a woman's grief and worry with trivialities isn't in me. My mother, bitch that she is, did manage to instill at least a few manners.

"I can't disagree with you, Mrs. Riley. But can you tell me what you hoped Mother could do for you, and more to the point, why I'm here?"

"Honestly, I wasn't sure what could be done, even by a senior witch. I'll be honest and say it is likely that nothing will be done to save my husband and those miners if we don't do it."

"Stella, I've informed Mrs. Riley that we can't just get the earth to vomit them forth," my mother says. "Also, we are limited in our ability to manipulate the ground, especially to the depths she is claiming they are at. And as to your presence here, I hoped that maybe you, with your hellfighter associates, might be able to come up with something."

I think this is one of the first times she's mentioned the *Dos Campanas* without using her snobbish version of profanity. She feels they have stolen me away from her and society. Of course, she didn't call them out individually or even use their name—a subtle dig to mask her mentioning them at all.

"Well, I'm having them to my home for dinner tonight. I can ask them and get back to you, Mrs. Riley. Where will you be staying?"

Her face goes slack. I read it as one more problem in a sea of the same. "I don't rightly know—"

"I'm sure my mother can put you up," I offer.

"Actually, I can't, dear," Mother says. "I have a visitor coming over who is somewhat secretive about his business."

I wonder if that business has anything to do with my mother's bloomers. I've never caught her in anything untoward, but lately, I've been wondering.

"Well, then, Mrs. Riley, if you don't mind sharing, I can put you up at my home. It is quite spacious," I offer.

"That is most thoughtful, Mrs. Ochoa."

"No trouble. Now, Mrs. Riley, if you might forgive me while I am discourteous to my mother for just a moment."

"Why would you be discourteous?" the auburn-haired woman asks. "She has been nothing but a gracious hostess."

My mother sits there as if butter wouldn't melt in her mouth. The look on her face is as if she were being defended by the entirety of Boston against a false accusation.

"Mother is always courteous and amiable to guests. However, she never does anything without recompense. I just want to find out where the body is buried. So, Mother, while Mrs. Riley is quite charming, that isn't enough to get you to let her in your home, much less go to some lengths for her. Confess." Both she and Mrs. Riley look at one another silently. So, they both know. "I'm not leaving without an answer, Mother. While Mrs. Riley also seems to know, she doesn't owe me anything."

"And you think raising an ungrateful girl to be a pernicious woman doesn't entitle me?" Mother fires back.

"Maybe if you had given me half the maternal care you seem to believe you have, I would give you that credit. Now cough it up."

Mrs. Riley shrugs at Mother.

"Alright. You win this round, daughter. You know I feel strongly about family—"

I cough to show my scorn for the entire notion.

"Whether you think so or not. I'm doing this for my niece, Luciana Riley."

I don't know whether to laugh or scoff. "You have no brothers or sisters, Mother. So don't feed me this cock-and-bull story about a niece."

"No, it's true, Mrs. Ochoa. I'm the daughter of your father's sister."

I'm sure I'd make a good flytrap as I sit there with my mouth open. My mother has only ever told me that my father left her, not the circumstances or anything else substantive about their relationship. I've never even known his name, and now I find I have relatives. "So, you know who my father is?" I ask Mrs. Riley.

She looks hesitantly at my mother, and then some unasked question and answer pass between them. "Yes, I do," she replies.

"What is the big secret?" I ask.

"Well, we should probably leave that for him to answer since it was his *hostia* idea," my mother says.

"Mother?" I've never heard her curse, much less make the vile implication she voiced.

"Oh, *se folla un pez*," my *madre* curses again, storming out of the room. Mrs. Riley is blushing, but I suspect she's heard much worse living in a mining community.

"Mrs. Riley ... Cousin, I guess," I say.

"Yes, Mrs. Ochoa?"

"Now that my mother is gone, I think we can drop the formality, Luciana."

"That's probably a good thing, Stella. I'm not used to all these etiquette rules. We live much simpler in Centralia. And it's Lucy to my friends. Only my mother and husband call me Luciana."

"Lucy. Got it. But I will warn you, my mother leaving you deprives you of your ally. I intend to get everything from you about my father that I haven't gotten from my mother in twenty-four years as her daughter."

Lucy looks unconcerned. "Wouldn't you rather have the information from the horse's mouth?"

"Whose horse?" I ask, wary of a potential avoidance.

"How about I arrange a meeting between you and your father."

I smell a rat. "When? Where?"

"How about tomorrow afternoon, after church services?"

"Won't that delay our saving your husband and the other miners?"

"Even if you come up with a brilliant idea to save them, the dirigibles won't leave until Monday morning."

"What about the train?"

"Wouldn't help us. There is only one set of tracks that is used by the coal trains exclusively. It measures a special narrow gauge to get through the mountain passes, so no other locomotive can use it."

"Well, how about by carriage?"

"Four hundred miles of twisty mountain passes? It would take weeks. Dirigible is the only practical transport to get there in good time."

"Good enough. And I'll be more than happy to receive my father on the Sabbath. It just might prevent me from killing him."

# # #

"Where are the horses?" Luciana asks after I have her climb into the poderabile.

"Sorry, I'm so used to it now that I don't even think about how anyone else might see it," I say. "This is a horseless carriage. It doesn't need horses to move." My cousin looks dubious. "Seriously. Climb in and I'll show you."

I get in and wrap the safety belt around my chest and turn on the air valve all as part of my standard procedure now. It has lost its magic. Checking on all sides of me, I pull back on the levers. Lady Justice, the name I've given to Henry Helms's invention, eases backward with a chuff of high-pressure air.

"It's like magick!" Lucy says.

"Oh, cousin of mine, it gets much better." As I push forward on the driving levers, the poderabile leaps forward like a yearling colt at his first taste of the crop.

"Wow! Why haven't I ever heard of these powderbeels before?"

"Because, as far as I know, this is the only one. It was invented by my good friend Viscount Henry Helms. He gave it to me as a gift when I helped him unravel a serious issue involving demons."

"That's right. I remember reading about it in the papers."

"You must have been quite bored to have found my exploits in the news," I offer back with some volume to cut through the wind.

"Not at all. You are quite the heroine, Mrs. Ochoa."

"Please don't go all formal on me. I'm just Stella."

"Seriously, I read all about it and am glad your mother is having you help me."

"Not helping yet. Only looking into it."

"I'm sure you will come up with a solution," she says as if it is a forgone conclusion. I wish I had her convictions. She looks over the side at the wheels going around. "What makes it go?"

"Compressed air."

"What? How can air move something like this on the ground? You don't have any sails."

"Let me give you an example. Close your lips and keep them tight. Now blow into your mouth until your cheeks puff out. Blow hard. Put your hand out in front of your face. Now let it all out. Feel the power? Now imagine you could make that power turn the wheels around. The tanks behind us hold all that pressure inside them, like you did with your mouth, and let it out a little at a time depending on how I use my levers."

"That is ingenious. How fast will it go?"

"It'll race the devil. I don't take the speed too high because it is bloody dangerous cruising around three times faster than a horse could gallop."

"Mercy."

Lucy finally falls silent as she looks over Lady Justice. It gives me time to finally think about everything that has transpired this morning—a cousin, and after all these years, getting to meet my father. Boy, am I going to have some choice words for him. And few of them will be printable in a newspaper. But along with that, I have questions—many, many questions.

Why did you leave Mother? Why did you leave me? Where were you all my life, especially when I needed someone to cry on, someone to hold me, someone to care for me in the way my mother didn't? How many other mystery relatives do I have that I don't know about? Are you going to be in my life from now on? What is your preferred way to die for leaving me alone all of these years? Can I hug you?

It should be quite a lively discussion, especially with my contradictory feelings.

I pull up to my lemon-colored brick warehouse. With all of the young girls living beneath my roof, I've gotten quite a lot of beautification done to my home. I have every kind of reclaimed vessel supporting plants around the outside. Even after only six months, I have most of one corner of the factory covered in climbing ivy.

"That's lovely!" my cousin exclaims.

The young women we've housed have taken it upon themselves to make sure the Lemon Brickhouse is clean and pretty. They are ingenious about recycling materials in the most attractive ways. Sixty-eleven girls are milling around, playing games, or just lounging.

After building my dream home and boardinghouse out of an old brick-making factory, I'd given over the rest of it as something of a flophouse for the urchin girls who lived in fear on the streets. My right-hand gal, Mikey Byrne, bounces up to the Lady Justice as I come to a stop. She administers the girls with an iron fist inside a velvet glove. At maybe fourteen, she's about as physically dangerous as a goose feather, but her spirit is tough as nails. There is a group of larger girls who help her keep the peace.

"Mikey, will you please put the poderabile away for me? I won't be needing it the rest of the night."

"Yes, Stella." A bunch of the other girls look excited as well. From what I know, they have some sort of lottery system whereby they get to ride while Mikey stables Lady Justice.

Lucy and I climb down. I've added running boards to make getting out much easier than trying to hike my skirt up and showing my ankles. As we approach the door, I hear the piano playing—a halting rendition of "The Song That Reached My Heart." Susan, one of my lodgers, must be teaching the keyboard again.

"Cousin, I forgot to warn you that my home is a bit chaotic," I say before opening the door. Over the last months, the Brick Factory has turned into something of a big family, with the ladies, who are my paying boarders, taking a number of the indigent girls under their wings like mother hens guarding their chicks. My boarders seem to prefer this homey atmosphere. If pressed, I'd admit that I do as well, but it is somewhat like having too many cats underfoot.

"Chaotic?" Lucy asks.

I shrug and open Pandora's box. The living room is all but full of girls from the ages of eight to fifteen. All are sitting on the spotless floor because they understand that the furniture is for the women. Their clothes may not be more than rags, but they are all clean, something my housekeeper, Yolanda Simmons, and Mikey Byrne both insist upon. Susan Montrose sits on the piano bench instructing an earnest nine-year-old Hilda.

"Stella!" cries out more than one of the girls as I come in. Two of the younger girls jump up and wrap their arms around me.

"Jesus, Mary, and Joseph," I exclaim with the two leeches attached to me. There are so many girls who stay at our place that I can't possibly keep all their names straight. "Audrey and …"

"Penny, Miss Stella."

"Sorry, Penny."

"Tha's alright, Miss Stella. We knows you tries to 'member us all."

"Well, Penny and Audrey, let me introduce Miss Lucy Riley. She'll be staying with us for a couple of days."

"*Qué demonios?*" growls a thin crone coming in from another room. Yolanda Simmons, our charwoman, cook, and general keeper, waves her cooking spoon in my direction. Hilda stops playing the upright at the curse. "Are youse addin' yet another guest fer me to cook fer? What do youse think I am? A witch, that I can conjure food out of thin air?"

"Not at all, Mrs. Simmons." Yolanda, a widow like myself, is the only person at the Brick Factory who insists on her last name and honorific. Despite her bark, she is a marshmallow in the middle. "You always have so much food left over that I assumed we could sneak one more in."

"G'damned selfish *zorra* ..." The rest of her grumble is lost as she turns her worn, leathery face away and leaves the room. Even the youngest roll their eyes at the woman's antics.

"Hello, Miss Lucy," Penny says. "It is a pleasure to meet you." She performs a moderately acceptable curtsy.

The rest of the room echoes her with, "Welcome, Miss Lucy."

My cousin's eyes widen at this universal show of respect to someone they've just met. "Thank you all!"

Hilda begins her lessons again. "It may be crazy," but we teach them all to at least emulate ladies," I say to Lucy, patting Audrey on her bright blond hair. "Come with me, and I'll show you where you'll be sleeping."

"Stella, what be meaning em-you-late?" Audrey asks. Lucy laughs.

"It means you try to look like something even if you aren't there yet."

"So, like Mrs. Simmons emulates being a bear with a thorn in her paw."

"You got it right the first time."

I take my relation down the hall before I can get pulled into any more questions or discussions. Two more girls are scrubbing the floor. "Hello, Miss Stella!" they say.

"That's a good job there, girls. Glad to have you."

"Thank you, Miss Stella."

As I lead Lucy up the stairs toward my room, she asks, "Are you in The Salvation Army?"

"Heavens, no! What gives you that idea?"

"Well, you've taken in all of these orphans and abandoned girls."

"Pshaw," I spit out. "The girls pay their own way. I mean, yes, I lose just a little bit of money, two bits or maybe four a week, but that's nothing. Effectively, my other boarders are helping pay for the youngsters. I mean, I won't let any girl sleep rough and at the mercy of any male's illicit attentions if she is willing to work. I'm lucky that as a witch I am a weapon and can defend myself. Many of these girls have no recourse other than to submit and hope they can live another day."

"So they all pay?"

"Mikey and I charge three ha'pennies for a cot to sleep in and a satisfying meal. Even if a girl doesn't have a penny to pay for a night's sleep, for two hours of work, she will be given a cot to sleep on. For another hour, Yolanda will give her something warm and filling for her belly. This is another reason I wasn't worried about my housekeeper's *quejumbrosa*—complaining about having another guest. She always has a huge pot of stew, or the equivalent, on the hearth.

"If I'm honest before God, for want of anything else to do, much of the work these young ladies end up doing is repeating what someone else did just hours before. But if make-work is all there is, at least it is value for value, and it keeps our house spotless, our clothes freshly laundered, and a cheerful visage on our building."

"You are amazing," Luciana says. "I can barely keep my three kids under control, food on the table, and my little home clean. You seem to do so much more."

I open the door to my room and usher her inside. As I close the door behind me, the cacophony of cooking, piano, talking, and just general moving around is completely shut off. "I can't take full credit. I have good help, and most of the rest of it just happened. 'Is it not to share your bread with the hungry and bring the homeless poor into your house; when you see the naked, to cover him, and not to hide yourself from your own flesh?'"

"Isaiah 58?"

"Very good. 58:7 actually. So you can sleep on the couch," I say, pointing at the area I have set up as a sitting room. "We can make up a pallet for you on the floor, or you can sleep on the bed with me."

"This room is all yours? It's bigger than our whole home."

"Yes, Lucy, all mine. This is my retreat when things get too crazy."

"And look at that bed!" Her excitement is palpable as she sees things I've begun to take for granted. "A whole herd of cows could sleep there."

I laugh.

"What's funny, cousin?" she asks.

"If I took offense easily, I'd be angry. You just compared me with a herd of cows."

Luciana's face drops as if she's been kicked. "Oh, I'm sorry, I didn't mean ..." She sees the big smile on my face and bursts out laughing herself. "That is the first time I've laughed since the accident. Are you a healer too?"

While I do have crude white witch powers, it isn't something I advertise. Witches with multiple talents are about as rare as snakes with legs, at least the nonhuman kind. "No. I'm just a garden-variety earth witch."

"Hardly, Stella. But in any case, thank you."

"I promise that the bed is plenty big enough for two if you want to risk being considered a bovine."

"I'll risk it," she says with another laugh. "Stella, could I use your water basin? I haven't been out of this dress in three days, and I certainly smell."

"That door over there is my own private water closet."

"A water closet?"

"Think of it as an indoor privy. This one comes with a bathtub."

"A bathtub?"

"Yes. We have running water indoors here, both hot and cold."

"Really? I haven't had a real bath in ... We have to boil water all day to get everyone clean." She looks through the door into the water closet. "Good God! You must be rich."

"No, I just have a good friend who knows how to advise me. It allows me to get a few of the nicer things in life."

There is a knock at the door. From the rap, I assume it is Mikey. Sure enough, when I open the portal, she says, "Stella, can we talk? I had to throw out Marcella again."

"Hold on a second, Mikey. Lucy, go on and enjoy a soak. But don't stay in there too long if you want dinner. Those late to the table get what the hogs won't eat. Dinner at seven, sharp."

"And there are a lot of hogs," Mikey chimes in.

#

The smell of roasted flesh has me simultaneously anticipating and on guard. "Stella, duck!" calls out Donny O'Sullivan, one of the *Dos Campanas*, my demon-fighting team. The projectile sails just over my pulled-down head.

"Now inch forward," someone hisses from behind me. There is the quick and the eaten. I move. I feel someone pass behind me.

"Maxwell, get with it. And don't let it bunch up so much!" Carlos de Aldana, our fearless leader, bellows from the far end.

"Sorry," Max Parker says, his voice breaking in the middle from the vocal cords the pox damaged when he was young. Chaos reigns even more than normal at the Brick Factory. I wonder who will take permanent injury today.

Bea Media uses her ice witch talent to cool the pitchers of buttermilk and lemonade on the table.

A possum pokes its questing nose out from underneath Raquel's seemingly unkempt hair. She offers the furry critter a tidbit from her hand.

"Oh no. There are limits. Not here, Menaj," I snap, using the shortened form of her nickname, Menagerie, for the animals she always seems to have on or near her. She prefers it to her real name, Raquel Ruiz. I've never found out why.

"Have a heart, Stella," she says.

"Not in my home you won't! Take scraps to it later, but not during the meal." I'm now firmly regretting my decision to invite the entire team to dinner at once. "And what happened to giving thanks before eating?" Their lack of manners would make my mother go pale and leave the table.

Carlos stops with half a biscuit in his mouth. He at least clears his mouth before answering, "Sorry."

"Max, if you please." My team—all eight of my boarders, my cousin Lucy, two of the orphan girls, Mikey, and Yolanda Simmons—all link hands around the dinner table.

"Lord, we thank you for the bounty of your love and the provender that you have cast upon us. We praise you in the comradery of new friends, old friends, and those who are family. May we use this abundance to put forward your words and works. In the name of the Father, the Son, and the Holy Spirit, amen."

"Amen," echoes through my dining room.

"Mrs. Simmons, you have done yourself proud this evening," I say, pinching a slice of medium-rare roast as I pass the platter on to Felicia Wolfe. "I think I've gained at least an inch around my middle in the last six months you have been cooking for me."

"That's 'cause that cow you done lived with 'fore ain't never cooked good enough to even feed the hogs." Chapman's Boardinghouse, my address before I earned the relative riches to purchase my own home, kept many a woman just above the line of respectability. Its cuisine barely could have been considered acceptable.

My boarders, all but one of them former renters at Chapman's Boardinghouse, nod in agreement around the food. "And if you'd get off your lazy backside, you might just keep your precious figure."

I admit to not getting enough exercise. The hellfighting team of the *Dos Campanas*, Two Bells, have had little to do but drink and make merry, with Mark Carlton and Heinrick Meier having both been thrown in prison, along with a few other members of the NPP. That alone relieves me of much of my worry. The rest of their ilk have gone deep underground. This effectively ended the mass of demon escapes all up and down the East Coast.

Because of his cooperation, Mark Carlton is serving only twenty years of hard labor. Due in no small part to my own testimony, Heinrick Meier didn't fare as well. He will get the noose next week. I've been torn if I want to see his ignominious end or not.

I decide not to interrupt everyone's enjoyment, so I don't rise to Yolanda's goad. Instead, I tuck in as well. I am not kidding about the danger the meal presents to my waistline—with garlic roast beef, creamy potatoes au gratin, biscuits that I swear will float away, honey-candied Brussels sprouts, and a big plate of fried squash and onions. If that weren't enough, I smell the apple pies cooling in the kitchen. I don't know how she manages on the household allowance I give her.

Oh, I'm not stingy. I want my renters to have good meals, not the crap that old hag Chapman handed out. But every night seems like a feast to outdo the last.

For the next forty minutes or so, the table is silent except for the occasional request to pass a bowl of food and scrapes of utensils on the stoneware. Many minutes later, Carlos, a barrel-shaped man, announces the end of the meal with a belch that would rock the palace itself.

"Good grief, man. Are you trying to deafen us?" Donny O'Sullivan says. His name is confirmed by his orange-red hair.

"Nope. Only making room for some of that pie."

"Wait for the rest of us to let this fabulous meal settle," I order as hostess.

"Sure. So, Stella, what is this secret you've been hinting at all night?" Maxwell says with his voice breaking in the middle of the sentence.

"Well, I introduced you to my cousin, Luciana. Her husband is one of the poor miners trapped in the Centralia Coal Mine collapse."

Exclamations of concern and sympathy erupt around the table.

"Oh, I'm sorry."

"Is he alright?"

"Are they digging them out?"

"Can we help?"

Menaj and one of the girls get up and hug Lucy. This isn't the false empathy she might receive at a court function or dinner party. My cousin leaks tears in response.

"Well, that is the secret," I say. "I'm going to investigate and see what can be done. Can I count on you to help out if I need it?"

"You can count on us."

"In a heartbeat."

"Unmodified yes."

"Just tell us when and where."

Even people not members of *Dos Campanas* and those not even witches are calling out in the affirmative. I feel an overwhelming sense of belonging. From my cousin's sobbing, I can tell that she does as well. My family surrounds her, comforting her. Mrs. Simmons is in the kitchen making tea because according to her worldview, it solves all ills.

It takes a good hour and several cups of tea to get settled. Luciana finally arrives in a place where she can talk without tears. Over Dutch apple pie and whipped cream, we continue our discussion.

"My husband and as many as two hundred other miners are trapped down at the three-thousand-foot level."

Donny whistles low. "That's deep."

"And Luciana has untrained white witch powers," I say. "When she left, she knew that her husband and at least some of his coworkers were still alive. What I want to know is if any of you have any brilliant ideas about how we might get them out."

Menaj says, "That deep, there aren't any plants or creatures. Not even moles. I could bring some animals with us who are used to earthen homes, but I don't know that I'd have any ability to help. I mean, I'd love to, 'cause without any demon escapes, my finances are weak at best. I've actually considered joining the army because of their extravagant claims for witches who sign up." Several in the group nod.

If it has gotten that bad, I'm surprised that the group as a whole hasn't turned their displeasure on me long before this. My work against the NPP and its puppets put the kibosh on demon escapes and the *raison d'*être of the *Dos Campanas's* existence.

"As powerful as Lord our God is, I don't see how the skills he's given me would help those poor miners." Maxwell gets out in a rare full sentence without his voice breaking. As a group, we nod.

"Well, water jets can erode and cut through earth, but it isn't fast," Donny offers from his own specialty.

"I agree," I say. "But I need you to cover my job of emptying the naval refit dry docks while I'm gone. They are doing three shifts, and we can't let them down."

The Boston Naval Yard is where I make my living. Once a new ship is in dry dock for refit, I empty the water out of the dock so the vessel can be worked on. I perform the job in a fraction of the time that it takes steam pumps. I imagine Donny is the only one of our group other than myself who has a regular income, since I got him working there as well. It not only pays quite well but it is also patriotic. The threat of war with England and France looms like a sword of Damocles over the whole civilized world.

"Got that handled, Stella," Donny says.

"Other than the skills of our fearless leader, do you know of any other witches in the area who might have the powers to help?" I ask.

"The reconstituted Canons have an earth witch," Carlos offers in his low, rumbly voice.

"I'm sorry, but I wouldn't trust one of the Canons as far as I can throw him. It may be unfair of me, but after dealing with Baron Cardiff, our resident murderer and demon releaser, I'm not sure I could work with someone from his coven."

"I don't blame you," Menaj says with a wink to me. "Once burned, twice shy." My friend knows how sensitive I am about the burns down the side of my body. She is making a joke at my expense. I stick out my tongue at her.

"Any other good ideas?" I ask. "Come on, friends. Think as if a demon were on our tail."

"Well, if they can be retrieved, I can help any injured if they don't have a white witch in Centralia," Max offers.

Lucy speaks up. "We do have an herbalist, but I'm the closest we have to a witch doctor. The Coal Syndicate won't pay for one despite all the injuries."

"That's not good," Max says unnecessarily.

Menaj adds, "If Stella can dig a hole, I can stabilize the sides with kudzu or blackberry, or both. It will reduce the need for shoring."

"And a water witch will help make the hole and eliminate the influx of water into the mine," Donny offers. "But I'm staying here."

"Ah, but I might know of a water witch who may help. But then, I'm getting ahead of myself," I interject.

"What about our fearless leader?" Raquel asks.

I look over at our pockmarked *jefe*. His face looks like the surface of the moon. "Carlos, I'm assuming that anything we do, we'll need you," I say. "If not for just leadership, then for your ability to bring good air underground."

I have never before seen Carlos hesitate as he does at the table. He tries to hide it by taking a bite of dessert. "W'ar did you 'ay it wa'?" he asks around the apple and cinnamon pie.

"Pennsylvania. An overnight trip by dirigible," Lucy offers.

"No way in by train?" Carlos asks her with his mouth clear.

"No. The trains only run when there is coal to deliver. With no one mining, they are sitting waiting to be loaded."

"And coach?"

"There isn't a decent road into the valley. It would take a week or more to get in even on horseback," my cousin confirms.

"I'm out," Carlos professes, standing up from the table. "Thanks for the meal, Stella." He walks out the door, leaving behind a roomful of gaping mouths and people looking at one another in confusion.

I jump up and run out after the man I've looked up to for a good portion of my life. "Carlos?" He ignores me and stalks out the front door. "Carlos, wait." He is halfway down the block before I get to my front door.

I have a special bond with the earth of my home. It is something that develops over time. I don't need to touch it or even taste it to urge its assistance. I lift up a clay wall in my mentor's path. "Carlos, wait!" The squat man turns back and glares at me. In his gray-green eyes, I see something that has remained hidden until now. His complexion couldn't be whiter if he'd been emptied of blood. "I just want to talk," I urge as I hurry toward him before he goes around my semi-circular barrier.

"Stella, don't," he pleads as I get close. "Just let it go." His hands shake as he puts them out as if to hold me at bay.

"What's wrong, Carlos?" I whisper to him as I get close. A crowd of people have gathered at the doorway of my house, but none are coming closer. A quiet conversation can be kept between the two of us.

"I can't. Just leave it at that."

"Carlos, we've been through hell and back together. I've never known you to back down from anything. I've never met a braver or more solid person. What's wrong?"

Carlos mumbles something too low for me to catch.

"What was that?"

His head falls forward as he whispers, "I'm afraid of heights. Now you know! Are you happy?" He sounds like a rather petulant seven-year-old.

My eyes go wide. An air witch, someone who can call the winds to his side and fly, can't for fear. What a crime! "My friend, I will take your secret to the grave if you wish. To prove it, I'll tell you about my two greatest fears—that I might somehow be left destitute, and that my mother might somehow get control of me again."

"Stella, no one likes their mother, and everyone fears being broke."

"Not like me. I have nightmares of waking up old, alone, and in a debtor's prison with bugs crawling all over my skin through my tattered and torn shift." I shiver in revulsion as I remember my old schoolteacher in just such an end. "And then my mother comes to pay me out, and I end up her slave. I'll do whatever it takes to make sure I don't wind up in that place. I'd whore myself out a hundred times a day to prevent it if necessary."

"OK, so we are both damaged. What now?"

A spark of inspiration hits as I see a stumblebum down the street, probably from the Good Time Saloon around the corner. "Would you go if you didn't have to fly? Or maybe better said, if you weren't aware you were above the ground?"

Carlos looks at me suspiciously. "What are you thinking about?"

"Well, what say we get you so drunk that you pass out, or we get an herbalist to put together a sleeping draught? Then we tote you on board the airship like freight."

"That could work if you make sure I'm out for the whole flight and that I don't know when it is going to happen. I don't think I could stand the strain of anticipation."

"OK, I'll assume your cooperation and me pickling you in enough booze for a dozen men. And to protect your reputation, why don't you just walk away? I'll tell them that you are afraid of dirigibles—too many of them catch fire."

"Yeah, that will work," he says without much enthusiasm.

"There is nothing bad about being afraid."

"You don't know what it's like, Stella. I have always wanted to fly, to soar through the air like a bird, but if I even think of myself more than about ten feet off the ground, I throw up. Imagine being able to use only a small fraction of the power you have, Stella. Really think about that."

I do, and it makes my stomach sour. "I'm sorry, Carlos. Just never forget that you are the one of us we look up to, fears or not."

"But would they if they knew what a coward I am?"

"I can't speak for everyone, but I have, I do, and I will follow you into nearly anything you can name. They would be idiots if they saw you as anything but what you are and have been—the rock that holds us together." I can see some color coming back to his face. "Now go home and collect yourself. I'm going to need you."

"Yes, your highness."

Turning to the assembled throng, over my shoulder I offer him a teasing "*Pendejo.*"

# # #

As the clock strikes eleven, Luciana and I lie on my bed looking up at the ceiling mural of a stylized lily painted in enormous size by one of our girls, Anna Taylor. At eleven, her art already provokes strong feelings. The flower wavering in the candlelight reminds me of a woman's anatomy, usually making me horny. But it has been months since I've done anything but masturbated, and even that, infrequently. I've even spurned the advances of my best friend and sometimes lover, Daring Karie.

So, Viscountess Adrianna Helms stole my heart half a year ago. She remains the only person other than my husband who has had my love. The Church and even my own priest have forbidden our relationship. It isn't because we are two women, but because she is already married.

Please don't think of me as a home-wrecker. Her husband, Viscount Henry Helms, is one of my best friends. His marriage to Adrianna is one of power and doesn't include carnal relations, as Adrianna prefers her loving in the arms of a woman. But that doesn't matter to the Catholic Church. She is married, and that is all that counts.

"That's a pretty flower," Lucy says, lying there in the flannel nightdress I loaned her. She erupts with an enormous yawn. As they are contagious, I find myself following suit. "Sorry," she offers.

"Nothing to be sorry about. If you can't yawn in bed, then when can you?"

"True," my cousin says, falling silent for the first time in hours. "Thank you again for coming to save my Adam."

"Lucy, we don't even have a plan."

"That doesn't matter. Hellfighters think on their feet. That's what Donny told me."

Blast that idiot, I think. "We do. We have to when dealing with demons. But that doesn't matter when you face something impossible. It may be no easier for me to reach Adam than for you."

"But you can make earth move for you."

"Yes, but we are talking the depth of ten football pitches. Over half a mile. Even I have limits."

Yawn. "You'll find a way, cousin. The white powers and my faith in the Lord let me know you and Carlos will succeed." Yawn.

"With all of my capabilities, I may accidentally cause the cave to collapse upon him. Lucy, I don't want to be a doomsayer, but we don't know that we will be able to get anywhere near him."

Snnnrk

"Lucy?"

Lady-like snores answer me. She sleeps the sleep of the righteous and ignorant. While I'm tired, her slumber eludes me. My mind spirals into the chaos of too many things going all at once. My mental kaleidoscope jumbles together—war, death, love, longing, questions, flight, and excitement. I ponder on Carlos's fear of heights, the lives of two hundred miners, meeting my father for the first time, my unfulfilled love with Viscountess Helms, my first trip in a dirigible, and even the possibility of hostilities against France and England.

Sometimes I just want to be a normal, mundane housewife with one partner to love and problems primarily around getting the laundry clean and dinner on the table before my spouse comes home from work. My mind grabs ahold of this and fantasizes about being Adrianna's partner until it becomes a dream.

2—Sunday, November 18, 1888

The Sabbath is my quiet time. On the Lord's day, I leave the usual chaos of the morning—girls coming in and out, women chattering about the day, and Mrs. Simmons's gruff attitude—to them. I take my breakfast in my room, along with the Sunday edition. This morning I invite Lucy to share my respite.

My guest comes out of the bathroom after her morning ablutions in a rust-colored gown with white lace trim. Mikey and my seamstress, Paula Simpson, both did me proud managing to get that dress here in time for church. Poor Lucy hadn't come with more than her one dress and two pairs of undergarments, so I brought her some gifts.

Lucy swirls around. "Oh, Stella. This is the most wonderful dress I've ever owned! You really didn't need to do this."

"Cousin, you can't go to church in your shift."

"True as that may be, I did wear my best dress here." If the patched dress is her best, then I'm happy I splurged twenty dollars on a couple of simple dresses for her. "But this is just wonderful. It feels so stiff and formal. Thank you ever so much. Wait until Adam sees it. I hope he doesn't think it's charity."

"No charity. I insist. Think of it as birthday and Christmas presents for all of the years we haven't known about one another. Now come over here and break your fast. I'm starving."

Lucy blushes and curtsies to me. I see a twinkle of mischief in her eye but put it down to the burden of worrying about her husband. "Yes, Stella," she says in a way that makes me wonder what she is plotting. She sits next to me and takes my offered hand.

"Lord God, please keep this woman's husband safe, along with his colleagues, until we can rescue them. Bless this food so that we may remain strong as we go about your work. Amen."

"Amen."

Our morning meal isn't grand—slow-cooked oatmeal with dried apples, cinnamon, and brown sugar.

"Do you have a preference of what section of the paper you like to read?" I ask.

"The Home pages, if you don't mind, Stella."

I unfold the *Boston Herald* and hand her that segment. I turn to the front page.

"Explosion Glider Takes Maiden Flight," screams the headline. *Intriguing*, I think and read the byline, "by Susan Queensbury."

She is the reporter who interviewed me after I was stabbed on the church steps. Her article about me being stabbed by a homeless Germanic immigrant was tasteful. It remained on the salient points and did not draw false conclusions about those without a situation, new citizens from other shores, or even those who had no place to rest their heads. This makes her article about powered flight doubly interesting.

This morning, with a thunderous roar and tongues of flame, the *Graceful Flyer* leaped into the sky off its cannon-like stand with Herbert Henry Dow at the controls. The craft was propelled by nothing less than a nitroglycerine-based detonation. It glided two miles before another explosion sent it hurtling faster and higher into the clear morning sky. Two hours later the glider landed safely in the beach sand at Kitty Hawk, Tennessee.

Mr. Dow remarked, "This is the first powered flight of heavier-than-air craft. The speed and versatility of such a craft must be obvious to everyone."

When asked how soon the vessel would be ready for trips around the monarchy and to Spain, he said, "Plenty of problems to work out first. That first kick is a doozy. Most people won't want the headache I have just to travel from Ohio to the palace. Besides, the military wants it for their purposes. And honestly, I'm aiming a lot higher than a new transportation method. I want to visit the moon."

Mr. Dow's enthusiasm intrigues me and manages to excite me in a way that takes away my dread of meeting my father for the first time this afternoon. *The moon!*

# # #

May's papal visit has done more than just make us American Catholics happy. With just a few months of proper funding, St. Leonard's Church shows the benefits. Scaffolding covers the exterior stonework. Where once there had been nothing but the tiny old rectory and but a few blocks laid, all of the walls now stand twenty feet or more. In some places, they are being topped with ceiling beams. It is beginning to take on the grand shape of the house of God that it was intended to be.

"How did you sleep?" I ask my guest as I park the poderabile in the churchyard.

"Guiltily."

"I'm sorry? Guiltily?"

"My husband's life is in jeopardy, and I slept like a babe. I should be thinking and doing something for him."

"Is there anything more you could be doing than you have already done?" I ask, piercing her faulty logic.

"Well, no."

"Then take guilt when you deserve it, not any other time."

"You sound like a preacher," Lucy says.

"Stella sometimes talks like that," Mikey, my other passenger, says with some sarcasm. "She don't let you wallow atall, even when she be doing it herself."

"When did this become pick-on-your-hostess day?" I toss back with a scowl.

"I will keep bein' as long as you tell us 'Do as I say, not as I do,'" Mikey says in a pretty good mockery of my own voice. Lucy giggles. I know when to throw in the towel.

"So you were saying, Lucy?" I ask, trying to deflect the conversation. Mikey laughs at my transparent ploy. Luciana smiles before answering.

"Well, I'd love to be able to afford a bed like that someday. It was so soft that I just sank into it. And you were sleeping next to me. But it was so big, I didn't notice at all. My bed is so small that when my husband and I sleep together and one of us turns over, we have to be careful not to push the other one out the other side."

"I knows what you means," Mikey says. "Sometimes, Stella lets me be sleepin' with her. Never sleep so good."

"I can't disagree with you," I say. "It's better than I've had before this. Mikey has my old bed, serviceable but not in the same class."

"Definitely not," Mikey says.

In respectful silence, we walk together up to the doors of the church. Father Juan Dubois y Cantonio isn't at the door. Instead, Father Miguel issues greetings to the church congregation.

"Morning, Miss Stella, Miss Lucy, and Miss Mikey," he offers with a dignified half-bow. Mikey giggles at the greeting, as she usually does. The padres insist on calling her Miss, but she never wears anything but breeches. Maybe they think one day she'll get out of the tomboy phase that many young girls go through.

My charge confided to me once about her choice of attire in a late-night hen session. She started wearing them as a form of protection against the boys, both as camouflage and as a barrier. Later she just found she got used to them and liked them better than petticoats and skirts. To each her own.

"And to you, Father Miguel. Is Father Juan ill?" I ask.

"Not at all. He is making preparations for his sermon and asked for me to invite all of you lovely people into God's house."

Damned unusual. Father Juan has never missed the greetings except on the high holidays, when his workload rivals the tasks of Hercules himself.

Lucy pauses at the back row of the church benches. "Don't we have to sit in the witches' pew?"

"Not at St. Leonard's," I say with a nudge for her to move forward so as not to be trampled by the people coming in behind us. "Father Juan did away with that nonsense months ago. Father Church hasn't gotten around to recognizing us, but here, we are family. We may sit anywhere we like."

"Really? This will be fun. I always feel left out of things when I sit back so far."

I smile at Elizabeth, a young air witch who has recently passed her first solo flight. She looks so happy sitting with her parents instead of inhabiting the back pew as we used to do. She waves wildly and gets a stern rebuke from her mother for unladylike behavior.

"We takes the third pew on the left," Mikey says from behind us. We three slide in.

I smile and nod at Earl Robert Clark III and his wife, Edda. She sniffs at me, and the earl doesn't quite scowl. Part of me is hurt, and part of me understands them holding me at arm's reach. I'd been the messenger of bad tidings.

Their daughter, Fredricka, was riding the Pony Express with Patrick O'Donald of the Los Lobos hellfighter team. It hadn't helped that the earl ignored that Patrick existed. Pat, a good friend of mine, and Fredricka were very much in love. I made it clear to the Clarks that if they didn't get the relationship under control, they would end up with a grandchild with no father. That fit into the earl's social stratum even less than a marriage with a lowly hellfighter who lived like a Native American. He relented to Patrick's suit for his daughter's hand. The marriage is planned for May, as I recall.

The nave quiets as Father Miguel walks up to the lectern. *Again, no Father Juan.* Padre Miguel performs the rites about six or seven times a year, but coupled with the absence of our normal priest at the greetings, it makes me wonder. Curiosity flits quickly, as I have too many other things to worry about in my mind.

I absently perform the Penitential Rite, *kyrie*, and even the *Gloria*. While my body and mouth go through the rituals, my mind focuses on the fact that I'll be meeting my father after services. My emotions whipsaw back and forth.

I'd always wanted a father I could go to and whose lap I could climb into when things went wrong, especially with my mother. I'm a bit old and big for that now. I had wanted someone to teach me the ways of the world—to show me how to whistle with a piece of grass between my thumbs, to vet my dates, to teach me all about the world and life. To hug and love me. But I know those are only my fantasies.

The lector talks, and I ignore what he has to say.

Another part of me wars with the anger about being abandoned, left to the nonexistent tender mercies of my mother. I want to grind him into a pulp and flush that down the water closet. On how many birthdays did I blow out my candles, wishing for someone I could call Pa? And to know that he is so close that I can see him on a day's notice aches in my chest and burns in my brain.

Father Juan's voice pulls me away from my ruminations. His sonorous preaching voice projects to every corner of the nave and well out into the street. Up in the pulpit, he looks like a profit from the Old Testament. Juan Dubois y Cantonio's flowing black hair merges with his cassock to the point that you can't tell where one starts and the other ends. His thick, full beard almost blocks the white of the starched collar of his office. His bushy eyebrows are knit together in concern.

"Today's lesson isn't from the Bible."

A collective gasp comes from the congregation. People ask their neighbors if this has ever happened before.

"That's right, my friends." Father Juan holds out a copy that at least from my vantage point is clearly printed with HOLY BIBLE on the front. "The Bible is not the sole source of wisdom. Don't misunderstand me, fellows. It is the ultimate word on most topics, but in some cases, other writers have been inspired by God to provide an even clearer truth.

"'The quality of mercy is not strained; it droppeth as the gentle rain from heaven upon the place beneath. It is twice blest; it blesseth him that gives and him that takes. It is the mightiest in the mightiest ...'

"Some of you might recall the words of the immortal Shakespeare in his classic *The Merchant of Venice*—act 4, scene 1 for those who want the specific citation.

"While in the original play, a disguised Portia tries to dissuade Shylock from vengeance in his duty to God, even the god of the Jews."

Yes, if I take just the right pound of flesh within my pa's chest, I can empathize with the villain. As in many Sabbath services, I wonder if the sermon is directed at me, especially when his deep-brown eyes lock with mine. I have so much desire for vengeance on my father for leaving me with my cold mother. I want the pain to go away, but I'm not as strong as God would wish of me.

But the moment passes as Father Juan continues. "There is so much more. 'It blesseth him that gives and him that takes.' Shakespeare's words are a pointed note that we travel through life dealing with those both in better and worse stations than ourselves.

"Doesn't the Bible state, 'Carry each other's burdens, and in this way you will fulfill the law of Christ?'"

My mind automatically fills in, *Galatians 6:2. Where was my dad to help carry my burdens?*

"Or 'My command is this: Love each other as I have loved you. Greater love has no one than this: to lay down one's life for one's friends.' John 15:13.

"How many of our husbands, sons, and sweethearts have been killed supporting our brethren in Ireland? We showed them God's love!" Father Juan says, slamming his fist against the pulpit. People in the congregation jump. As a priest, Señor Dubois y Cantonio isn't a thunderer, so it shocks nearly everyone. "Every one of those who sacrificed themselves is at God's right hand.

"But stop not there. 'Do not withhold good from those to whom it is due, when it is in your power to act.' Each and every one of you has the power to act.

"Take God to your heart and do good. Help others." Father Juan ends in an urgent tone. "Let us pray."

As the service ends, my stomach churns. It feels as if I've swallowed a full block of ice all at once. *What will my father look like? Will he be worthy?*

"Confession, Miss Lucy?" Mikey asks after a moment or two. My young friend has told me many times that I sometimes get a look on my face that means I'm totally lost to the world. She must be recognizing it now if she is taking away our guest.

I once saw a steam-powered mixer in a commercial bakery. The questions in my mind feel like the different fixings they put together for that dough. Watching the ingredients whirl around, I know eventually something good will come out. But in the meantime, it just makes me nauseous.

I find I've walked out and planted myself out on the edge of the shallow church steps. *Right about here*, my mind says about where I was knifed some months ago. You can't see even a dim mark on the stone. *Time and wear eliminate all stains*, I think. *Will I have to do that with Adrianna? Let time wear away that pain—that stain? What about my father?*

I watch other parishioners leave in a flood as I wait for Mikey and Lucy. They descend the stairs like the slow dropping of my mood. I'm wondering more and more if I even want to meet my father. It seems like a fool's errand. I can never get my youth back. I can never unfeel the pain. "This is stupid," I say to myself.

I've been oblivious to my surroundings. Father Juan tucks his cassock underneath him and sits next to me on the steps without even an invitation. As many times as he's saved my life and soul, I guess he has earned that privilege.

I look at him with more than a little puzzlement. "Not listening to confessions, Father?"

"Only one confession matters today, Stella."

"Mine?" I chortle without any mirth. "For a change, I haven't enough sin to interest even a new priest, Father Juan."

"Nope," he says, staring straight ahead at the street traffic. "Not yours. Mine."

I join him in staring at the people passing by in their Sunday best. "I thought you confessed to the bishop?"

"I have many times, but this one I have to confess to you. Forgive me, my daughter. It has been twenty-three years, four months, and twenty-five days since my last confession."

My head swivels toward him. "No! It can't be." I bolt upright when he doesn't deny it. "No!"

"I'm afraid it's true, my daughter."

"Don't call me that! Don't ever call me that again, you ... you ... fraud. Liar!" I find myself standing there shaking, but it isn't only me. The entire front of the church is rocking back and forth. Bricks are falling off the top of the unfinished walls. My breaths come in bursts. Tears run down my face.

"Stella, control yourself!" the man, who is my father in more ways than one, barks.

"Control myself? You dare order me to control myself?!" My despair is changing to rage. "You judge me in the confessional. You preach to me. All the while knowing I'm your daughter?"

Bricks are no longer falling but exploding into white and red dust. I feel the shrapnel hitting me. Father Juan stands still despite several of the shards slicing wounds into his face. His voice goes soft. "I don't order you, Stella. I ask. I plead. I beg. Not for me, but for all of the other innocent people around."

The people on the street are running away. People farther down the lane are staring in this direction. I look around to find foot-wide cracks in the stairs. The front of the church has completely collapsed around us. Everyone inside is cowering against the altar.

I hate to admit it, but he is right. I close my eyes and think of Adrianna and the love for her that still wells within my heart. My memories allow me to transition my anger into simple sadness. It is working. The ground is no longer shaking underneath me. I suck in three deep, slow breaths before opening my eyes again. People within the church are now streaming out in a rush, but they mean little to me at the moment. My focus pierces my father—the man who lay with my mother and fornicated with her to make me. A Catholic priest. Ha!

"So?" I prompt him. "This is your confession, priest. Confess."

"How detailed do you want me to—"

"Just tell me!" My exclamation echoes in the very earth beneath us.

"This may take some time. Would you like to sit?"

I let him walk me over to the sanctuary, where we sit on one of the only slightly broken pews.

"I met your mother when she was on a trip to Spain to study." Hell, I didn't know she'd ever been out of the Monarchy of America once her family immigrated. "It was the fall term of 1859. I was a student of languages at the University of Rennes when she arrived to study witchcraft under Master Warlock Ivrea y Alba."

I find myself grinding my teeth. I want more and I want it all *right now!* My intellect understands that all of the detail I want can't come out quickly. My mind barely contains my emotions, which chafe at tearing down the entire church around his ears.

"Josephine was dark, beautiful, and mysterious. I fell for her pretty much the first moment I laid eyes on her. She claimed that my studious nature attracted her to accept my suit for her hand. For five years we courted until between us we agreed to be man and wife.

"We traveled to the monarchy in order for me to officially request permission from her father. Unfortunately, he died of smallpox after his last letter to your mother. Without a near family member, we moved ahead with the wedding.

"You were born twelve months after the nuptials. I was never happier in my life. Piney ... Sorry, my nickname for your mother. Piney and I struggled. She had just started her earth witch practice. I found work sporadically as an interpreter."

"Stella?" comes Mikey's tentative voice.

I don't even bother to look around. "Take Luciana home in Lady Justice. I'll make my own way."

"But do you nee—"

"GO!" I bark at my young friend. I make a mental note to apologize later.

I hear rustling behind me. Sometimes, I think Mikey knows my moods better than any spouse ever could.

"Go on, *Father*," I say, turning his title into a slur.

"When your mother got pregnant again right away, our excitement multipl—"

"But Mother's womb detached when I was born."

"No, Stella. I'm sorry if I'm contradicting what Josephine has told you, but that didn't happen until your brother's stillborn delivery."

"I have a younger brother?"

"Had, Stella. He survived less than two minutes despite everything a witch doctor could do for him."

I give him a hand gesture to continue. The difference from what my mother has told me is meaningless.

"Grant's death and her inability to have more children crushed your mother. We'd both eagerly looked forward to as many as possible. She began to slip into melancholia. I wasn't much better. I sought solace in the Bible in solitary study. The more I read, the more I questioned, and the closer to God I got. At the same time, your mother and I grew apart. She eventually picked herself up and put her entire attention on her business and improving our social standing. Probably to further her career, but I'm not certain.

"You were well cared for, primarily by me. Your mother definitely was the breadwinner of our pairing—something that hurt my ego as a man."

"So your ego drove you to divorce?" I say, picking the least of the things he'd offered.

"No ... Yes ..." After a few seconds, he says, "No. Did it matter? Yes, Stella, it did to me. In my Spanish heritage, a man takes care of his family. I hadn't, and now I had a wife who was taking care of me. I can't say this made up no part of my decision. But in the end, God called me. I can't describe it any better than that.

"I knew I had to follow his path for me, and that path was in the clergy. It wasn't an easy decision. I knew I would have to leave behind all of my worldly possessions if I took orders. I would have to leave my wife and my daughter behind. It tore my heart apart."

"What did Mother say?"

"What do you think? We fought bitterly. I think she threw every breakable item in our small house at me. She wheedled, pleaded, threatened, and even begged me not to go. But by then, my heart had hardened against her. You, on the other hand, caused me tears every night over my decision until I left for the seminary."

I tried to imagine my mother begging anyone. I couldn't raise the image. It didn't make any sense.

"How old was I?"

"Just turning two. The day I left, your mother put you in this pale-yellow dress with a matching hair bow. It looked like you were going to Easter services. It was a parting shot at my heart."

"And so you requested Boston to stay close?"

"It doesn't work that way, Stella. The Church sends you where you are needed. When I was posted to Boston, I actually begged to be sent anywhere else. I explained the situation and got told in no uncertain terms that St. Leonard's needed my talents."

"It took me nearly a year after being here to realize that it would be good for you and me, both. I've been able to give you at least some of a father's love through the years."

"Ha!" I snap in response.

"Say what you will, but who did your mother send you to when you were bad or needed guidance?"

I can't bring myself to say the obvious, so I nod instead.

"I watched you grow up, giving gentle nudges here and there. Your mother deserves credit—"

"Stop right there. My mother deserves credit only for keeping food in my mouth and a roof over my head. NOTHING. MORE."

Father Juan, my father, looks at me silently for the count of about ten heartbeats. "I won't disagree with some of your assessments. But before you judge her too harshly, look at it from her point of view."

"Go on. This should be a hoot."

"Seriously, Stella. I joined the priesthood. Remember that the Church doesn't believe in priests being married or in divorce. For me it was easy. I denounce my former life. For Josephine, she can't get out of being married to a ghost of my old self. She can't remarry. She is left without a caregiver for you, someone who reminds her of the wounds I caused by leaving. I'm sure she saw me in your eyes every day of your entire life.

"Imagine your pain with your viscountess and magnify that by seeing her every day. You can never move on. As much as I feel for you, my daughter, the one I really feel for is Josephine. Think about that the next time you want to despise her for something."

I frown at him but don't say anything. I swallow hard. My life takes on a different shade. My mother's actions and lack of emotion take on new meanings.

"So, Stella, my story is pretty much finished. I am ready for any vengeance you feel is necessary for my fraud and abandonment."

"So was that sermon pointed at me to make sure I didn't take a pound of your flesh?"

"It was pointed at you, but it had nothing to do with saving my own skin. I am like Antonio of the play. I made the bargain. I am forfeit. I just wanted to make sure that you help your cousin Luciana."

I snort. "I had already decided to do that, if it is possible, priest. You wasted a good sermon."

"While I targeted you, it will return manifold, daughter."

I still flinch at the term like it's a hangnail being brushed the wrong way, but it annoys rather than hurts.

The tweet of police whistles penetrates the overall ache that still resides in my chest. There is still pain, but with explanations, I at least understand somewhat. The clang, clang of the Royal Firefighters is heard over the shrill toots. All of them seem to be coming this way. Of course, someone just all but destroyed a church.

"I need to think about this more," I say.

"Stella, I'm not going anywhere. If there are any questions you want to have answered, all you have to do is come by and ask."

"Wait a minute. How did you know I was coming to talk to you? Lucy has been with me all the time."

"Piney. Your mother. She came over and read me the riot act, chapter and verse. She told me the time for secrets was over."

My mother. Who'd've thunk it?

"But over all of this, Stella, remember—I still can't publicly identify myself as your dad. Father Church does insist that we sever that tie. It shouldn't matter much, as I have nothing to give or leave to you other than my friendship."

"I understand, Father Juan."

There are sixteen firefighters and a dozen constables just at the edge of the damage I've caused. They are all looking around for victims. They look at us sitting in the middle of the mess, relatively unscathed.

"I guess I'd better help clean up the mess I've made."

"That would be a good start, daughter. You might also do twenty Hail Marys and donate six new pews to repair the ones that are damaged."

I twist my face at him. "Right now, I don't like you very much."

"My job as the shepherd of your soul has never had being liked as part of the job description."

# # #

"Is my uncle still alive?" The question is called from the kitchen the moment I trudge into the main door of the ex-brickhouse. Oddly, the house is deadly quiet. No girls run about. No one is playing the piano. Come to think of it, no kids were playing outside when I arrived. My household must have informed everyone that I might return in a mood not conducive to good health.

"He was when I left," I offer without much in the way of emotion. I make my way into the kitchen to find Lucy in her original dress and an apron, kneading dough. "What are you doing? You are a guest. Yolanda, how could you!"

My cook has her fingers engaged tying up a roast. "I done tried to shoo her off, but she wouldn't be listenin'."

"I was nervous, Stella," Lucy interjects on behalf of my friend. "I've been feeling like a fifth wheel today, and I couldn't just sit still while I worried. I insisted."

I sit down, taking one of the cinnamon jumble cookies out of the big earthen jar. Biting into the sweet treat in a kitchen that smells of simmering stew, chopped garlic, and pickles centers my still-churning mind.

I had chosen to walk home to give me time to think. While the spot in my soul under the heading FATHER has been filled, my emotion about it all hasn't completely settled. The burning anger I bore has tempered, as has the joy in finally knowing. It makes for a volatile mental state. I am still but by no means calm.

"Well, you will be happy to know that Father Juan Dubois y Cantonio is in excellent physical health apart from a few scratches."

"You clawed him?"

"No. I didn't mean it that way. I didn't touch him except for a hug just before I left."

"So how did he get scratched?" Lucy asks as she sprinkles a bit of flour on the dough before kneading it more.

"There was an accident." I can feel heat in my cheeks at my less-than-completely-truthful statement.

"OK. Now what about you, Stella? Did this make you feel better or worse? Your mother was certain it would hurt you more than help."

"I think the jury is still out, cousin. Say, that makes me wonder. How many other relatives do I have that I don't know about?" I take another cookie.

"Youse keep at them cookies, and I won't have none for no others, and them pretty dresses of yorn won't fit," Mrs. Simmons barks. I smile at her concern and gruff love.

Lucy twists her head in thought. "Well, my parents died years ago—"

"Really? I'm sorry to hear that," I offer in automatic condolences. I realize that I have no feelings about her parents, but I'm sincere in my concern for my cousin.

"Thank you. They were on the Pittsburg Unlimited when it derailed outside Altoona. Three hundred fourteen dead. Wasn't anyone's fault. A piece of track buckled by the summer heat. They've been gone for what? Eleven years now. I've mourned them well," Lucy says, moving on. "So, my parents had no other children. I do have Grandma Ree." Lucy smiles. "She is quite a character. Pinches the bottom of any male who gets within her reach."

"I can't say I disapprove," I spit out around a mouthful of confection.

"Nor can I. There has been more than one bottom I would have liked—"

"Miss Lucy," interrupts Mrs. Simmons. "Don't youse go sayin' nothin' nasty, or I'll wash yorn mouth out with soap."

I nod when Lucy looks at me.

"Yes, Mrs. Simmons," Lucy replies. "Anyway, Grandma Ree was from my father's side of the family. My mother has three other brothers and a sister in Spain. I really don't know much about them. I think my family Bible has their names, but we've never connected."

"What about your kids? I'm certainly related to them," I toss in, giving the proud mama the chance to brag about her offspring.

"Well definitely. Sometimes I think I'd forget my head if God hadn't nailed it on." She wipes her hands on her apron and fetches her handbag. She pulls out an old tintype photo of her family. Her husband, Adam, looks solemn but handsome. He is thin, but even under his best Sunday suit, I could see the muscles in his chest and arms. Lucy is in the same dress she is wearing right this moment. Two chubby-cheeked girls, maybe three and five, look cute in store-bought dresses. The boy, maybe fourteen years old, bears his father's looks but is gangly, not yet reaching his full height or maturity. "That's Adam Junior. He's fourteen, Holly, six, and Gretchen, four. They are all good kids, but Gretchen, wow. I need three of me just to keep track of her. She insists on doing everything her brother and sister do. I even caught her trying to pee standing up in the outhouse once."

I chortle. "Sounds like she is a handful."

"I love her to pieces, but yes, she is."

In the relative silence of the Brick Factory, I hear the front door open. Mikey saunters in. "That were quite a show you put on at St. Leonard's, Stella."

"I'm not proud of that, Mikey," I say, feeling the embarrassment deep in my gut.

"If I was meetin' my father fer the first time, I'da done squashed him under one of those walls," Mrs. Simmons adds, being as helpful as if she'd dropped dynamite into a fire.

"That's why witches are trained," Lucy says before I can retort. "With their powers, they can be dangerous to everyone. Half of what they learn is how to control their temper." I look askance at my cousin. She returns my gaze and says, "Just because I haven't taken formal training doesn't mean I don't know about it. I wanted to, but raising children and caring for a husband took precedence."

"Miss Lucy is quite right," I say. "We learned breathing techniques, body control, and self-hypnosis. And between all that, my mother threw tests at me that would have gotten her shot in other cultures. Her crowning achievement was when I was recovering from being burned by Gazzunreep in my early witch training. She not only told me that she knew I was summoning something too powerful for me, but also that she let the demon burn me to teach me a lesson."

"How comes she is still being alive?" Mikey asks.

"That was the point of the exercise, Mikey. Could I keep my temper even when I was provoked beyond endurance? But she didn't poke me after that."

"She done figured out that she went too far?" Mrs. Simmons asks.

"Kind of. It might have had something to do with the threat I leveled at her."

"Ain't that the same thing as losing yorn temper?"

"No, Yolanda. I didn't do anything. I just made it clear what would happen if she did anything like it again. I buried it deep, one of the things we were taught. That it simmered there doesn't matter."

"What did you threaten your ma with?" Lucy inquires.

I just shake my head. "No. That is between her and me. Even more importantly, the intimidation shouldn't have been voiced in the first place. Intellectually, I know she did what she did to teach me. Emotionally, it is something else entirely. Let it be."

The conversation dies. Mrs. Simmons puts the roast into the oven before Mikey pipes up with, "So, Miss Lucy, you packed and ready to go in the morning?"

"No, Mikey. I came with only the clothes on my back. I don't have a trunk or suitcase to carry the wonderful new things my generous cousin bought for me."

I quickly clear the cinnamon, sugar, and flour from another cookie from my mouth. "Mikey. Take Lucy upstairs. In my armoire, you will find a trio of carpetbags. Use one for my cousin's things. Lay out things on the settee for me to pack in the other two so I can check them. Lucy, you can help her because I don't know what the weather is in Centralia."

"Ankle deep in snow and mud when I left. Winter came early again this year," Lucy says.

"Mikey, add my second pair of boots."

"Yes, Stella. C'mon Lucy. This is going to be fun. I love seein' all of Stella's pretties."

"I thought you didn't like dresses, Mikey," I tease.

"No, I likes 'em alright. Just don't like to wear 'em."

3—Monday, November 19, 1888

In the nautical dawn, a milk wagon pulled by an old nag trundles into sight along Newbury Street. The milkman darts back and forth between his slowly moving cart and customers' front doors with his morning deliveries. Five of us wait until his wagon rattles out of sight over the railroad tracks.

The railroad is part of our plan, actually. Our target lives right next to them, and thus strange noises aren't unusual.

"You know what you are supposed to do?" Puffs of white clouds punctuate my words in the cold. Pinching a piece of dirt from the empty planter next to the door, I lick it and taste the acrid bitterness of played-out soil.

"Yes, Stella," Mikey says after her sergeants in arms around the yellow factory—two big girls, Victoria and Helen—nod. I look at Luciana. She nods too.

"Be ready to switch up if something goes wrong," I say, then get a confirming nod from my four other ladies. I take a deep breath. I've never taken on this kind of commission.

I pound on the door. There isn't an answer. This doesn't surprise me, as our quarry would be likely to sleep until noon. I pound on the door again and nod to Helen. She yells out, "There is a demon loose! Mister, everyone says you is the man to see."

Carlos, in only a worn nightshirt, slams the door open. "Did you say—"

I convince a tentacle of the earth to come up and wrap around his body, arms, and legs.

"Hey!" he cries out. Victoria knocks him over onto his back and grabs his nose. "W'at ya doin'?" he cries out in a nasal version of himself.

Mikey uncorks the tincture bottle. This is going smoother than I'd hoped. The winds that form behind me belie my thought even before it completely forms.

"Helen?" I direct. Helen is no little fainting stick of a girl. At fifteen, she out-masses Carlos and me together. She's stocky and solid like a butt of wine. Any man who marries her had better either be big too or plan on being on top to keep from being crushed.

Helen gets a bit of a running start through the forming whirlwind. She forces Victoria, Mikey, and the recumbent Carlos en masse inside Carlos's home. I step in through the pelting pebbles, dragging Lucy with me. She slams the door shut behind us. The wind batters the outside, but the small flat inside is too small to allow much of a whirling dervish.

Carlos thrashes around, fruitlessly trying to break free of my earthen bonds and Victoria's steel grip on his nose. As Mikey starts to pour the black goo from the bottle, Carlos clamps his mouth shut.

"You are going to have to breathe sooner or later, Carlos. Just take your medicine." I dictate. His head jerks back and forth just a little bit. "Helen, would you help Victoria?"

The biggest of our girls grabs Carlos by the chin to force his mouth open. Mikey is ready when our victim gasps for air. She pours the rather thick liquid into his mouth. Vicky reaches around, grabs his chin, and slams it shut. Lucy wraps a clean rag around his mouth and the back of his head. Between the pair, they manage to keep the liquid in. My friend and mentor finally has to draw breath again only to find he must swallow to get the air he needs.

After he has ingested the sleeping draught, Carlos's eyes roll up before drifting closed.

"Sweet dreams, Boss," I say.

We probably could have done it with one less person, but Carlos always taught me to be prepared. Who knows what he might have been able to do if we hadn't caught him by surprise.

"Mikey, pack a valise for Carlos. Then we better get moving because we don't want to allow the constables to mistake our intentions."

# # #

The silver-gray dirigible floats above its mooring with the blood-red lettering *Majesty* on its flanks. Her sleek, and at the same time bulbous, form looks like a giant boa constrictor that has eaten an equally gigantic elephant.

In the last two days, I've read everything about her that I could find. Her form is burned into my brain. Right now, I'm so excited that I'm not sure if I should go off and find an outhouse or not.

Christened just four months earlier into the Boston and Seattle Airline, the *Majesty* bears all the latest technological advances. She has an external frame of the new shiny aluminum material. Three steam-powered propellers drive her through the air—one behind the carriage, or passenger decks, and two swinging wide on either side of the main body. Each engine is ducted to vent the coal-fired smoke far behind the main bladder. The ship's rudder is a complex x-shape maybe a third of the dirigible's body length, behind it.

It isn't until I see the flea-sized men loading the cargo hold that I realize the size of *Majesty*. I no longer wonder why she doesn't leave out of Boston proper. The bloody thing would have covered a considerable portion of the city, say from the northern wharves halfway to the Commons. Enormous!

As we stand in line to be weighed, I yawn. I would have rather gotten up a little later for our eleven o'clock departure, but we had our early adventure to collect the reluctant member of our crew. A handcart holds a small suitcase and Carlos, who snores like a train leaving the station. Helen attends to our sleeping beauty. Mikey has my bags.

Lucy paces three steps in either direction. Her lips draw tight together, and her jaw is working. Any calmness she achieved over the weekend has flown. I'd like to hug her and get her to calm down, but I suspect that if Adrianna were trapped somewhere, Church or no, I'd be chomping at the bit over any delay. We edge forward, but I'm paying attention to the entire process. Everything is so new.

"Juan Ortega. One thirty-five," says the loadmaster in his smart white uniform coat and black trousers. He stands next to a commercial scale that looks large enough to hold a moose. Instead, a small Spanish gentleman stands on it.

"Juan Ortega. One thirty-five. Under five," repeats someone, cross-referencing lines in a ledger.

"You may step down and get in line to embark," says the loadmaster in a pleasant voice and demeanor. "Your ticket, ma'am?" he asks the next person in line. "If you would, climb up onto the platform."

Someone in a uniform that reminds me of a bellhop's gives the woman a hand so she can steady herself up the single step.

"Pamela Ortega. One fifty.

"The woman delivers a scowl at the officer of the airline like her angry eyes alone could incinerate him. Having been at the other end of a demon who could do just that, I flinch just a bit.

"Pamela Ortega. One fifty. Overage ten."

"You may step down and get in line to embark, Mrs. Ortega."

She delivers a harrumph and climbs down, yanking her arm away from the bellhop. Mrs. Ortega storms over to her husband and gives him an earful, gesticulating as if she had just been accused of cheating at whist.

Even if Mrs. Ortega's antics amuse me, I lose interest in the process until it is our turn.

Helen wheels Carlos up to the platform.

"Ah, what is this?" the loadmaster asks.

I step forward. "A passenger, of course. Here is his ticket."

"Ma'am, we usually require that our passengers walk on board."

"We were assured by your ticketing staff that this wouldn't be an issue," I say. It is something I checked on when I purchased our fares. "He isn't feeling well and sleeps a good deal of the time."

"One moment," the loadmaster says. He walks forty feet to the side and talks to a man with a few more gold braids on his sleeve. He returns. "It seems that this is acceptable, but we will have to put him into his stateroom. We can't have nonticketed people on board."

"That's fine. He is a heavy sleeper." With that draught in him, he'd probably sleep through the Second Coming.

The cute bellhop helps Helen wrestle the handcart up onto the stage. There they unbuckle the straps and lay Carlos down on his side as Helen leaves with the trolley.

"Carlos de Aldana. One seventy-seven."

"Carlos de Aldana. One seventy-seven. Under seventeen."

I'd had to guess at his weight. I figured guessing over would be better than under.

Three porters wrestle with Carlos's unconscious body before getting him on a cart. The trio trundle off with my slumbering friend and mentor toward the ship.

"Ticket, please?" Excepting his starched uniform, the loadmaster is so normal that he would be a statistician's delight—average height, average build, brown hair, brown eyes. He reminds me of Henry Helms's accountant, Mr. Olds.

"Mrs. Ochoa, would you please step up onto the platform?" the loadmaster says.

I climb the single step on the arm of a downy, fresh youngster who, beyond any reason, gets my lust brewing.

In men, I tend to prefer the brawny types. My Aaron, God rest his soul, could have made two of the loadmaster and four of this fledgling. He could have snapped either of them like twigs in just one hand.

The demon-stoked sex bomb inside me must have reached its awakening hour. Yes, I discovered six months ago that I'm part demon. My g'g'g'grandmother copulated with an incubus. Among other things, this means I am randier than ten billy goats or three mares in heat. Normally, Daring Karie, the grand dame whore of all of Boston and my best friend, keeps my carnal fires banked. We enjoy an unusual relationship that includes friendly sex. Karie loves sex, maybe even craves it sometimes—all the time. Think of it as a person who enjoys their work so much that it is also their only hobby.

All that aside, I've not had even that outlet, as Karie has been on a vacation with a gentleman friend for the last month. I also have been avoiding her because I feel every time we tip the velvet that I have somehow been unfaithful to my Adrianna. Of course, that is the problem—she isn't my Adrianna, according to the Church. She belongs to Henry. My feelings are so messed up that they could be served as spaghetti.

I step onto the scales and put the rest of it out of my mind.

"Stella Ochoa. One hundred ninety-eight pounds."

"Stella Ochoa. One—"

"Wait, what?" I ask, dumbfounded. I mean, I know my bosom is large, but that's out of bounds.

"—hundred ninety-eight pounds. Over forty-three pounds."

"I'm sorry, Mrs. Ochoa, but you are significantly over your allotted weight. We can't fly the ship if there is too much mass. That's why we ask for your weight when you purchase a ticket."

"But I don't weigh two hundred pounds!"

Mikey comes over and looks at the dial. "Stella, that be what it says." Her eyes light up, and she pats her tummy. It then dawns on me as well—my metal girdle-cum-armor. Back when I was the target of an assassin with a long rifle, I'd taken to wearing iron underwear like a corset. As an earth witch, I can form it to me. It has saved my life more than once. Since then it has become like any other garment I put on. Over my bloomers and chemise, but beneath my dress.

"One moment, sir." I've worn it so long that the metal bends to my will easier than my own muscles. The entire constrictor-like length uncoils just enough to fall over my hips and out from under the dress. It hits with a thud and a jangle both. I wave to it, and it rolls itself into a ball and off toward Mikey, right in front of the loadmaster. He leans back with his eyes wide.

"Now, that isn't something you see every day. Reweigh!" he calls out. "Stella Ochoa. One sixty-nine."

"Stella Ochoa. One sixty-nine. Over fourteen."

"Thank you, Mrs. Ochoa. If you'd climb down and embark, you can start your journey."

I turn to my young friend. "You are in charge, Mikey."

"I know, Stella. I'll do you proud."

"You better!" I say with a wink to soften my tone. At thirteen, this young woman has more intelligence and native street smarts than anyone I've ever met. I know I don't have to worry. I can focus on enjoying this first air flight.

But, fourteen pounds over? Maybe Yolanda is correct. I probably should lay off the cookies.

# # #

"G06. This is your stateroom, Mrs. Ochoa. You'll find your luggage inside," the porter says.

The room is stunning, decorated in the latest revival style—dark-blue walls punctuated with matching built-in bookcases full of books. But the most impressive part of the room is the blue-framed windows that dominate one entire wall. Out of it, I can see Boston in the distance. The king-size bed covers match the walls, as if the paint had flowed right off the walls and onto the bed. There is a small sitting room with a zebra-skin rug and an aluminum table topped with a lacquer vase full of colorful asters.

"You will also find a map of the ship, which I suggest you either memorize or carry in your purse. Decks C and above are for crew only. If you need anything, the purser's desk is—"

"Deck F," I say. "One deck up and midships."

"Very good, Mrs. Ochoa. And the first-class dining room—"

"Deck I, on the very bottom of the gondola."

"Amazing. Have you traveled with us before, ma'am?"

"I haven't. This is my first flight, but it has always fascinated me. I studied plans of the *Majesty*."

"You are ahead of most of the people aboard, then, Mrs. Ochoa. In the first-class dining room, they are serving champagne cocktails and hors d'oeuvres. You can watch our launch from there."

"Excellent. Thank you."

"You're welcome. Let us know if we can help you in any way." I hand the youth a dollar. "Thank you, Mrs. Ochoa," he says, leaving with a smile.

"Stella! Where are you?" I hear Lucy's voice call from the hallway.

"In here."

"Where's 'here'? There are dozens of 'heres.'"

"G06."

"There you are," she says, coming in wearing the blue gown I bought her. I'm so pleased that it highlights her blue eyes. It isn't a designer dress or anything, but it does flatter what she has.

"You settled in?" I ask her.

"Settled in? Do you want to tell me why I have a first-class cabin? I came steerage, in a shared inside cabin right below the steam engines."

"So why shouldn't you go first class? I put Carlos in your steerage berth. He won't know. Now, stuff your guilt and let's go get some champagne."

# # #

Lucy and I stop at the edge of the sunken dining room. I don't know about Lucy, but I can't believe my eyes. The entire room is floating on air above the ground. At least that is the way it looks at first. Red carpeting winds between tables to a parquet dance floor, where the vast majority of the people congregate around a pyramid of crystal flutes of champagne kept upright by a spiderweb of silver railings. But everything is on a floor of glass. In between chairs and carpet, I can see the ground crew twenty feet below preparing to release our ship.

"I feel like we are in a crystal goblet," I say.

"I don't know if I can go down there," Lucy says, looking not at the parts that seem normal, but rather at the emptiness and the space below. I feel somewhat the same.

"Ladies," says a pair of the ship's officers, who are walking up behind us in full dress uniform, including swords. Both of them look good enough to eat, I decide, and my middle gets gooey. Hanson, as his uniform's badge names him, is a tall drink of water with the dark skin of a Cuban islander. The other gentleman, D'Oro, is a solid man about two inches taller than me. But what strikes my fancy are his long, aristocratic fingers. I'm trying to decide which man should be the main course when Hanson speaks up. "A bit daunting, isn't it?"

I'm still in my fantasies when my cousin comes to my rescue. "Quite. Is it safe?"

"Absolutely, Miss ..."

"Mrs. Riley, Captain Hanson."

He laughs. "Sorry, Mrs. Riley. I'm only the first officer. I'm around in case Captain Pérez gets thrown overboard by pirates."

"Pirates?" Lucy squeaks.

"That's why we still wear these ridiculous things," First Officer Hanson says, patting his sword.

"He is just joshing you, Mrs. Riley," D'Oro says. "There are no air pirates. It wouldn't pay."

"You take away all of my fun," the first officer snaps back. "Ladies, could we escort you into the room? We'll support you."

"Certainly," I say, latching onto the arm of D'Oro. Underneath his uniform coat, I feel a forearm as hard as a steam pipe and about four times as big around. I look up to see his clean-shaven chin. It looks as if it were cast from iron. What captures my attention is the intensity of his gaze.

"Mrs. Riley?" First Officer Hanson says, offering his arm.

"And what is your position, Mr. D'Oro?" I ask, trying not to look below us as we walk down the half stairs.

"I'm the chief engineer, miss."

"My name is Stella Ochoa, Engineer D'Oro. You seem young for your position."

"And you seem young for a Mistress Witch, Mrs. Ochoa." Our tone is conversational but unlikely to carry beyond us. I can't even hear Lucy and the first officer talking.

"*Olé*, Mr. D'Oro," I say. "He nods graciously accepting his victory. "You are well informed."

"I followed your exploits in the newspapers, Mrs. Ochoa." There is no hero worship in his voice or manner, unlike many who claim me as one of their own. As an engineer, he would keep everything quantified in numbers, and heroines don't add up as supernatural.

"Good grief, but they did exaggerate everything."

"I don't doubt it. But if you erase ninety percent of the stories as applesauce, the remainder still is impressive."

I was right, numbers.

"I do want to thank you. My parents have a demon installation, and I'm glad they are much safer now," he says.

"Tell it to Viscount Helms, the owner of Forever Power. He is the one who made it happen."

Engineer D'Oro raises one eyebrow in disbelief, but he doesn't contradict me. A change of subject is called for.

"So, as chief engineer, don't you have important duties on takeoff?"

"Well, as you can imagine, we have a large crew complement. Even during critical evolutions, we rotate out some members of the team. This allows the crew to expand their experience just in case there is an emergency. As such, those who aren't directly involved take turns with our paying passengers. Normally, I find this an onerous task, as I'm much better with machines than people. But I have to say I find you delightful."

I laugh. "Why, Engineer D'Oro? I've not said a dozen words. Are you saying your only interest in me is based on my figure?"

"My given name is Robert, Miss Ochoa."

"Are you evading my question, Robert?"

"Not at all. Would it be so bad if I did find you attractive?"

My middle goes to mush. *Keep your bloomers on, Stella*, I think. "Not at all, Robert. But a woman like myself does like to be measured by more than just how shapely her ankles are."

"I'll keep that in mind." The flat delivery of the line makes me look at him more closely. The twinkle in his brown eyes makes me realize I'm being teased.

"As any gentleman should." My reply is equally toneless and just as much of a lie. I'm feeling shivers that are definitely telling me I've been celibate too long.

The officers take Lucy and me down to the dance floor, where we can stand on solid wood and not be acrophobic on the glass. Unfortunately, our escorts excuse themselves to mingle with the rest of the passengers. I'm conceited enough to believe that I see Mr. D'Oro glancing my way from time to time. I do manage to get a glass of that pink champagne. I sip it slowly, as I get drunk easily on the bubbly wines.

To take my mind off my own lusts, I edge over to where the parquet floor ends. We must be close to launching, as below us all of the dirigible's lines are only held by big, brawny men rather than being tied down.

I hear a high-toned bell ring three times. Bells, as you might imagine, have a special import to me. I scan around, looking for it. I find a glass box over the doorway with four different-sized handbells inside. The top of each has a small wire attached, leading into the bulkhead.

Behind me, I hear First Officer Hanson tapping a glass for attention. "Guests, an airship launch, especially of the *Majesty*, is quite impressive. We are about to lift off. I suggest you look out the windows and watch."

As there are many windows, we all seem to be looking in different directions. There is no bad view as the linesmen release as one. The nose of our ship lifts up, tilting the floor. Several of us stagger, but no one falls. The vertical speed is less than impressive. I know some of my girls can climb a tree faster than we are rising. After the poderabile, I expected to be smashed to the floor with its movement, not having to comfortably deal with the marginal angle of the floor.

The room starts vibrating with a low rumble. A couple of the women squeal in fright.

The chief engineer speaks up. "No cause for alarm. It's just the engines starting up."

The shaking increases in speed, its tone going higher but volume dropping. This increases our rate of ascent, but it is still underwhelming. Two bells ring again.

"Folks, you might want to hold on to a railing. Those two bells you heard mean that we are about to release our grounding ballast. There will be a jolt," the first officer says.

This is the first I've noticed the railings around the room. I walk up the incline and take hold of the banister fastened to the wall.

A cascade of water, ballast, releases for the space of five seconds at the bow and the stern like twin waterfalls. The champagne glasses rattle, but their gilt framework prevents them from moving. Officer Hanson's jolt dumps the three people who fail to heed his warning. They slide down the tilted floor before being stopped by some object solidly attached to the floor, like a table's leg. It makes me wonder if the crew strapped down Carlos. I'll have to check on him later.

A man in a uniform, to whom I've not yet been introduced, tends those idiots who refused to hold on. The caduceus on his sleeve identifies him as the ship's doctor. Fortunately, he treats only a few bruises and one minor cut. I give the half-wits the attention they deserve for not following instructions—I ignore them. It isn't hard with the view of the countryside streaking away from us. Buildings, trees, and people grow smaller by the second.

As the ground recedes, the natural order of the solid, stabilizing earth lessens until it is no stronger than a single strand of a spider's web. My head spins like someone has realigned the universe's planes.

"Mrs. Ochoa, are you alright?" Robert D'Oro asks as he catches me tilting.

I concentrate on the metal in the ship around me. Through it, I realize that the earth hasn't completely abandoned me. It firms my mental location, making the dizziness evaporate. "Yes, Robert. I think so."

"Some people are afraid of the height."

"No. Not that. I ... Well, I don't know what that was, but it is gone now."

"That's good. Not nauseous?" the engineer asks.

"Not at all, Robert. Thank you for your concern."

"So, not likely motion sickness," the doctor says. He has come within earshot as he checks the rest of the passengers.

"I think it has to do with being too far away from the ground," I say. "As an earth witch, it seems I'm somewhat susceptible to its absence."

The doctor digs around in a small black bag. "I don't think I have a tincture for earth witches being away from the ground," he jokes dryly.

"I guess you will have to remedy that oversight in the future," I tease back.

Mr. D'Oro steps in with, "Doctor Aurelius Hogue, would you please meet Mistress Witch Stella Ochoa. I thought you should be at least introduced if you are going to throw barbs at one another."

"I like strong women," Dr. Hogue says, bending over and kissing my hand. In my lustful state and with the shivers his lips send through me, I'd have pulled him to the floor and had my way with him if he were even ten years younger. As it is, I'm concerned that I'd break him. *Control, Stella. You are the one in control, not your body's demonic desires.*

"Very nice to meet you, Doctor. But if you don't stop tasting my hand, you'll have to perform more first aid."

"A shame to have to give up on such a tasty meal," Aurelius says. He's a harmless puppy as long as I keep my distance, and more dangerous than a wild puma if I don't. "Well, in that case, I should see if anyone else has suffered any other ill effects. Mrs. Ochoa, I must warn you about our chief engineer. He is the worst Casanova. Be on your guard."

The engineer snorts.

I reply with a knowing smile. "Doctor, that is like the cougar warning the sheep about the coyote. But I will be on my guard with all of you *gentlemen*."

"Very well, m'lady. You have a nice flight. If you need my *services*, my office is D-4 inboard, near the stern."

I'm certain the only thing the doctor offers in his office involves taking off my bloomers. "Thank you, Doctor. I'll keep that in mind." *As a place to avoid*, I add to myself.

The doctor, with his smile and his white teeth, slides off to another knot of people.

"So, Mr. D'Oro, are you going to leave the doctor to have the last word on your character?"

"Not at all, Mrs. Ochoa. He is too aggressive. I just let things flow naturally."

I'm sure you do.

My ears feel stuffy and a bit painful, which sidetracks my flirtation. I rub behind one of them.

"Yawn, Mrs. Ochoa. Up here the air pressure is lower."

"Yawn? I'm not even sleepy." But I do yawn involuntarily. And not a little ladylike sigh behind my fan, but one that engages my whole jaw to open to the size of a melon. My ears give a pop and now feel normal. "Hey!" I exclaim in surprise and relief.

"Works every time. If you feel any more pressure or pain, just work your jaw back and forth." Two lower-toned bells from the glass case sound, and Robert adds, "It shouldn't get any worse. We are at our cruising height of twenty-five hundred feet."

Out of the corner of my eye, I catch Lucy staggering. She looks not at all steady on her limbs. "Oh, it seems that my cousin may have imbibed a little too freely of the champagne. I think I should collect her and a plate full of goodies, and retire to our cabins," I say, emphasizing the plural. "Thank you for your assistance, Mr. D'Oro," I say with a curtsy.

"You are quite welcome," Robert says with a bow.

# # #

"Ib nebber ha' champ ... champ ... tha' stuff 'fore," Lucy announces about three times louder than necessary over the muted thrum of the engines.

"You don't say," I say as I keep her from careening off the walls. "What room are you in?"

"Effffffffffff ... Tha's fun ta say. Effffffff." She sprays the hallway with her second attempt. I know she is staying on the F deck somewhere near the stern, but not specifically which room.

"'Wenty 'ooooooooo."

I've dealt with more than one inebriated soul in my time, myself included, and speak fairly fluent drunk. "So F22."

"Tha's right, cous'n."

I find her berth easily enough, but my relative and current charge has passed out. I pin her up against the wall while I dig through her handbag to find the key. Any woman will tell you that I've just committed sacrilege. A woman's purse is sacrosanct. But I consider it a better option than leaving her to sleep it off in the hallway. I ignore anything in there except the key. Thankfully, I see nothing that might give away any of my cousin's secrets. We all have them. Oddly, it makes me wistful about Adrianna—not that my ex-love drinks, but that we have that secret love betwixt us.

I pour Lucy, boiled after just three glasses of champagne, into her bed. I make sure there is a glass of water and a tincture of willow bark on her nightstand before heading back to my own cabin. Give her three or four hours, and she'll be back up, probably only a bit the worse for wear.

I return to my stateroom to watch the scenery flow by beneath me. At first, I wonder why the cotton balls are green and vibrating until it dawns on me that I'm half a mile in the air and those puffs are actually trees swaying in a stiff wind. Horses and wagons present as fleas moving along lines between matchboxes of homes and businesses. It feels like being God looking down at the world.

The exhilaration of being the queen of all I survey wears thin in short order, but I haven't lost my amazement completely. The impressive man-made structure that is the *Majesty* still awes me. I'd love to crawl all over her and poke into every nook and cranny to understand how she does the miraculous, controlled flight that even birds and air witches are jealous of. But that is unlikely as a mere passenger. Instead, I take off the shelves a book that I've not had the privilege of yet reading, *A Tramp Abroad* by Mark Twain. I curl up on one of the couches and engage with Twain's magical words about traveling through Latin America.

# # #

A steward walks by outside my room, ringing a bell for the first late-luncheon seating. I set aside my book.

Looks like I'll have to wake up my cousin. Not only that, but the engineer wolf has disappointed me. I expected to need to bar the door against him, and instead he hasn't even shown up. A somewhat disappointing afternoon.

There is a knock at the door as I'm freshening at the china washbasin. "Come in!" I call out.

Lucy stumbles in. "What hit me?" she laments, holding her head.

"Never drank champagne?" I ask in a volume three levels lower than I'd normally use. I understand her delicate condition, having worn it more than my fair share number of times.

"I don't drink much at all. Even then, it is only a part of my husband's beer."

"That would do it."

"I didn't even know it was alcohol. It tasted so mild."

I chuckle. "I can drink most Irishmen under the table, but there are two things I am very careful with: champagne and absinthe. Both are sneaky."

"Wow, you can say that again. I was going for my fourth glass when you took me away. I don't remember much before or after that. I didn't—"

"No, you didn't embarrass yourself. I got you well away before something like that could happen."

"Good. I remember thinking how cute the first officer is. Me, well married with a husband in danger, and I'm thinking about another man. Does that make me a bad person?"

"Lucy, you are worn to a frazzle with worry, and you were drunk. Nothing you would do or could have done would surprise me, or even make me think the less of you. Well, maybe four men in your stateroom at once might raise my eyebrows."

Lucy blushes. "Stella! How could you even say such a thing?"

"Probably the bad company I keep. You see, my best friend is Daring Karie."

"The famous Whore of Boston?"

"The very same. She is a wonderful person, even in her vocation."

"We've heard of her even out in Centralia."

"I guarantee that any story you've heard about her is likely too tame by half."

"What a hussy!"

"No, Lucy," I admonish. "She doesn't plot after men." *Or women*, I don't add. "She doesn't lure men away from their wives. She doesn't keep them or even spit them out. She gives them sex and loving. Oftentimes, those she beds gain a better appreciation of love and take that back to their partners."

"You sound as if you approve of whoring," she says with a stern tone.

"I don't approve or disapprove. It is a job just like any other, as long as it isn't forced or coerced. Karie is her own woman. She has no pimp. She rents her body and her caring to men—and yes, sometimes women—because she enjoys it. No, she revels in it.

"But not all women do it because of pleasure. Some do it because that is all they have to sell. It isn't wrong, just sad. And for those forced into it, I say there is a special place in hell for their pimps."

Thoughts run across Lucy's face. She listens well. "Something to think about, cousin."

"Yes. In my book, loving is right if all parties are loved—not forced, not coerced, and not threatened. As a religious girl, this definitely puts guilt upon my soul, but it is my personal belief. Of course, this comes from a woman who has been censured by the Church for one of her liaisons. Take it with a grain of salt."

Without seeming to agree, Lucy changed the subject. "We should probably make our way to luncheon."

"Agreed."

# # #

The strains of a string quartet waft down the hall as we are two of the last to arrive. I guess being late is normal for women. It makes me feel bad, however.

The luscious chairs, which had been bound to the walls by velvet ropes during our ascent, now surround the tables. Place settings in fine white china are highlighted by the gleaming Revere silver utensils and crystal goblets. White napkins are folded like swans in the middle of each plate.

Waiters in full tuxedos stand at attention behind the head and foot of every table. The maître d' comes up to us. "Mrs. Riley and Mrs. Ochoa. You are seated at the captain's table. Please come this way."

I've never met the man, and he knows our names and where we belong. Of course, it could be because we are the only ones left to seat.

"The captain's table?" Lucy asks with just a hint of incredulity in her voice.

"Yes, ma'am. The captain was quite insistent, although it may have been the first officer's suggestion."

"Thank you, Mr. Martin," I say, reading his name off his badge.

"You are welcome."

An officer I've yet to meet holds out the chair for Lucy near the foot of the table. Mr. Martin performs the same service for me next to the captain.

The string quartet stops playing as Captain Pérez, an older, swarthy gentleman, stands. Just his presence dominates the entire room. I think that King Fredrick II probably has that same air of command. "Gentlemen and ladies, welcome to the *Majesty*," he says. A round of applause greets his deep voice that, for a Spaniard, is remarkably vacant of the Castilian accent. "My crew and I will do everything in our power to make your flight not only comfortable but as posh and blissful as possible." More applause greets him. "To the king!" he salutes in the traditional manner.

"The king!" everyone replies.

"Please serve."

The lunch served rates slightly below that of the Viscountess Adrianna's cook, and not a patch on Mrs. Simmons or even Karie's cook. Don't get me wrong, it is tasty and beautifully displayed, something Mrs. Simmons could take a lesson on. But I guess after having the best on a regular basis, great just isn't up to snuff.

Other than the food, I find luncheon at the captain's table tedious. My mother would be in her element. The other guests are also snobbish society types. I can't even really relate to what they are talking about. Parties, soirees, and balls. Who gets invited to which? Who is courting whom? The rising star of this or other noble. Court etiquette. New knights dedicated by our king. It's like a different language. One I can't even speak, as the only nobles I know are Viscount Henry Helms and his wife, assuming you ignore the dead baron, of course. After fifteen minutes of listening to this rubbish, I'm ready to shove one of those beautiful table knives into my ears so I don't have to hear it.

I mean, here we are on the most beautiful machine in the world, and they are worried about who danced with whom at the ball because someone dropped a hat. I'm about to excuse myself when I'm saved by the captain himself.

"Miss Ochoa, I understand you are a hellfighter."

His statement gets attention. Half of the long table now focuses on me. Up until now, I've been nothing more than a silent attendee who hasn't one-upped anyone at the table. I've gotten some stares for being seated at the captain's left, but nothing more than idle curiosity until now.

"That's right, Captain Pérez," I say. "I'm a member of the *Dos Campanas* in Boston."

"Then you have captured many demons in your young life."

"Quite a number, sir."

"You may call me Gustavo, Mrs. Ochoa. At least in the drawing room."

"Then you may call me Stella."

From down the table, a man rudely interjects himself into our conversation, asking, "So, how many, Stella?"

I want to boil over at the way the speaker, a rude man about a hundred pounds overweight, assumes that the permission I'd given to Gustavo to use my Christian name has somehow transferred to him. Especially after the same said blowhard earlier lectured the table on manners at court for ten minutes.

"It isn't something I've ever calculated or kept track of. It isn't like a soccer score—subdue three demons and you win, or hellfighters two, demons nil. We deal with every. Single. One." I glare at the question-asker. "But, to answer more fully, my team has dealt with over a hundred demons."

"That's quite impressive, Stella," Gustavo says. "I have to say that I don't think I've ever met a witch."

"We aren't thick on the ground, like nobles," I say, once again glaring at tubby. Witches aren't universally loved. In some ways, we are like the nobility itself. We have an ability, a gift that allows us to excel at something that many can never possibly obtain. If you aren't born to it, you must just envy those who are. Maybe one in a hundred have the capability, and only one in a thousand of those can actually do anything useful with it.

"Miss Stella, if I might ask, and you may decline if you wish," the ship's master says diffidently.

"Yes, Captain?"

"Can you demonstrate your power here in any way?"

I'm not a fan of random displays of my powers. But declining the simple request of the captain of this wonderful vessel seems ungracious. I pick up my silver spoon. I put it into my mouth, taste the silver plate, and feel the base iron underneath.

Sometimes I describe my ability to manipulate the earth as a symbiosis, but it is much more a partnership. I hold the spoon out on my palm and will it to flow like butter on a hot day. It happily agrees. I roll my hand around as the metal melts over my hand. A woman down the table gasps.

"Does that hurt?" asks the man sitting across from me.

"No. Why would it?" I respond.

"It's not hot?"

"No." Now, by rotating my hand and allowing gravity to act, I coat my hand with the metallic ooze. I order it to solidify.

"She's an illusionist. She palmed the spoon, and that's just quicksilver," fat man declares.

I hold out my hand. "Jab it. Take your knife and put it through my hand."

"I don't want to hurt you," he says, backing down.

"Captain, would you like to take a stab?"

Before he can respond, a woman to my right cries out with some vehemence. "I'll fix that witch," she cries. She reaches around her escort and jabs a steak knife down on the metallic skin protecting my own. The blade ricochets off my armored hand and pierces the tablecloth, then buries itself in the wooden surface below.

I turn toward the hate-filled woman and show my hand. The only damage is a shining scratch where the knife struck. She glares at me. I wonder what she has against witches. The event spawns some dark whispering at the table.

I offer my metallic palm to Gustavo. He shakes his head in confusion as he reaches forward. He raps at my pewter-colored hand. When his knuckles bounce off, he squeezes the tip of one of my fingers to find it solid.

"Amazing," the Captain Pérez says, leaning back. I urge the silver and iron to regain their former shape. This is harder than making it flow, as now I'm the artisan. My skills as a sculptor rank right up there with my ability to cook. That is, not much. What it produces is a mockery of a spoon. I hand the ragged utensil to the ship's master.

"That is impressive, Stella."

"Sorry about the spoon."

"No, Stella. I'm going to keep this to remind me of your skills. Can I assume that you won't abuse my ship with your powers, ma'am?"

"Captain, I wouldn't dream of damaging this glorious craft. I'm in awe of her."

"She is a beauty," Gustavo mutters in a way a romantic newlywed might talk about his wife.

Thankfully, the conversation turns away from witchcraft to cooks and servants. I take the opportunity to look out the room's surrounding windows. We are lazily turning to the right.

"Isn't that Salmon Falls down there, Captain?" I ask. From this height, the stone next to the flowing river is pockmarked with pinpricks.

"Very good, Mrs. Ochoa. Are you training to be a navigator?"

"No, sir. Just, I remember it from one of the few outings I had with my mother as a young girl. The power of ice and water to carve stone is simply amazing."

"Too true, Stella. I guess it is a lesson that nothing is too tough for someone with patience."

Remembering the geography of Massachusetts, I realize that we are quite far north, and the bow of *Majesty* continues to edge even farther northward. "Captain, why are we going so far north? Isn't Centralia well south of us?"

As sweet as the old man is, he dismisses my question with condescension. "Probably the bridge edging us around a storm."

I absently accept the reason and put it out of my head. My patience for any company has worn off, as even the captain is grating on my nerves. I can feel a nap in my near future.

"Captain and guests, if you will excuse me, I'll take my leave," I say.

"Me, also," Lucy says from the other end of the table.

As I walk by, I whisper to Lucy, "Stay if you are having fun. I just need to rest."

"I am enjoying that they think I'm a rich woman. Little do they know ..."

"Then go back. Just be careful of the champagne."

"I learned that lesson quite well, thank you, cousin."

# # #

A solid, no-nonsense knock at my door wakes me. I open my eyes just in time to see my privacy invaded by a young naval rating stepping inside. "Mrs. Ochoa?"

I thank my prescience for sleeping fully clothed. I push my skirts down over my petticoats. "What are you doing in here? This is my cabin!"

"My apologies, Mrs. Ochoa, but the captain requests your presence on the bridge."

"This couldn't wait until I answered the door?"

"Captain Pérez insisted that he wanted you as soon as possible. He authorized me to wake you if necessary."

OK, so I'm slow. "So this isn't a request, is it?"

"Of course it is, ma'am, unless you decide not to accede to it."

"Young man, you should go into politics. You'd make a great debater." I slip off the bed and reach for my boots. I realize I'm flashing my ankles to this young stud. He smells good even this far away. "I think I can get dressed by myself. Tell Gustavo that I'll be along presently."

"Yes, ma'am. I'll wait for you outside."

As I button my boots, I try to figure out what the captain could possibly need from me. Did Lucy commit some *faux pas* that requires that I bail her out of jail? Maybe she fell overboard? Maybe Carlos woke early and is terrified. I'll get nowhere just inventing ridiculous scenarios, so I hurry out to the youngster. "Lay on, McDuff."

"And damned be him that first cries, 'Hold, enough!'" my guide replies.

"Very good."

"I'm studying theatre at Boston University. This job is just to keep a roof over my head until I graduate."

"Very nice. Do you know Professor Xena?"

The boy-man blushes, but I've no clue why. "Yes, Mrs. Ochoa. I am well acquainted with her. Where might you have met her?"

"She has interviewed me for her witchcraft treatises." I keep to myself that she is the one who has defined that I'm part demon and that my lusts would gladly take this young boy's virginity multiple times over, as unstable as I am right now.

"Quite a force of nature, isn't she?" he asks as he leads me up the stairs to a door that says "Crew Only." He pushes through. Luckily I'm used to climbing steps to my bedroom in the Brick Factory. Even with that, I'm starting to get winded after the fourth flight of stairs. A society woman wouldn't have made it one. My guide must be part mountain goat.

"No question of that," I wheeze out, thinking of Xena's intensity. "What is your name?"

"Bradley, ma'am. Just two more flights of stairs, Mrs. Ochoa."

"Easy for you to say," I offer as I stand on a landing. "Give me half a second. This is worse than wearing a corset." Bradley giggles but waits patiently. "OK, let's finish this."

"Yes, ma'am." Good as his word, it is only two more flights to a door labeled "Engineering – Danger – Keep Out." "Put these in your ears, Mrs. Ochoa." He hands me two wax plugs. "They will help protect your hearing, as it is quite loud inside."

I do as I'm told. My escort opens the door to a burst of heat and steam. Even through the plugs, I can hear the engines much clearer here. My guide says something that is lost. He waves me into the steam bath. It's hotter and wetter than a public bathhouse. I'm damp all the way down to my bloomers, and not for the normal reason. The fog makes it nearly impossible to make out anything except what is two feet in front of my face. I can feel every thrum and clank of the engines as I walk the twenty feet to the bridge door. I know what is around me only because I've studied the layout.

Bradley opens the door and walks in, waving me to follow. "Civilian on the bridge," he announces.

The fog reduces as the youngster closes the door behind us. He removes his earplugs, and I follow suit.

In the clearing air, I see two of the six men on the bridge using special leather coverings to conceal dials and controls. This, more than my own work in the naval yard helping refit ships, makes me realize just how close America is to war. If they are being secretive about the capabilities of a nominally civilian craft, my king remains steadfast against the bloody English and their French allies. Loggerheads like this mean only one thing—the deaths of tens of thousands of men and boys, all to appease the vanity of that English bitch, Victoria.

"Captain Pérez? Mrs. Ochoa, at your request," the young boy says.

"Back to your duties, Bradley."

"Yes, Captain."

The bridge is a room with glass on three sides, like the dining room below. Controls line the walls in banks. I'm pleased that the archaic swords have been left at the door. Each man does wear a revolver at his waist.

A giant wooden ship-style wheel dominates the middle of the sixty-foot square room. A naval rating holds the wheel in place, but as I look out the windows, I see we are drifting to the right.

"Mrs. Ochoa, I apologize for the intrusion. But Engineer D'Oro specifically required your presence for our discussion. He will be along shortly. As some background, we have experienced an engineering failure."

"No! Your beautiful ship!" Thus, the reason the wolf of an engineer hasn't been chasing his prey. I feel better about the fact that I've been left alone.

"Yes, quite. You may have noticed that we aren't flying straight but are executing some rather unusual turns."

"I'm sorry, Captain, but I've been sleeping and haven't noticed much of anything."

"Actually, you noticed the issue at luncheon, but back then, we just thought it something we could easily fix."

D'Oro comes through a cloud of steam and a cacophony of noise as the door to the control room opens. "Excellent. Thank you for coming Mrs. Ochoa," he says.

"My pleasure, Mr. D'Oro."

The engineer turns to Captain Pérez. "Captain, I've inspected the rudder. The pinion gear, the part that allows us to turn port and starboard, has been damaged and jammed. It is severe."

"Time to repair?"

"With the proper replacement gear, four hours. Without it, never. The closest replacement is Dayton, Ohio."

"It isn't repairable, even if pulled out of service?"

The engineer shakes his head. "The pinion itself weighs close to a ton. None of our auxiliary support equipment can handle that heavy a device. And even if we could jury-rig something, we don't have the heat or the machining capability to straighten it. The *maldito* thing folded under the pressure of our takeoff. I've never seen anything like it. *Infierno*, but I've never even heard of anything like it."

Our captain clamps his jaw tightly enough to reveal the muscles bulging there. "Navigator, what is our ETA to Centralia at our current rate?"

His female navigator, in a smart uniform dress, says, "Assuming our continued skew turns, two days, fourteen hours."

Up until now, I've just been following the conversation, still wondering why I'm here. At her words, a shot of ice goes through my body. Carlos will wake up in the morning and still be in the air. This isn't good. I wonder how long I can keep him safely unconscious with our sleeping draught.

"And to Dayton?" the captain asks.

"Same assumptions and that we stop in Centralia, six days, three hours."

"Too long," the captain mutters. When the navigator starts to say something, the captain interrupts. "I know, Sidney. It isn't your fault. Nor is it Mr. D'Oro's, even though I'd like to horsewhip you both. So, Mr. D'Oro, you wouldn't have had me bring Mrs. Ochoa to the bridge just for her beauty."

"I think Mrs. Ochoa could repair the gear in place if she is willing."

Still daydreaming about how I'm going to deal with a berserk air witch, I am caught off guard. "Huh?"

"Out of the question!" Captain Pérez barks.

"One other thing before you rule out of hand, Captain. The damage to the pinion may have an effect on our attitude control on landing. I can't see any damage, but as you know, just getting to the rudder is challenging. I may have missed something critical."

"You'd have me risk a first-class passenger in the hope that she could do something?"

"Captain, Mrs. Ochoa is a hellfighter and used to taking intelligent risks. Why don't we ask her, Captain, sir?"

"First things first. Pull the drawings of the gear."

D'Oro has them in his hand and spreads them over a high table.

"Mrs. Ochoa, can you read engineering drawings?" Captain Pérez asks.

"Somewhat," I say, sidling over to the two men. The drawing shows what looks like a lady's fan—a quarter of a circle with large teeth on one end and a shaft on the other.

The engineer says, "It is folded nearly in twain along this line." He draws with his finger a ragged spar from midway along one of the straight sides to about a third of the way around the arc.

The captain holds out the spoon I'd played with earlier. "Could you straighten that, Mrs. Ochoa?"

"How big?"

D'Oro points at the five-foot human scale that is dwarfed by the lady's fan, and I begin to think about it. "Jesus, Mary, and Joseph. That weighs only a ton?"

The engineer flips another page to the top and points at another view. "See, fluted on the bottom. Not totally solid."

"I probably can iron that out, but I'll have to be in direct contact with it. I can't do it at a distance."

The engineer raises his eyebrows at the captain. Something in their eyes conveys silent communication for just a few moments before the captain asks, "Mrs. Ochoa, would you consider assisting us in our hour of need? I can assure you that the airline will be appreciative."

"Why not? Where is this pinion gear?" I ask.

"Mrs. Ochoa, are you afraid of heights?" the engineer asks.

# # #

Engineer D'Oro takes me back to my cabin so I can change. When I come out in my denim work dress, he looks me up and down. "While quite fetching, Stella, do you have a pair of trousers?"

"Why would you ask that? What woman would wear trousers?" I have visions of Xena Xavier, the demonologist at the Boston University who does just that.

"Well, the women who work in the engineering gang wear pants because of our safety equipment. Parts of it go up between, well, your limbs." He coughs and looks away.

"I don't have any. Can I make do without them?"

"Probably, but you will need something to cover your limbs unless you enjoy exposing them to the whole world, almost literally."

"Hmm," I say in a prelude to thinking over what I brought with me.

"I think Ensign Cortez is about your height. We can borrow some from her. Let's go. We have to get this done before dark."

D'Oro leads me through the engineering decks. I'm pleased with my insistence to change, as my clothes attract grease like a magnet might iron filings. I don't know how the engineer keeps his uniform without a mark on it. Whenever I dodge one of the machines, I come away dirtier. The engineer remains spotless.

"Cortez!" D'Oro's voice penetrates over the background noise that sounds like an orchestra all tuning their instruments at the same time to a different key.

"BOSS!" calls back a young black woman who is climbing down out of the pipes and aluminum girders like a panther picking its way through a jungle canopy. A smear of grease decorates her forehead, a splash of oil makes several lines across her uniform, and a smudge of soot is on her tight, narrow bottom.

"We need a pair of your pants for Mrs. Ochoa here. I need to get her into a sling."

The curly-haired woman looks me up and down. "Boss, you are an idiot."

"What did I do now?" he asks rather than attacking his subordinate for her insolence. I am liking him even more.

"While we are about the same height, I doubt she could squeeze into my pants. I mean no offense, Mrs. Ochoa. I actually envy you that you don't need to wear a bustle. *Maltido* things always make my bottom itch in a totally unladylike way."

"Well, what do you suggest, Ensign?"

"GEORGIA!" she shouts.

Another, somewhat portly, woman scrambles out of the machinery and steam. "What's up?"

"We need a pair of your pants."

"Give me two minutes." She dashes off with the speed of a rabbit chased by a coyote.

"Sorry, Mrs. Ochoa. It's not gonna fit real good, but it's best we got that's going to go over your hips," Cortez tells me.

"I think in this case, function over form is more important. Just don't ever tell my mother I said so. She insists there isn't any reason for fashion to be trumped by reality."

"This one is a firecracker, Boss," Cortez says to D'Oro. "Where did you dig her up?"

"She's standing right next to you. You can ask her and stop being rude."

"Sorry, Mrs. Ochoa. I'm more used to steam fittings, wrenches, and gears than people. They keep us hidden in here for a reason 'cause we ain't fit for real people."

"I'm not offended, Miss. Cortez. I was a working woman myself. And I do have an ample caboose."

"How tactfully put, Mrs. Ochoa," the engineer says.

"Hell, I must be slipping," I offer. "I've never had any tact, or at least so my mother claims."

Georgia comes running back, yet she doesn't seem winded. In her hands are a rather wide pair of trousers and a leather belt. "I sees that you weren't near as wide as me, miss. This should do you."

"Got somewhere I can slip them on?"

"Not really," D'Oro says. "I'll turn around."

I look at him sideways. "Cortez, help me." Georgia and Cortez take a canvas tarp. By holding it in their hands above their heads, they create a dressing screen. I sit down and slide on the pants under my dress. Georgia is very right. Without the belt, they'll just fall down around my ankles. I tighten them enough to hold them in place over my bloomers. I drop my skirts back down over them.

"Done, ladies. Thank you. Mr. D'Oro, you can turn around. I'm decent."

"Excellent," he says, but his face doesn't agree with his words. "Let's get out and repair my ship."

"Your ship?"

"Well, I let the captain run my baby around, but goldang it, I keep her running. I make her go. And right now, *Majesty* is in pain."

OK. The wolf exhibits some hidden depths.

"I'm in your hands, good sir," I offer.

Engineer D'Oro leads me and his two assistants toward the stern. There, two leather nets, or harnesses, hang from the wall. D'Oro pulls one down. "Watch me put this on. You are going to put on the other one."

"Excuse me?"

"He are tellin' the truth, miss. Ya need to wear it to go out to the rudder. Ain't no other way," Cortez says.

D'Oro puts his legs into two straps. One goes tight up into his nether regions, and the other he buckles around his thighs near the knee. Then he shuffles the rest up over his shoulders, very much like the modified belts Viscount Helms installed in the poderabile. One strap goes over each shoulder, each of which splits into two. One of each meets at a brass buckle in the middle of the chest; the other two wrap around the shoulders and triple button to similar straps coming from the back. Next, he brings a wide belt around his waist, with three pawls, and cinches it tight above his hips. Finally, he pulls the two straps that run up through his crotch to weave through a buckle and pawl on his waist belt.

"Mrs. Ochoa, I want you safe. Wearing a maintenance sling and getting it on you correctly isn't simple. I can help you, although it means taking some liberties with you. Or you can have Cortez and Georgia help you, or both."

"While I think I could enjoy liberties you would take, for the sake of my reputation, I believe I'll have the ladies help me."

"As you wish."

The engineering women pull all the straps tighter than my mother did on my corset at my coming-out ball. I think the kindest thing I say is "Ow." After several minutes as a dressmaker's dummy, I offer, "I'll never complain about a bustle, a brassiere, or even a corset ever again."

The women laugh. "We gots to make it tight, miss. We don't want you falling out. If'n you did, the captain would whale on us something fierce," Cortez says.

Georgia agrees by nodding.

Once the two sadists get done abusing me, D'Oro looks me over. He can't leave well enough alone and tightens the turnbuckle over my right shoulder. "Now to hook you up," he says. "I'm going to go first so you can see for yourself that we aren't asking you to do anything we don't do."

The women use clips on woven metal cables to connect to six different steel circles built into his leather harness, one at each knee, one on either side of the waist, and one on each shoulder. He looks like a marionette with his lines going up to a scaled-down, flatcar—at least that is what it looks like. Two train rails run overhead and through slots in the door in front of us. The small car has wheels on top of the tracks, and all six of D'Oro's wires go up and connect to it. The engineering assistants connect similar cables to me. I feel like I'm wearing multiple tails, as they swish with every movement.

If it weren't for the fact that I could control the metal wires, I'd worry that I was being trussed up for some ritual sacrifice. D'Oro pulls a string next to the door in an obvious pattern—three long, two short. We are so close to the engines that I hear the chuff, chuff of them winding down slower and slower. Soon there are no mechanical sounds. Many noises of escaping steam and popping of boilers, but nothing of movement.

Two short bursts of a steam whistle sound, followed by three long. "That's our cue. The captain has stopped the engines so that we can have minimal wind while we are out," D'Oro says. He opens the door to show an expanse of nothing.

Well, that isn't quite true. I can see the stern of the gas bladder and frame curving up and away. The lower two-thirds of the rudder cross shows below the balloon. But below that is nothing but a panorama of the countryside, half a mile down.

D'Oro gets into the doorframe and leans forward. All I can think of is what he will look like to anyone who might find his remains. D'Oro makes a fist with his thumb up. He jerks it up, and his crew haul on some ropes, which actually shorten his metal cables so that his thighs and hips are level with his head. He is lying facedown over nothing. He reaches up behind himself and does something until he swings all the way around to face me.

Speaking a little louder over some incidental wind gusts, he says, "I'm not crazy when I say I want you to come into the doorframe and lean out."

Part of me wants to tell him to go hang. The other part sees him flying like a bird and is excited by the prospect. I stand in the doorway.

"We will lift you up now, miss." The next thing I know, I'm floating up near the railroad tracks on a car of my own. Looking down, I see nothing but an abyss. Tiny creeks run between the crenellations of a rumpled green-and-brown napkin. At least until it sinks in that the tiny creeks are raging rivers and they aren't folds in a napkin but rather hills and mountains.

"I think you can tell the captain that I am now!" I call out.

"You are what?" Robert asks.

"Afraid of heights."

All three of them laugh at me. I'm not paralyzed in fright but suffering from a sinking feeling in my gut and acid filling my belly. "We all go through it, Stella. You are doing great. Look at me. Focus on me."

I look at the handsome man, and more specifically his intense gray eyes. It helps. My stomach stops sending emergency messages. *I'm just lying on my bed about to get raunchy with this man*, I think. That turns the feelings in my gut in a much different direction.

"Now, my team is going to pull us out to the rudder. Just let them do the work. It won't be very fast." The engineer makes some symbols with his hand, and we both begin to move up the curve of the dirigible's stern in small, jerky motions. I look up and see the pulley wires being used to drag us up the incline. Mild winds buffet me side to side. I'm pleased that there is no strong wind. I can't imagine being tossed around like a *piñata* in anything more than a gentle breeze.

"Do you really do maintenance up here?" I shout.

"Often. Painting is a regular occurrence. Sometimes we have to adjust the rudder mechanism. Every trip, we inspect the entire gas bladder and superstructure!" he yells back.

"Why not do it on the ground?"

"Ladders would be too long. Safer this way. Sometimes we have so many crew members in harnesses that the *Majesty* looks like a floating ant hill."

"Goodness."

We pass the stern of the main balloon and structure. Another thirty feet, or maybe a skosh more, ahead is the rudder. Think of a massive weather vane about thirty feet high. From the side, it looks like a V, but on the end, where I am, it has the shape of a plus sign. The narrow end of the V is connected to a proportionally large ball joint.

Just below the ball joint is a big, round wooden pulley, maybe ten feet across below the fan-shaped brass pinion gear we are here to fix. And it is obvious why it needs fixing. About a third of it has folded down and been pulled up under the wooden pulley. It even seems like the wooden disk sits at a slight angle. Even at this distance, I can feel the bad pour of the brass that caused the original weakness. It feels like someone started to fill the mold of this gargantuan device and then stopped. Then they added more metal later, expecting that cold joint to be as strong as the rest.

Out of the lee of the dirigible's main body, the wind is a bit stiffer. "Can you fix it?" Robert yells.

"As long as you can get me close enough to touch, it shouldn't be a problem!" I shout back. He nods.

We haven't stopped our slow, lurching movement toward the tail. I hope there is a barrier at the end of our railing. Otherwise, we might just be pulled right off into space. Despite the dark thought, I am beginning to loosen up and enjoy the sensation of flying. I wonder if I should have been born an air witch. But, alas, I'm an earthbound type. Nice as this is, I don't think I'd like a steady diet of it.

Five more minutes see us to the gear. The tracks take us right below it. "Can you reach it, Mrs. Ochoa?" he asks. It is at an awkward angle above me. My arm and body can't quite touch the surface. I think about the problem for a moment.

I kick my foot over my back. With some extending and contortions, I can unbutton the shoe. Tucking the boot down my blouse, I reach back again and rip a hole in my stocking. Now, by kicking up as far as I can stretch, my bare toes and feet touch the cold metal. The earthen metal welcomes me. My eyes close as I feel its sense of purpose and the ache of its badly forged self.

First, to iron out the bend. Mentally it is no more difficult than unfolding a piece of paper. The metal thanks me, as it has been forced into an unnatural position, like someone with their arms twisted up behind their back. I hear a wooden creak above me as the pressure on the wooden reduction gear is removed.

"You know, I can feel you doing that," Engineer D'Oro says to me.

"You can?"

"When you released the metal and made it spongy, it felt like the entire structure was made out of taffy, and I wasn't even touching it. It's like I could hear you beckoning it to go limp."

My eyes snap open. I look into his, and my middle melts. Even floating in the sky four furlongs over anything resembling solid earth, my lusts are getting the better of me. It's been much too long since I've felt another person's flesh against mine. I feel like what opium addicts claim to have without their dragon—a longing deep in my soul, blotting out anything but the need to satisfy it. I want nothing more than to tear off his uniform and perform aerial sex acts in front of the entire world.

Xena Xavier warned me about my increased lusts. They've never been so intense before.

I bite my lip hard enough to draw blood. It drives off the craving enough for me to say, "That's remarkable. Sounds like you may be a latent earth witch. You should investigate that."

"Do you know anyone—"

"I can give you several earth witches who teach. Let's finish this, first."

"Agreed."

I've lost the connection to the metal. I have to do contortions again to touch it with my bare foot. I must look foolish twisting and stretching in odd ways.

The brass doesn't quite reach for me in its eagerness. The metal no longer feels cold to my toes. I can once again feel the form in my head. The removal of pressures within the brass structure lets me know that the gear has found its original shape again.

Now to solve the weakened area of the gear. Imagine a good meat pie, one with a hard, crusty outside and a liquid inside. That's what I do to the plate of brass. I turn the middle to liquid, leaving only the thinnest skin intact to hold in the gooey center. I now mentally whisk up the middle of the pie so it no longer has a boundary, and thus a weakness. I release the metal to resume its natural state. It returns to a solid, but a uniform solid that won't break.

I take a big breath before opening my eyes. No matter how much sense of self I get from communing with earth and metals, it still drains me and excites me at the same time. "All done," I sigh just above the sound of the thin wind.

"That was incredible," Robert says. "I don't know what you did there, but it had me tingling all over." He yanks on a cord. Some form of signal. I feel myself going backward a little faster than I'd gone outward.

"That definitely sounds like an earth witch power," I observe. "It could be very useful to you in this trade."

"If I can do that sort of thing with metals, you're damned right it would!" Robert is like a little kid who's eaten a few too many sticks of candy right before bedtime. I find his enthusiasm stoking the fires in my belly, and I'm wondering if he would be that excited all over my body. As a result, neither of us is paying any attention to what is going on around us.

Honk, honk! comes the sounds of a gaggle of migrating, cackling geese. I barely see their classic V formation before they are on top of us. The black-white-and-gray goose leading the V flies right between us.

"Ahh!" I screech in surprise. Face-to-face, they are as big as a mastiff.

"Don't worry, they won't—"

Ironically, my left shoulder support wire gongs like a bell as the bird crashes into it. Then it snaps like a dried twig in a windstorm. Feathers explode as the dead carcass of the bird lands on my back. The fowl following behind its mate performs a death dive that sheers the wire of my left hip.

The world slows down as I find my left shoulder plummeting. Falling yanks at my gut with a primal urge to scream, but I don't even have that length of time. The boot falls out of my bodice and disappears into the distance below me. My body twists and is caught by the remaining wires, hanging mostly head down on my left side. The bird carcass slides off my back to disappear below me, its lifeless wings fluttering in the wind generated by its plunge.

"HELP!" I yell, my arm groping for any purchase. Somehow, Robert is suddenly right next to me. He latches onto my flailing arm and rights me.

"Don't panic, Stella. I've got you. I won't let you go. Any one of those wires will hold you up."

"Tell that to the damned geese!" I yell.

"They are all past us now." He's right. The ragged chain of birds, with two links cut out of it, flies off into the distance, honking even more than before.

"I think Carlos may have had this right. Heights belong to the birds. I don't think I like this anymore."

"I'm sure you don't. Let's get us back as quick as possible. Hold on," he says, reaching up over my head with his free hand.

"Hold on? What do you mean—" The feeling of falling returns, if not quite as severe. Instead of moving back toward the door in short jerks, we start accelerating like a toboggan down Flagstaff Hill. My mind is too frazzled to think straight. "Ahh!" I screech again.

"I've got you, Stella," Robert says. He moves closer and wraps his arms around me. "You're safe."

I'm quaking with his arms around me. I'd rather have his legs around me, but I'll take what I can get. I lean my face forward and kiss him, smack on the mouth. He might think I'm being thankful for him saving me, and there is more than a bit of that, but my intentions are much more direct. My meaning can't be mistaken for anything else as I shove my tongue between his lips.

My fear dissolves as another portion of my mind flares.

Our dangling ride speeds up for an unmeasurable length of time during our kiss. His mouth responds with a passion that I'd hoped for. Swirling around mine, his tongue replies in kind to my invasion. His head turns to the side to give each of us a better angle into each other's mouth.

As much as I want his hands in other places, I'm happy to feel the steadfastness of his grip and support. It brightens the fire in my crotch. I want to mount him. I want him to mount me. Anything. I'll be his. Anything, just to put out this fire in my belly.

The carts jostle as they, and we, slow—in more ways than one. Unfortunately, I lose the attention of my engineer's lips. I open my eyes to find us sliding through the doorway we left from. Over Robert's shoulder,

I can see the distant rudder and even a small cloud of drifting feathers below us. The man knows how to kiss if he kept me centered for that long. I wonder if they have a course in oral loving at engineering college.

"What happened, Boss?"

"*Maldito* birds flew into Mrs. Ochoa's wires and snapped them."

"Are you alright, Mrs. Ochoa?"

I take a shaking, deep breath as they lower me. "I think so."

"Luckily they hit the wires instead of her," D'Oro says.

"Luckily?" I ask with an air of incredulity.

"Yes. The kinetic energy of one of those birds is high. Say a ten-pound bird at forty miles per hour. Energy is one half the mass times the velocity squared. Mass must be in slugs. So, say ten divided by thirty-two, or about a third of a slug. Forty miles per hour is roughly sixty-four feet per second. Put those together, and get six hundred fifty-three foot-pounds. Your standard pistol bullet has roughly two to three hundred foot-pounds. Imagine what the bird would do to your lovely body."

"You figured it out that fast?" I ask, as my feet thankfully touch down onto the deck. Sure, I can do my figuring as anyone else who graduated grammar school, but Engineer D'Oro completed it as fast as he could talk and knew all the formulas.

"Yeah? What of it? It's relatively straightforward."

"Well, I want to thank you for rescuing me."

"You are quite welcome, Mrs. Ochoa, on all counts. Thank you for fixing my broken ship."

I'd like to wave it off as nothing, but my heart still hasn't stopped racing at about eight thousand beats a minute—from two different causes.

"Boss, the bridge messaged four times. They want an update after those jolts," Cortez says.

The naval engineer replaces the glorious man who saved me. He turns to me and says in a stiffly formal manner, "Mrs. Ochoa, I hope you won't be upset if I leave you to the tender mercies of these two of my crew. I must report our success."

I reach up and wipe some of my lipstick from the corner of his mouth. "Not at all, Mr. D'Oro. May I expect you at the captain's table for dinner?"

Robert blushes. I see a smirk on Cortez's face. The two female engineers focus on the task of unhooking me instead of the tableau with their boss. "Very likely, Mrs. Ochoa."

"I'll be happy to receive you." The coldness of the wooden planks beneath my bare foot gather just a bit of my attention. "Oh, and tell your captain he owes me a new pair of stockings and boots."

#

The note on my dressing table is on a naval message form that says, in short, that the captain desires the pleasure of my company at dinner. It isn't quite an order but as close to one without him exercising his full authority. *Damned and double damned.*

My appetite isn't for food. My libido races away, dragging me behind it. I never asked to be part demon. Why can't I have levels of desire like a normal woman? I feel like a steam engine with the safety valve stuck. My throbbing sex calls to me. I really just want to lie in my bed and rub the little man in the boat until I'm fit to be around the rest of mankind—say sometime next week. I feel like nitroglycerine in an oven, right on the bare edge of exploding.

With a heavy sigh, I manage to curb my passions enough to dress for supper. I am keeping my composure for the walk to Lucy's cabin only by counting each vibration of the engine through the floorboard. This unfortunately makes me think of piston thrusts, which makes me think of another kind of thrusting.

I wish my Aaron were here. All of this would be moot. In our short life together, he kept a lid on my lusts—not tamped down like a frigid dowager, but at least held in check.

I need to be in someone else's presence. It will keep me at least ladylike in act and deed if not in mind. I knock on my cousin's door. She opens it with a smile.

"Stella. Are you ready for supper?"

"Absolutely, cousin of mine. I could eat a horse."

"So, how was your adventure with the rudder?"

"I don't think I will ever exactly love heights in the future."

"Oh?" Luciana asks as she takes my arm and starts off for the banquet room.

"Well, dangling over a mile of empty space by your toenails doesn't exactly make one love the empty space."

"No! Seriously?" she snaps in astonishment. "They wouldn't do that to you!"

"Relax. I'm exaggerating, Lucy. With the exception of the goose, I was never in any danger."

"Goose? What does a goose have to do with anything?"

"Haven't you seen those black-white-and-gray migrating birds out the windows?"

"Of course. At first, it was really fun being up near them. Taking the flight to Boston, I went steerage. I didn't get to see anything. But I still don't understand how a migrating goose matters to your repairs."

"I'll tell you. Two of those crazy things honked their way right into my support wires. Broke them like a bit of thread."

"Oh, mercy! What happened?" she asks. "I'm dealing with possibly losing my husband, and now this."

"I didn't fall, obviously. It just felt like I would. Rober— The chief engineer managed to grab hold of me and keep that part of my body up. Apparently, I was never in any real danger, but it sure didn't feel that way."

"Remind me never to go outside to try to fix a dirigible."

"You remind *me*, cousin."

We both laugh as we walk down the stairs to the dining room. At the top of the stairs that go down into the glass dining room stands the immaculately groomed and pressed maître d' next to his podium.

"Ah, Mrs. Ochoa," Officer Martin says with what below his waxed handlebar mustache must be a sneer. Now, I don't know if his mouth is always puckered like he's eaten a green persimmon, nor am I sure his tone is condescending. So I hold in my desire to read him the riot act.

"Well, I am here, Mr. Martin. And don't forget Mrs. Riley."

"Yes." I swear he looks down his nose at Luciana over his *pince-nez* glasses. "I see you ladies are fashionably late."

I turn my head to Lucy in question. She shakes her head and adds a shrug. I open my reticule and pull out my husband's pocket watch, the one I've carried since it was returned to me after his death. It announces five past the hour.

"Well, Mr. Martin, I see we are only five minutes late. We are obviously way too early. I apologize for our *faux pas*. We'll take a stroll around the deck to ensure we don't mess with the staff's plans." *More than one can play suet-head.*

"Absolutely, cousin," Lucy says, taking my proffered arm. We turn, but not before Officer Martin's face goes from sneer to consternation.

"Ladies, I think you've misunderstood."

"Oh?"

"Seven o'clock dinner is when serving begins, not when you are to be seated. The meal has actually started."

"Did you experience that on your other flight?" I ask Lucy.

"No, we just showed up around mealtime and managed a sandwich if we were lucky."

"In either case, I'm willing to offer a conditional apology to the captain for my tardiness," I say, handing forth an olive branch that this officious bumpkin can grasp.

To everyone's relief, he isn't a complete *bufón*. "Excellent. Captain Pérez is expecting you. If you ladies will follow me?"

The man walks in mincing steps that make me even less enamored with him. The captain's table is full except for the two spots for Lucy and me. All of the men at the table stand in unison.

"Mrs. Riley, if you would be so good as to sit to the right of Doctor Hogue," Martin says. Doctor Hogue holds Luciana's chair for her. "And Mrs. Ochoa, if you would have a seat at the captain's right." I find myself between the captain and the chief engineer. A brief war of facial expressions between them begins as the two vie for the boon of seating me. The captain earns a frown from Robert as the ship's master seats me.

"Welcome, Mrs. Ochoa," Captain Pérez says.

I don't try to duck anything. "I'm sorry for our tardiness, Captain."

"Nonsense," he says. From the scowls of the other passengers at the table, I feel I've committed a crime just below treason. The pompous nobles can stuff it into their pipes and smoke it.

My passions won't wait much longer. I reach under the table for Robert's thigh. The engineer snaps his head to search my face as I give him a tender squeeze. I wish I could slip my foot out of my boot and run it up his calf. I don't know any better way to let a man know my intentions short of unbuttoning his pants or taking off my dress.

Not knowing about me panting after his officer, the ship's master continues. "How can the guest of honor be late?"

The captain has gained my attention. "Guest of honor?" I ask.

I almost squeak when I feel Robert's fingers teasing my hand out of sight beneath the table.

Instead of answering me, the captain picks up his fork and taps his glass. What little conversation has been taking place throughout the room ends. The orchestra stops playing. "Guests, I want to tell you a tale of bravery and sacrifice. One of your number has gone above and beyond the duty of a mere passenger. In fact, she has done something that not but a small portion of our crew might have attempted."

Pompous and overblown. I just want to get out of here and follar *like a bitch in heat until I can seal away the infernal desires of my body.*

"Our ship, the *Majesty*, suffered some damage on liftoff." There are several gasps from ladies around the room. A buzz of hushed conversations begins. Captain Pérez stomps on it hard by raising his voice above the din. "I want to assure you that at no time were any of you in any danger. The *Majesty* was airworthy even with the impairment." More than one woman relaxes her shoulders. The male passengers nod as if they already knew this. Oh, my word, what *pretendientes* men are.

"But the engineering casualty would have delayed us by weeks on our crossing to Seattle. Fortunately for all of us, we have Mistress Earth Witch Stella Ochoa as a passenger. Our chief engineer, Robert D'Oro, took Mrs. Ochoa outside the balloon, where she was able to straighten our damaged gear."

When the captain says his name, my seducer pulls his hand away like a schoolboy caught with his hand in the cookie jar. The only way anyone can possibly see our less-than-socially-correct patty fingers is if they themselves are under the table.

"Even on the ground, this would be no simple task. But we made it even more difficult by suspending her from an engineering harness above half a mile of open space." The female guests put their hands to their mouths with eyes wide. The men, including some of the crew, shake their heads, indicating they wouldn't have been so brave. *Nobles and soft businessmen*, I think. Maybe I shouldn't have traveled first class. I'm sure that in second class there would be real people who understand work and reasonable risk.

"And, if that isn't heroic enough, two of her safety lines were snapped by migrating geese! It left her dangling above a certain death. In the process, she lost the boots right off her feet."

I'd have just as well forgotten about both of those. The rest of the room is now rapt with attention, half on the ship's master and half on me.

"But our heroine calmly let herself be pulled back inside."

Like hell I did. I just about peed myself and just about raped his engineer in the middle of the air.

"And because of her heroic efforts, we are now good as new. With a bit more steam, will arrive at our first stop, Centralia, on schedule. All thanks to Mistress Witch Stella Ochoa." A crescendo of applause ripples across the dining hall. The captain won't let it just die. "Let's all raise a glass to Mrs. Stella Ochoa. To the queen of the hour. Long live the queen!"

"Long live the queen," the room toasts in unison.

"And before our queen is deluged with well-wishers, I have to give you, Mrs. Ochoa, my heartfelt thanks. While I'm sure the Boston and Seattle Airline will be properly grateful, you may travel free on any vessel that I'm the captain of."

I get another round of applause. I never wanted to be a stage star.

"Speech! Speech!" some idiot calls out from the room. It grows until I can't deny it. I really wish I could properly thank the moronic prompter by dropping him through the floor. Unfortunately, my witchcraft can't affect glass, and I don't know which of them called me out. I stand up, releasing my finger's grip on my real prize.

"Let me correct the captain on one item. His gear is not good as new. I did the best I could, but please remember that spoon," I say, reminding him of the less-than-perfect return of the liquid metal to a mockery of its original shape. "I'm not an artist or an engineer. My modeling capabilities are only fair. I'd replace that gear as soon as possible."

The master nods to Robert, who nods back. Then the captain says, "Seattle. The engineer assures me we will have no issues until long after that time. We'll replace it in Seattle."

"Good. But I'm just going to say this. Heights are not for me. Next time, you are on your own." This earns some general laughter, allowing me to sit down and dinner to be served.

I certainly don't dine in a very ladylike manner. I gobble down each course. One would think that I'm competing against the table in some food-eating contest. I race so that I have time in between courses to paw the gentleman to my right. He moves his leg closer to encourage my attention. His fingers walk all over my lap and belly as well, enough that I can feel every callous and scar that make it clear that Mr. D'Oro earns his living with those powerful hands.

Jesus, but the dinner stretches interminably. My bloomers feel like a swamp, and my breasts ache for want of touching. I don't think my passions have held me in this much sway even the day before my wedding night. Just as I believe dinner will all end, the captain rings his glass again.

"Fellow travelers, we have one more gift for our queen of the hour."

Please let it be an engineer in my bed! I shout in my head in a most unladylike way. *Oh, and a guard outside to ward off people concerned about my cries.* The daydream lasts only as long as a soap bubble might. The waitstaff carries into the room an enormous cake in the fan shape of the gear I repaired. The kitchen staff have outdone themselves, as even the frosting resembles the golden hue of the shiny brass gear. The band plays "The American King Forever" by John Philip Sousa.

I lean over to Robert and whisper, "What an overblown bit of nonsense."

He replies out loud, "Nothing less than you deserve, Mrs. Ochoa."

The captain speaks as the music trails off. "Mrs. Ochoa, I agree with my chief engineer. You truly are the queen of the hour. We owe you a great debt. Would you be good enough to cut the cake?" he asks, handing me his sword, hilt first.

As I take the blade, it drags down in my hands with the tip hitting the floor. I reach up to the metal barrier between the handle and the blade, and touch it, communing with it. It becomes part of me and no longer seems as heavy. It feels as if it is nothing more than balsa wood. I lift the point up to the confection. The lettering on the cake reads, "To Engineer Stella Ochoa. More power than any steam engine. The passengers and crew of the *Majesty.*" It almost seems a shame to abuse the work of art, but applause breaks out as I make the first cut.

I hand the sword back to the captain, who passes it off to a steward, who cleans it. A pair of servers continue cutting the cake with a regular kitchen knife. One cuts, and the other delivers the lemon cake. I receive the first piece on a tiny china plate with a silver dessert fork. The captain's attention is drawn to his other passengers as he stops at each table in turn.

I sit back down, hoping this won't turn into a tedious after-dinner party. I have a leaden balloon of hunger in my middle, not for food but for lust. I can actually feel drips down my leg sticking my bloomers to my flesh. I'm surprised I don't have a visible cloud of musk around me.

Slowly the focus goes off me and onto the chef's masterpiece—both tart and sweet at the same time. The crumb is light and airy, so it tastes like I am eating a flavored cloud, not a stodgy mess many cakes can turn into.

"Your cook is quite skilled," I say to Robert. "I've had desserts from some of the finest chefs in Boston, and this cake tops them."

Robert, still sitting next to me, offers *en sotto voce,* "I certainly believe that there is a much tastier dish here."

There are more than one pair of eyes still on me. I dare not whisper back. I must keep things completely above board. "Mr. D'Oro, I'd really like to meet your cook sometime before I leave."

"I think that may be arranged," he says aloud before whispering, "I believe there is another request you might have fulfilled long before that."

I bite back a prurient and imprudent answer with clenched teeth. I stand up. The gentlemen all stand as I do. "Thank you all for your approval, but I believe I need to retire for the evening. The events of the day have left me knackered. I bid you all a good night."

"Room G06," I whisper toward the brawny engineer.

"Stella!" Luciana exclaims at my brazen offer. I hadn't noticed her get so close to me. She pulls me away from the table to talk to me one-on-one. "What would Father Juan think?"

"Might just egg me on after my last partner."

"Stella!" she says, shocked.

"Listen, Lucy. I am my own woman. You aren't my mother, my lover, my husband, or my priest. I'll flirt with or even take to my bed whomever I chose."

A flow of emotions flies across her face. They race too fast for me to categorize. "I'm sorry, Stella. I am just thinking of how I can protect you. I want you safe and happy."

I laugh. "I've never been safe, but generally can take care of myself. As far as happy ..." I steal a glance at Chief Engineer Robert D'Oro. "Yes, happy is likely to be achieved."

"You could stay and dance instead?" she says, making it a weak alternative suggestion.

"You dance your way, I'll dance mine. And lay off the champagne."

#

I hustle to my berth as quickly as ladylike decorum permits. As soon as the door is closed behind me, I start peeling layers in the near darkness. I don't even make a pretext of being neat about it. After untying them, I step out of my skirt and petticoats at the foot of my bed. I unbutton my bodice and drop it on the bed. I sit on the settee to unbutton my shoes. Each of them goes flinging across the room, followed by my stockings. I slip out of my bloomers, which I can probably wring liquid out of. They smell like a whorehouse on payday. I undo my brassiere.

Naked as the night is long, I examine my clean clothes for something suitable to greet my suitor in. I hadn't been expecting company on the trip, or I would have packed the heart-stopping lingerie I had made by Paula Simpson, my seamstress. I had them made to wear for Adrianna. But because of our forbidden relationship, they have never left their original boxes.

I settle on my best bloomers and a chemise that does little to hold up my bosoms. My hair cascades down my back as I remove my jade *peineta*. There is a tad of guilt, as Adrianna and her husband, Henry, gave me that hair comb.

Now ready for my liaison, I run around cleaning up after my own chaos. My heart is pounding like a two-year-old filly's just crossing the finish line. My fresh underthings are already sopped. I'm looking for my second shoe when a knock interrupts me. I dash to stand at the side of the bed.

"Who is it?"

"Engineer D'Oro."

My chest tightens in the guilt of cheating on my dead husband and Adrianna, the lady love I can never have. I take two deep breaths. One to tell the unwanted emotion to peddle its wares elsewhere. The other I use to cast off some of my nerves. Belatedly remembering my scarred body, I turn my right side toward the door so that only it is visible in the pale light.

"Come in, Robert. The door is open."

The door opens, and he comes through into the dim light. I'm silhouetted like some cheap trollop in a fancy house. I hear a low whistle.

"I didn't want to mistake your meaning, Stella. You don't owe me anything. I can just—"

"There is no misunderstanding, Robert. I know I don't owe you anything, but you do owe me something. And I intend to collect tonight. Right now." I slip the chemise off one shoulder with a little shrug. Robert's Adam's apple dances up and down as he swallows hard. "Now shut that door before I give a show to every passing guest."

Robert closes the door, sealing himself inside with a wild, lascivious woman.

My lusts aren't going to let me take this slow, or easy. I walk up to him and unbutton his vest, and then his blouse underneath. He stands there like a prey animal hypnotized in place. I press my lips against his chest. His sweat and the few fine hairs he has there tickle my nose. I breathe in his scent as a drunkard guzzles his first pint after abstaining for months.

Robert loses his shock. His hands find their way to my loose top. His hands roam over my barely restrained breasts, seeking and finding my areolas. They aren't difficult to locate, as they stand out hard, like steel rivets.

"Yesss," I hiss against his muscular chest. He takes the hint and rolls them between thumb and forefinger.

I must have been with Karie too long. I immediately seek out his nipple with my mouth. I suck it in and nibble.

"Hey," he exclaims.

"I'm sorry. I just thought maybe you would like it as much as a woman does."

"I did. It just surprised me."

"Then shut up and enjoy!" I cover his mouth with mine, thrusting my tongue deep. His teeth are remarkably straight and smooth. He retaliates by exploring my mouth.

His hands wander around my waist to pull me closer. In the process, he stokes my fires as they move down to grab my derriere. Now it's my turn to moan, right into his mouth.

I break the kiss and make my way down to gnash on his other nipple.

I hear a growl in his throat. To his credit, he doesn't stop touching me. His big, calloused hands reach up under my top to maul my loose breasts more roughly than a dairy farmer milking a cow. I do like them handled in rowdy excess. I revel in the intimate touch as my breathing starts getting ragged.

I want him to be touching somewhere else as well. I have to be soaked through my bloomers by now. To get my mind off the heat down there, I slide down to my knees. I yank at his trousers, but they don't budge off his hips. He undoes the hidden button holding them in place. I all but tear them off him. A solid, fleshy member is my reward.

His beautiful penis rivals a hammer in length, even if not terribly big around. My Aaron was built like a horse and stretched me from our very first time. Of course, as long as it has been since I've had a man, I'm probably back to being almost virginal in my tightness. But that is for later. First I am going to taste it.

"Jesus, Stella."

4—Tuesday, November 20, 1888

Awakening is sharp and clear, even if I am languid about doing anything at all about it. The coolness of the bed announces that I'm alone. I don't even need to open my eyes. Sometime after midnight, he mentioned that he had to get up early to man his post for landing. Even before our third and fourth honeyfugle, I thanked him for pleasing me. Men somehow find it surprising to be recognized for their efforts.

Taking a deep breath, I let it out as a sigh of contentment. I take stock of myself. The need that gnawed at my middle for much too long has fled with one of either my three spends under Robert's pounding hips, the one on top of him, or the one he gifted me with his mouth. I hope our amorous antics didn't shock the neighbors too much. I wasn't particularly quiet or stinting of my praise for the man's attention.

A slight sting from my velvet doesn't surprise me. I'd forgotten how nice the roughness and weight of a man can be. My bosoms ache from being mauled by my lover. He apparently enjoyed them very much, placing love bites all over them, even the scarred edge. In fact, his discovery of my disfigurement brought caring tenderness followed by the rough loving I needed.

My completely nude state in this morning's bright sunshine makes me frisky again. "You've had quite enough," I mutter to my body. Besides, as tender as I am, I don't think I could touch the little man in the boat without screeching in pain.

I sit up and stretch, opening my eyes for the first time. I yawn in a very unladylike way. My ears pop. Wondering what time it is, I look around for the clock to see it is nearly ten in the morning. Looking out the window, I can see trees as something more than the puffballs they were when I hung out over nothing.

Goodness, but I need to get respectable. I crawl out of the bed to find a rose on the nightstand. *That romantic fool*, I think. After the loving he gave me, I really owe him something, not the other way around. There is a note scrawled in a man's hand. "I trade you this beauty for yours.

Your bloomers are my trophy."

Well then. As I stand, I smile at the tenderness of abused back muscles. Looks like we are even after all.

I take advantage of the washbasin to clean up the worst of my night's excesses. My nether lashes take a good deal of scrubbing, as I'd told him that we didn't need Spanish safes to couple. I didn't tell him why I can't get pregnant. Thanks to my demon-loving ancestress, I could take on a full regiment without swelling, but that is my secret.

I wipe down the rest of me, noting the handprint-shaped bruises on my chest. Damned man doesn't know his own strength. I pull up my bag and dig out my arnica tincture. With a bit of cloth, I rub it over the darkened patches. I feel one sting as I brush the alcohol-based liquid over a raw patch of skin.

"Whew! Probably best that I'm getting off *Majesty* today. I don't know if I could take another night like that."

If my body got a vote, it would probably like to try another one.

#

"There you are, Stella. I knocked on your door three times this morning but got no answer." Luciana stands on the dining room floor with about sixteen other first-class passengers.

I don't reply, as I have a mouthful of bagel with schmears and lox. Sex takes a lot out of a girl. I need to stoke my boiler. When I manage to clear my mouth, I offer, "Dead to the world, cousin," before stuffing my mouth with another bite that is anything but ladylike.

Lucy sneaks up next to me and murmurs, "Did you ... You know. Last night?"

This time I mumble around my food. "Which answer do you want to hear?"

"Stella!"

"Be nice. We have your husband to save, remember?"

My cousin's demeanor on this trip has been one of a giddy traveling companion. My comment eliminates the girlish in Lucy, with worry lines forming back on her face. Now I'm sorry I brought it up. It had to come out sometime, but there's no reason to steal someone's happiness.

"Mrs. Ochoa?" comes a new feminine voice. I turn to find someone I recognize, but now my addled brain won't dredge up a name.

"Yes ..." I let my voice trail off.

"You may not remember me. I'm Susan Queensbury of the *Boston Globe*," she says, offering her hand. Susan stands at least four inches higher than me but hasn't got more than a hundred pounds on her prominent bones.

"Miss Queensbury! You did the article about my stabbing and that piece on the explosion glider. I didn't know you were on the *Majesty*."

"Yes. I'm on my way to Seattle to do an article about the corruption in the local governments."

"It's nice to see you again. May I introduce my cousin, Luciana Ri—"

"Riley, yes. We met earlier in the trip. Hello again, Mrs. Riley."

"So why haven't I seen you before now?" I ask.

"Oh, I don't get to travel first class, Mrs. Ochoa. My paper sends me second or sometimes steerage if I insist on going via dirigible. They'll pay for first class on the transcontinental railroad, but as that is mostly freight, it would get me there sometime next century."

I smile like I even have any experience in what she is talking about. I've rarely left Boston.

Lucy says, "Not that I'm looking down on anyone, nor would I tell anyone, but how did you get into the first-class dining? I would have thought Officer Martin would have porcupines in breech position."

"Oh, that is very simple. I bribed him."

I look at my cousin, and we both nod. Sounds like the pompous little creep in taking advantage of his position. Offhandedly, I wonder how much it cost her. "So you aren't here on just a social visit."

"No, Mrs. Ochoa. I wondered if I could have a few minutes of your time. I wanted to get your firsthand account of your death-defying repairs to the *Majesty*—for the readers back in Boston."

I screw up my face. Lucy laughs. She must know me better than I've given her credit for. "Miss Queensbury, I want more notoriety like I'd like to be burned at the stake." Funny I should pick that choice, but I've had that happen.

"I don't know if you've realized it, Mrs. Ochoa, but you've become a popular folk hero in Boston."

"For doing nothing more—"

Susan interrupts me. "For already being a hellfighter, a glamorous profession in and of itself. But also for dealing with a reigning prince of hell, for imprisoning people releasing demons, for escaping multiple attempts on your life."

"But, Susan, I didn't do any of that for fame or fortune. I did it—"

"Because you are a heroine," Susan insists.

"In most cases because it was either that or die. I'm not Calamity Jane or Wild Bill Hickok," I emphasize.

"No, Mrs. Ochoa, you are not. You are more important than either of them. You do good works."

"Like any good Catholic woman," I rebut.

Susan takes a breath that about doubles her pencil thinness. "Mrs. Ochoa ... Stella, this story is going to get out. It is already the stuff of wild tales among the passengers and the crew. When we land, it will spread like gossip usually does, getting more and more exaggerated in each telling.

"You know me. You know my reputation. You know my writing. Let me tell the real story. It should put the wild rumors in their place."

"Damnation!" I exclaim. "You have a way of getting under a woman's skin, don't you, Susan?"

"That's my job, ma'am ... Or should I say Mistress Witch."

I look out the window at the scenery, trying to make a decision that is already made. *Majesty* noses down, heading directly away from the morning sun toward a town at the bottom of an east-west elongated bowl made by the surrounding mountains. Calling it a town may be stretching the term. The shake roofs of the three hundred or so cookie-cutter homes that make up the vast majority of the area are leprous with patches. White winter snow covers the ground except for the muck-churned streets.

A knot of larger merchant buildings clusters up against railroad tracks at one edge of the sprawl. In front of one, a six-horse team knee-deep in the quagmire struggles to drag a loaded wagon. At our two hundred or so feet above the ground, the sticky, gray mud glistens even in the leaden, overcast sky. A horde of children skip and jump around the worst of the muck, but they and their ratty clothing are coated as if they had been dunked in the stuff. The only building that absolutely announces its function is the church. But even this is a pine clapboard affair with a small spire on top. As we glide by, I can see that there isn't even a bell in the steeple.

Surely, this poverty-ridden hellhole can't be the mecca of Centralia, Pennsylvania. Hundreds of thousands of dollars come from this place every year.

"Is this the whole town?" I ask Lucy.

"Yes, cousin." In order not to insult her, or her town, I shut myself up by cramming more bagel and schmear in my mouth. "Over there is my house. Third down Main Street on the left." None of the roads, in either direction, looks any more significant than any of the others, so I can't pick hers out. "That's Syndicate Hill," Luciana continues, pointing to a tall wooden structure that covers the mine entrance, a quarter mile away from the town. It sports a massive metal pulley on top and a conveyer out of its upper reaches leading out to the tailing pile. A fan of railroad tracks at the bottom of the prominence holds hundreds of coal cars. As we float over them, I can see that most are empty. It surprises me to see very little activity at the mine or railroad marshaling yard—especially this soon after a cave-in.

My cousin indicates, "Over there is Dirigible Mound, where we will land."

I swivel my head to look where she indicates. A much smaller hill west of the town has a tall metal tower on the top that reaches up dozens of yards. Along with the line handlers, there are dozens of women milling about at the base of the hill, where the disembarking stairway stands.

I feel tension creeping up the back of my head the closer we get to landing. It must be the worry that I may be able to do nothing. Rubbing behind my ears at the ache, I say, "Looks like we will be landing in a few short minutes. Susan, come with me. I'll give you what little there is to tell while I finish getting my bags ready."

"You won't regret it, Mrs. Ochoa," her thin lips say.

"I do already."

#

Stepping down onto the stationary platform from a floating airship gives me the willies. It seems strange coming from a woman who dangled over nothingness from just a few ropes, but I wasn't exactly thrilled then either. Tiny motions move us back and forth, making the gap between the dirigible and the platform one to three inches. It makes me feel like I might fall between them, even though the ship is tethered. After my derring-do, it wouldn't be seemly to get squashed by falling now. I hesitate. With no real reason behind it, I give a small jump to hop over.

Lucy has already gone down the stairs and is swallowed up by the mass of women in dresses that have been laundered a few years beyond their nominal life. There are a few ship's officers at the bottom of the steps, but not the captain or Robert. I guess my engineer is to be a very brief affair. Probably best for all. I certainly don't need a man controlling my life. I mentally thank him for the relief and pleasure he brought me.

Even after a tincture of willow bark against my loving pains, the muscular ache where my head meets my spine becomes stronger with each step down I take. It feels like a horde of gremlins hoeing at the base of my scalp. They become more and more insistent as I go down. When I finally put my shoe on the rocky ground, I buckle under the anguish and pain radiating from beneath me. I collapse like a sack of flour.

Women rush around me.

"Stella?"

"Who has smelling salts?"

"Damned city woman. Probably has her corset too tight."

The very earth beneath me cries out in agony, the kind of damage that can never be recovered from. The mine has ripped the ground asunder and left it to bleed out. What is normally the solid, reassuring support of the earth feels no more substantial than spun sugar. I don't even want to stand up for fear of breaking through. Who could perpetrate such a crime?

Like anything in nature, the earth repairs itself from incursions. Like a stream where too many trout are caught, other fish fill the void and then procreate. Air polluted with smoke will spread it out, making it dissipate. But here, no healing has taken place. Men have torn out its liver and kidneys, and now are reaching for the lungs.

I can tell that no earth witches live within a hundred miles of here. They would go mad with the throbbing, incessant suffering. If I cut a finger, I would feel my hand in pain. Even if it were severe, I could point to the pain and wish it would go away. Here there is no location of the pain. Rather, everything feels like it is being ground into sausage.

The earth's screams have turned into a dagger within my breast and head. I weep as I lie there. I try to wrap myself around the dirt, to cradle it as one would a hurt child.

"Stella? What's wrong?"

"It hurts. They've raped it."

The women look back and forth at one another as I curl up into a fetal position and moan. I can't stand the anguish.

#

"Mommy, is she really my auntie?" asks a young girl.

"Shhh. Yes, honey," Luciana answers in a hushed tone.

"Why is she sleeping, Mommy?"

"We don't know, Holly."

My eyes don't want to open. It's like they are glued shut. I rub at one of them until the grit flakes away.

"Mommy, she's awake."

"Stella?" I hear Luciana ask in a low tone.

"I'm here." I realize that the overwhelming pain I suffered before is still there, but muted, like a shout behind a locked door.

"Are you alright?"

I rub the sand out of my other eye and sit up. I find myself on a pine pew in the middle of a church. "I think so. I wasn't expecting what has happened here."

A redheaded little girl, just old enough to start primary studies, stares at me with the most intense green eyes from under her mother's arm. Luciana hands me a china mug of water. "I don't know what you are talking about."

I down about half of it, remarking on the odd use of earthenware. The cup is hand-painted with bright-blue cornflowers around the outside.

"It's the ground, Lucy. The mining has been too intense, too far spread. As I'm attuned to it, the earth passed its pain to me. I guess it overwhelmed me."

"And now?" my cousin questions.

"I still feel it, like a nasty headache."

"Auntie Stella, are you going to save my daddy?" the little girl asks from the safety of her mother's arm. I look at Lucy for guidance.

"She knows. Even as a child, you can't live in a mining community without knowing."

"So, are you going to do it, Auntie Stella?"

I don't know what troubles me more—her innocent stare, the pain in the earth, or that I don't know if I can save him.

"I'll do my best, sweetie. I really will."

Lucy saves me any further consternation. "Honey, why don't you go tell Auntie Melissa to bring all of the others here."

"Yes, Mommy." The young girl in her blue dress, which is cleaner and newer than most I've seen, bolts out of the church.

"Thank you," we both say to one another.

"How long was I asleep?"

"About an hour."

"What's the situation?" I ask as I take stock of the gray mess that my red dress has become. "And where is Carlos?"

"We carried that big galoot down to the pub. He woke up about twenty minutes later, demanding food. Last I heard, he was on his third meal and still eating," Lucy says.

"Doesn't surprise me. He was out for a whole day. I'd be hungry too," I admit. "What about the rest of it?"

"We lost two of the trapped miners, but not my Adam."

"What about the mine owners? What are they doing?" I ask.

"Darrin Jasperson said—"

"Jasperson?" I interrupt.

"You know him?"

"I know his accursed brother, Bruce," I say. I want to spit the bad taste out of my mouth, but this is a house of God.

"Darrin isn't much but a pompous puppet who does everything his brother tells him."

"That doesn't sound good," I remark. Saving Lucy's husband and his colleagues will be hard enough without the Jaspersons looking over my shoulder.

"It never is, especially when he is the boss."

Somber women enter the church. Lucy leads me up to the raised dais area, which holds a lectern and some straight-backed chairs under a simple wooden cross twelve feet tall.

"Let me do the talking," Lucy admonishes me as she directs me to a chair. Her tone and actions seem so different from what they were last weekend. In Boston and on the *Majesty*, she seemed so diffident. Now she acts like a strong woman who controls her surroundings, rather than the other way around. It's clear that she is in her element here in Centralia.

"Yeah, speaking of that, why are we having a meeting? Can't Carlos and I just get on with things?"

"We need as many on our side as we can have."

"I thought bringing me here was unanimous," I snap.

"Well, no one objected, but not everyone was behind it."

"Jesus," I blaspheme. Things keep getting better and better. And as a cherry on top, I'm sitting here covered in mostly dried mud.

Carlos strides in and plops down next to me. "I have to admit, that is the only way to travel. Go to sleep in one place, wake up in another with a big, hearty meal."

"Even though you went by air?"

"If I can convince my mind that it didn't happen, then yes," he says, picking his teeth.

"Hypocrite."

"Love you, too, Stella."

"Bah, you don't love anyone but yourself," I tease him.

"Probably why I can't keep a woman in my life except you and Menaj," he says, rather more seriously than I would expect. His pockmarked face seems to be more of an issue than I realized. A good portion of my body bears the fire marks of a demon prince. I understand the emotional pain because of such mutilation.

When I don't reply because of my own inner demons, he adds, "First time I've been in a church in nearly twenty years."

"Well, I don't think there is going to be any praising God here," I offer in a dark tone.

"Oh? Trouble in paradise?"

"I'm not sure. Let's listen in and find out."

The room has almost filled up, primarily with women and children. Most look listless, with black circles of sleeplessness or the red of crying grief around their eyes.

"Ladies," Lucy says, quieting the murmuring in the nave. "And gentlemen," she adds for the few men in the crowd. "Per our agreement, I've returned with an earth witch." She points at me. "What's more, I bring you Mistress Witch Stella Ochoa. Many of you have read about her exploits in the newspapers."

I wish the damned reporters, Susan Queensbury included, would have kept their stories to themselves.

As one, the room looks at me. I read despair, anger, fear, and even hatred on their faces. Only on a few do I see hope. Most of the attendees have had their emotions drained from them through their ordeal.

Lucy tries. "She is here to save the day!" No applause comes from the group. Most are stiff jawed. "Stella, maybe if you can explain what you have planned." Lucy invites me to the podium.

"Oh, dingblasted," I offer in a soft voice to Carlos.

"The joys of leadership," he whispers back.

I stand up and walk to the lectern. "Folks, I believe my cousin has oversold my capabilities." People talk low with one another, causing an almost growl of disapproval in the room.

"Ladies, what I promised to do is to come and evaluate if I can possibly save your loved ones. Right now, I don't know. But my fellow witch, Carlos, and I will do our best.

"For now, I need to know what is going on with the rescue efforts and have a map of the mine to see where we might be the most useful." They turn to one another and ignore me. I catch some of the talk in the seats up front.

"Stupid bitch faints at the sign of a town that ain't got paved streets."

"Lucy's got a lot t' answer fer, bringing us this worthless cow."

"What's one fancy lady gonna do in them pretty clothes in the middle of the Pennsylvania clay?"

"That prim 'n' proper society auntie ain't never savin' my Edward."

"Gots as much power as a twig."

I've had enough. Maybe it is the low level of pain from the earth around me that leeches my patience. I'm tired of being thought of as a charlatan, or even a member of the aristocracy with no redeeming value. I start by ordering the dirt away from my gown in the most violent way possible. There is a loud pop, and I'm surrounded by a fog of gray.

The sound startles everyone, bringing their attention back to me. To ensure I have their focus, I seek out the mud from the street. I form a three-foot-wide snake of sticky goo that oozes through the doorway and splits into two smaller pythons that wrap around the outside of the congregation.

Now the angry, accusatory voices have turned to fear. Several people cross themselves or thrust forth a crucifix in my direction. One woman tries to flee, and I form a massive cobra head to block her escape. I let the muck engulf my legs and lift me up for a moment. People look up at me, wondering if I'll hurt them. Ignorant people. How many of them even graduated third grade? I have the gray clay deposit me on the floor, not the dais. I send it retreating from the building. Nothing of the earth touches another individual.

"I am a woman, just like you! But I have skills that may possibly be able to save your miners. Now, stop behaving like naughty children who have been told they get no dessert!"

I go back and plop down next to Carlos. Half a dozen people have fled from the building.

"Not bad," he says to me. "Damnation, if it had been me, I'd have just let loose a zephyr in the center of them. Not enough to hurt but maybe tear a dress or rip apart a hymnal."

I reply with a less-than-ladylike grunt. At that point I notice Susan Queensbury standing in the doorway taking notes. *Sweet Mary, please send her away*, I pray.

Lucy takes her place at the podium. "Now that we've witnessed just a bit of Witch Ochoa's powers, can we assist her instead of running her down?"

The crowd give shaky, nervous nods of assent and sit down. Two or three more nervous Nellies leave the building.

Lucy pushes forward with, "Emma Grossman, can you please tell us what has happened while I've been away?"

A heavy blonde woman stands with a *bebé* on her hips and four others of varying size, up to maybe five years old, clustered around her. Her pinched face reminds me uncharitably of Mrs. Chapman, my former landlady. "We lost six rescuers 'cause of additional cave-ins. The company stopped further attempts."

"They what?" Lucy barks.

"What else was they supposed to do? Throw good men after bad?" claims one old biddy in the back of the room. "Besides, there is the rumor."

"What rumor?" Lucy asks.

"That no one can even go into the mine. The supervisor who went in after they stopped came back out bloodied like he'd been in ten bar brawls," says Emma.

"But what about those still down there? Are we just supposed to give the last rites to the ones buried?"

"We only got your word that they are still alive!" another woman says.

Lucy's face bunches up. I can almost see the steam jetting from her nostrils. I reach over and tug on her dress. When she turns, I say, "Don't do it, Lucy. We need their help." I see her jaw working.

When she speaks, it is in level tones. "How many of you have I healed? Janice, didn't I heal your little girl's leg when she fell from the boulder? Esther, didn't I take the fever from your Bobby? I've helped many of the men of the mine with serious injuries over the years." The same words could have been spit out in spite, but she is reminding them with the calm of a saint. "Despite that, if I am a fraud and don't know if our men and women are still alive, then you risk nothing. If the company won't do anything to save them, then they are already buried in their grave. Working with Stella, Carlos and I can't hurt them. But we may be able to retrieve them."

I stand up to add, "Helping us costs you nothing. Won't you at least try?"

My friend and leader of the *Dos Campanas* offers, "And where else but a church is the best place to have hope of our Lord's mercy?"

The faces in the crowd change from ones that would be expected at a funeral to showing belief. Hope.

"Someone fetch a mine map," a woman calls out. Everyone mills around to welcome Carlos and me.

# # #

"I'm sorry, but Mr. Jasperson is booked," says the secretary at the administration building. Her bright eyes don't show the stern tone her voice takes. She mouths to us that he isn't booked and hooks her head in the direction of the office.

Carlos and I have been warned that Minnie Farmer is on our side but needs the job to support her children after her husband died in the mines two years back. She has to at least appear to be her boss's doting servant.

"The soonest he could see you is next Friday."

"It is very important," I add.

"Mrs. Ochoa, with the cave-in, you can imagine he is quite busy." She shakes her head, indicating he may be doing nothing more than playing solitaire.

"It is about the mining accident that we wish to see him."

"Oh? Well, I'll—"

A short man wearing a suit without the coat bursts through the door. He isn't nearly as fat as his brother, but I see he got the family pomposity trait. "Let them in, Minnie. I might as well get this over with."

"It appears Mr. Jasperson will see you," she says with a wink.

Our meeting with the wives and husbands of the trapped miners set many things straight about Darrin. Even though a director of the Coal Syndicate, Darrin Jasperson wouldn't button his shoes without his brother's approval. He also regularly gets telegrams giving him very explicit instructions for even simple tasks.

Carlos and I stroll into the mining overseer's office. It has none of the grandeur of his brother's. While a decent size, its walls are pinned with the mine diagrams, copies of which we've poured over for the last three hours. Most of these have penciled markings on them. One of the walls is covered in cabinets. The desk is well inlaid with several colors of wood but has so many papers, tools, ore samples, and the like that it is impossible to determine the pattern. There is a telegram on the top that reads, "2x Armadillos en route. Expedite mine opening. Flow of coal paramount."

His opulent chair is the one thing that I find out of place. The green velvet upholstery has the sheen of being heavily worn but eminently serviceable. The supporting wood shines with the patina of long use. It is big enough to be a throne, dominating the space.

"Have a seat, Mrs. Ochoa and Mr. Aldana." The chairs we are offered are without any cushioning. The leg on mine has been repaired numerous times, as has the back of Carlos's. They look like items liberated from a cheap bar after a brawl.

"So, you know who we are?" Carlos asks. We decided that he should speak for us, as I am probably *persona non grata* to the Jasperson family. One of their extended family members is serving twenty years of hard labor because of my testimony.

"Yes, I do. I have here a telegram from my brother." The little pig tosses the yellow form haphazardly in our direction. "As the president of the Coal Syndicate, he tells me you would arrive today by dirigible."

"You are well informed, sir."

"Yes. I assumed you would eventually end up in my office, as Mrs. Ochoa seems unable to keep her nose out of other people's business."

"I won't say that you aren't right about that," Carlos says with a smirk. I throw my friend a dirty look.

"Cat got your tongue, Mrs. Ochoa?"

"I thought we might get beyond personalities if Carlos spoke for us."

Darrin leans back in his chair. It squeaks under his weight. "Unlikely, Mrs. Ochoa. While not excessively fond of Mark Carlton, I'd just as soon spit in your face as look at, much less talk to, you. Only my culture is keeping me in check."

I almost laugh at his suggestion that he has any culture. But it wouldn't help my case, so I just lean back and try to keep the distaste I have for the entire Jasperson clan from showing on my face.

"As Mrs. Ochoa is keeping her counsel, won't you tell me, Mr. Aldana, why you have come to speak to me?"

"We are here on behalf of the wives and husbands of the trapped miners. We believe we may be uniquely capable of saving them."

"In what way?"

"As you know, Mrs. Ochoa and I are both witches—Stella earth and myself air. If we could get down into the mine, we should be able to burrow to the miners and lead them out."

"No."

"Excuse me, Mr. Jasperson?" I say in visceral reaction to his flat rejection.

"I said no. I thought even Mrs. Ochoa would be able to understand that two-letter word."

"Can you explain why?" Carlos asks. "It would be much easier to reach the victims from the interior of the mine rather than going from up here all the way down."

"Oh, I can give you many reasons, Mr. Aldana. The mines are extremely dangerous. I'm sure your friends have told you we've lost seven men trying to get to the others. Your skills won't save you from a tunnel collapse."

What a load of horse manure, I think.

"Next, those miners are already dead. The number of rescues from a mining disaster after this long is effectively nonexistent.

"In addition, the mine contains any number of proprietary methods and tools that we don't want to share with the outside world."

Like we don't know what a shovel looks like, I fume to myself.

"If those aren't reasons enough, I don't like Mrs. Ochoa, in any way, shape, or form. Even if those miners were somehow miraculously still alive, I still wouldn't let you anywhere near. You might just perform some feat of legerdemain to get them out and be the heroine one more time.

"And in the end, I have instructions from the president of the Coal Syndicate, and incidentally my brother, specifically denying you any rights here in any way.

"As this entire valley belongs to the Coal Syndicate, you are trespassing. I'll give you forty-eight hours to leave, or I'll have the sheriff arrest you."

"And there isn't anything we can do to change your mind?"

"HA!" he bursts out.

"I see," Carlos says as he stands.

The plump Minnie walks into the room. "Mr. Jasperson, you have a telegram waiting for you."

Still seated, I look at Darrin Jasperson, narrowing my eyes as I purse my lips. "You are an evil little man, Mr. Jasperson—you and your brother. This world would be much better without you both. You can count your luck that the witches' law of three makes it unwise for me to remove you."

"Are you threatening me?"

"You heard every word I said, putty-brain. You decide."

We walk out, leaving the pompous ass sputtering.

My cousin waits for us on the building's porch. "What did he say?" Lucy asks as we come out of the administration building.

"About what we all expected. He told us to go boil our heads and lick his arse," I curse.

"Stella!" she exclaims.

"Come now, Lucy. Living in a mining community, I'm sure you've heard worse."

"Yes, but that doesn't mean I like it from a lady."

I consider it and offer a conditional apology. "True enough. I'll try to watch my viperous tongue. What's more important is that he called us trespassers and threatened to send the law after us."

Carlos remains quiet as he studies the surrounding area.

"He wouldn't! This is a town," she tells me.

"Yup, it is. It's a company town. I figure Darrin is contacting the sheriff right now. We are likely to have an escort to make sure we behave and leave like good little schoolchildren."

Carlos says, "Well, if we are going to do anything to save those folks, we best take a shot now, Stella. We may not get another one."

"True. Let me change into my working dress. Lucy, if you can locate a spot as nearly overhead to where the miners are trapped as possible, that would be helpful."

"Come to my house. That will give you a chance to change and have a place to put yourself up."

"If you don't mind, I'll just wait at the pub," Carlos says.

"We'll meet you in an hour," I add.

"Thanks. See you there," he offers as he walks down the split logs on the sides of the streets used as walkways through the mud.

Lucy turns to me as I watch him walk away. "Stella, I've got a map of the mine there, and we can decide on next steps."

"Good."

# # #

"Welcome to our home," Luciana says as she opens the door of a tiny house. Unlike the other paint-peeling, cookie-cutter homes along the street, this one wears a recent coat of happy green.

As we stand at the threshold, a pair of youngsters darts from behind us and runs inside between their mother and my skirts. "Gretchen! Holly!" Luciana barks. The two screech to a halt in the middle of a combination living room, dining room, and kitchen that is half a size smaller than claustrophobic. While tiny, it is neat as any house with children can possibly be, and appointed with beautiful vases and tasteful ceramic sculptures. A large fired clay cross takes up most of one wall. I'm surprised to see a shelf with thirty-odd books on it.

"Wipe your feet and then clean up the mess you left." There is a trail of gray from the stoop all the way up to the young girls.

"Sorry, Mama." The pair slink back to the door to obey their mother.

I don't risk it. I scrape my shoes on the boot brush and on the doormat before going inside. A young man, wearing more of the mountain on his clothes than what still lies in the streets, snores on a blanket covering the sofa. I point to him and shrug at Luciana.

"Don't worry, Stella. Adam Junior won't wake to anything short of a stick of dynamite under the couch. He's been helping the workers with the rescue. He's too young to go into the mines, but he can fetch and carry. The other ladies say he hasn't stopped since they started. And he fired up the stove, bless him."

"Quite a young man. Sounds like you and your husband have done right by him," I say, taking a chair at the table.

Lucy blushes. "Thank you, cousin. We try."

Without ceremony, the young girl named Gretchen leaps into my lap. "Are you my auntie? I ain't never—"

"*Haven't ever*, Gretchen," her mother says, digging through a cupboard. "*Ain't never* isn't correct." She looks at me. "I've got to stay on these kids all the time. Otherwise, they pick up the muck the kids speak here. Before I met Adam, I was a schoolteacher."

Some things fall into place as I consider this information.

The girl continues. "So is you?"

"*So are you*, Gretchen," Lucy says.

"Yes, Mama. So, are you my auntie?"

The conversation whipsaws back and forth between mother and daughter so fast, I can't keep up. "Ummm."

Holly comes and sits next to me to listen, more like a young lady than her boisterous sister.

Gretchen continues with, "She doesn't talk very good, Mama."

"Don't be rude, Gretchen," Holly interrupts. "And it is, 'Doesn't talk very well.'"

I finally get my brain to work. "I think I'm your first cousin once removed, Gretchen."

"Who removed ya?" Before her mother can rebuff her, she changes it to, "Who removed you?"

"I really don't know, Gretchen. It is just what they call me."

"You don't look like my cousins. You're old," my lapmate says.

"Gretchen!" Lucy barks from the stove.

I hear something sizzling there.

"That's alright, Lucy. She is just a youngster," I offer, not being offended by a little slip of a girl.

"But if I don't correct her, she'll grow up thinking such talk is acceptable. Gretchen, it is never, ever a good thing to ask a lady's age or imply that she is old. Understand?"

"Yes, Mama," Gretchen says, jumping down off of my lap with as little warning as she mounted it. She skips over to a corner and picks up a home-sewn doll.

"You going to a funeral, a wedding, or a birthday?" the other little girl asks.

"Neither, Holly. Why would you think that?"

"You are wearing a fancy dress. That's the only reason someone would wear their best dress if it wasn't a Sunday."

I smile at her. "Actually, Holly, I'm about to go change into something a bit more robust for working."

Holly looks like she might ask another question but instead goes off and joins her sister.

"Stella, if you want to change, take the door on the right."

"Thank you, Lucy."

The door leads to a room where a double bed, covered in a stunning handmade quilt with a snowflake pattern, takes up almost the entire space. The chifforobe at the end of it leaves only a narrow walkway around the edge. Add to that, the ceiling is only about half an inch higher than my head. Changing isn't a trivial task in this environment. I find that if I put myself into the corner, I have a few more inches to work with. I must be getting soft as a lady of my own manor. I used to dress in a similar environment living in Chapman's Boardinghouse.

I struggle around but eventually manage. My denim overall dress has been well broken in since I got it made by my seamstress, Paula Simpson. Originally it was stiff as overstarched bloomers. Now the sturdy fabric is as supple as any other garment. I wear a heavy blue blouse beneath to maintain my dignity, as the simple straps over the shoulders definitely don't cover my chest modestly.

While the dress has proven itself to be as durable as I'd hoped, it hasn't caught on as I expected. Everywhere I've worn it, I get strange looks. Walking back into the living area of the house, I realize that today is no different.

The four occupants—Adam Junior now awake and rubbing his eyes—look at me as if I've sprouted a third arm out my back.

"Those look like overalls," Gretchen says. "Are you going to work in the mines?" Lucy just shakes her head in exasperation at her daughter.

"Kind of, Gretchen." Then I turn to the young man. "You must be Adam Junior. I'm Stella Ochoa. A distant cousin."

"Yes, ma'am. I'm pleased to meet you. Are you the witch they say wants to try to save my father and the other miners?"

"I'm going to try, Adam."

"Well, if you do half as well at getting the miners out as you did scaring the townsfolk, then my father is as good as home. Those clay snakes have them terrified."

Marvelous.

"Supper, everyone," Lucy says, dropping food on the table. When the smells hits me, I realize just how hungry I am. A bagel and schmear isn't enough to keep a good witch energized throughout most of the day.

Adam Junior says, "Mother, I should get back. The miners are getting together to convince the foreman to let us go back down. I should be there."

"Not without eating first, young man."

"Yes, Mother."

Luciana takes her place at the head of the table and indicates that I'm to take the foot. The children take, what I assume, are their accustomed places. "With your father absent, I'll say grace," she says.

We all link hands together. Adam's are rough and calloused already with the work he has been doing. Gretchen giggles when she takes my hand. Hers is as soft as the fur of a week-old kitten, even if her fingernails need trimming.

"Thank you, Lord, for bringing Stella and her friend Carlos into our midst, that they may be the tools of our salvation. May you keep Adam Senior, and all of the others trapped in the mines, safe and within your love. Praise be to this food that it makes us strong to meet your tests. Amen."

"Amen."

The meal on the table offers nothing more than I might have found at my stingy ex-landlady's table—a strip of bacon, fried potatoes, and fry bread with a teaspoon of cranberry sauce. That being said, the potatoes are seasoned with tart cheese, and the bread is cooked in the greases of the bacon. It is hearty, filling, and frankly, tasty—unlike that of my former lessor. Adam rushes through his meal as if a steam shovel is scooping everything into his gullet.

"Mother, may I be excused?"

"Adam, before you leave, is there any rusted metal around that no one needs?" I ask.

"Ah. Well, there are a bunch of old mining carts with broken axles down next to the dump. They are pretty rusted out. Some of them haven't been touched in years. The boys sometimes play in and around them. May I ask why?"

"Let's just say that I had to leave my armor at home and want to make a new set." The young man looks me over as if he isn't sure if I am cracked or just pulling his leg.

"As you say, cousin. May I be excused, Mother?"

"Yes, but come here before you leave." He moves close to her, and she kisses him on the cheek. "Do what you have to, son. But stay safe." She gives him another kiss.

"Thank you, Mother." He rushes out, pausing only long enough to slip on a heavy coat.

"Are you expecting trouble?" I ask Lucy.

"From what I've heard, the miners are very angry about having to stop. I'm hoping that they won't take matters into their own hands. Clashing with the sheriff and the Coal Syndicate's guards wouldn't be good for anyone." Her eyes tell a story all their own.

"I can imagine. That was an excellent meal, Lucy. I imagine that Carlos is waiting for us."

"Too true, cousin. Gretchen and Holly, clear the table and start on the dishes."

"Yes, Mama."

"Stella, if you will help the girls, I'll get the mine maps."

The two girls have already set up at the sink. One is pumping water into a big bucket while the other scrapes the scraps into another. Her sister sorts the dishes I bring. "You two are good at this."

"It's our chore, Auntie Stella."

"Of course it is."

Lucy climbs down off a ladder from a loft above her bedroom. "I've got them, Stella." She spreads a roll of parchments out on the cleared table.

"Here is the town and here is the mine," she says, pointing at the top sheet. "I'll skip all of these other pages and go right down to the level that is caved in. You see it is drifted off to the southwest, almost directly south of town." She digs deep into the thick stack of drawings.

"How far down is this?" I ask.

Lucy runs her finger down to the title in the lower right corner. It reads, "Thirty-One Hundred Feet."

"Good Lord, but that is deep. I'd hoped you'd exaggerated, cousin."

"Nary a bit. I'm sorry." She frowns.

I want to tell her that I'm not certain I'll be able to save her husband. From the tear in the corner of her eye, she knows. I don't need to heap more uncertainty upon her.

I flip page by page through the sheaf of drawings and goggle at the sprawling tunnels. They cover linear miles per map, and there is map, after map, after map. There must be more miles of mine than there are streets in all of Boston and her sister cities. No wonder the earth itself cries out for healing.

Gritting my teeth, I flip back to the main page and point to the elevation lines that indicate a hill with a building on the top, half again farther from the point above the miner's entrapment.

"What's that?" I ask.

"That is Bruce Jasperson's house. He lets his brother use it as his place of residence."

"*Cacafuego*. Either I'll have to burrow down at an angle or we'll be doing this right under their nose."

"Not quite. There is a copse of trees at the bottom of that hill. It will hide anything we do."

Holly steps between us and says, "We're done, Mama."

Gretchen pulls on my denim dress and says, "Both of us." I smile down and ruffle her curls with my hand.

"Good girls," Lucy says. "Now, I want you to go to Widow Manor's. I'll fetch you there when I'm done."

"Yes, Mama. C'mon, Gretchen." The pair walk out the door hand in hand.

"The Lord blessed you with two good girls," I offer to my cousin.

"True, but they do tend to get dirty."

"What do you think we are going to do? First, I need you to show me the dump."

# # #

"I thought our goal was to the south," Carlos says after we pick him up from the public house. To my surprise, he hasn't even been drinking—only swapping some stories with the bartender and a couple of the town's working girls.

"We are, but I need to make a quick stop first," I say, dodging a pack of kids.

"This way," Luciana says, her footsteps crunching on a crushed gravel road. The snow has been compacted down into the bed and doesn't give us any trouble.

"So why are the town streets knee-deep in mud and we got this nice road to walk on?" Carlos asks her.

"This is the same road they use to carry the coal to the railroad loading. It deserves the effort of being lined with rock, unlike the town streets. The Jaspersons say we can carry our own rock from the tailings, but we don't have the carts, time, or energy to do it fast. We might get one wagonload a week. It's slow."

"You know, if you get the kids to haul it a basket at a time, it might speed things up. They have plenty of energy," Carlos tosses out there.

"We did. We even offered a penny for every five baskets hauled. It worked great for about a week, until they learned just how much they had to do to earn the money."

"I'd make it a contest," my boss throws out there. "Find something they all want, and the one who hauls the most gets the thing."

"I'll keep that in mind. I'll suggest it at the next town meeting. What do you think the prize should be?" Lucy asks.

The two keep talking for the next five minutes. I let them natter on as the earth's pain gnaws at me. The ache doesn't go away. It just varies in intensity like the twisting cramps I have during a particularly bad time of the month. As a result, I'm not as observant as I should be as I'm walking.

"What is that smell?" Carlos asks, his face wrinkling up.

"Welcome to the dump," Lucy says.

Rotting food doesn't cause the foul odor. I saw the girls feeding the dinner scraps to their pigs. The stench bears the bitter chemical tang you'd smell walking outside a tanner's establishment. Additionally, there are yellow, red, and green patches of snow spaced around the refuse.

Off to one side are the skeletons of five mining carts coated in a liberal layer of snow. Under the white, the wooden boxes are mildewed and rotting, and the metal is well coated in rust. Perfect.

I skirt the worst of the nasty smell and oddly colored snow to reach the carts. I reach out and wipe snow from one of the small rail wheels. Beneath the ruddy exterior, I can feel the sturdy metal, despite the impurities that lined up to allow the axle to break. I call to the refined earth. The metal sheds the red exterior like a hound shaking off a spring shower. A silver snake slithers out from within the iron. It curls around, up under my denim dress and up my legs. I've been having metal climb my limbs like a serpent for almost half a year now. The first few times made me squirm as if I'd found a spider walking across the back of my hand. With my previous experiences, I expect this to be just another morning.

"¡*Hijo de la chingada!*" I exclaim through clenched teeth.

"Stella?" Luciana asks, rushing forward.

"*Maldito*, but this metal is cold. Especially under my dress!" Lucy looks concerned. Carlos laughs deep and heavy. It looks like he might fall over. The frigid touch against my skin doesn't make me want to laugh with him. "Oh, you're so full of yourself. Take a piece of it and put it down your trousers."

"No, thank you," he manages between fits of laughter. "I'm just fine."

The metal bands solidify around my middle like a corset that fits me from hip to just above my bosoms. The weight settling on my hips is comforting. Over the last year, I've found it useful in any number of ways, not to mention protecting my precious skin from bullets being fired at me and knives stabbing me.

The metal's chill sets into my middle and puts goosebumps all over me. "Lord!"

"Stella, do we need to go back and get you warmed up?" Lucy asks.

"Yes, but I want to test our burrowing first."

"Well, then let's go over—"

"No. I really mean a test, Lucy. Despite how easily I transformed that metal, the earth around us is damaged. I don't know if it will respond the way it usually does for me." Lucy frowns. I think she expected me to save her husband in the next five minutes. I wish it were that easy.

"Stella, is this a good place for that?" Carlos asks.

"Well, I'd like to move a bit away from the smell, but why not here? Unlikely anyone will be watching the dump."

"True enough. How about right behind those bushes? That will stop anyone from stumbling upon us," Carlos says.

"That's great. Lucy, just keep a watch for anyone. We won't be long. I'll pop back up and check before we surface." I shiver, as my body still hasn't warmed the metal.

"I understand, cousin."

With my boot, I scrape a trough in the snow to find gray clay beneath. I bend down and pick up a pinch of it. I reach up to touch it to my tongue but am interrupted.

"I've always wondered. Do you have to do that?" Carlos asks.

"Unlike an air witch, I don't breathe in the element I'm controlling. In some cases, I can do without it, but the closer I get, the easier it is to form a bond."

Carlos shrugs and waves me on. The sour grit of the clay spreads on my tongue. It's worse than chewing on a green persimmon. My face screws up in distaste.

"This is not going to be easy. Carlos, come over here and wrap your arms around me."

"You that cold?" he says with a smirk as he wraps his big arms around me. I'm very thankful for Robert D'Oro and how well he removed my cravings. I've never felt anything romantic toward the leader of the *Dos Campanas*. He has been more of a father figure, as I've never had one. Scratch that, I do now have a father, but I didn't for many, many years. Carlos gave me someone to look up to.

"No, silly. I want to make the smallest hole in the ground possible," I say to his forehead. Because of my boots, I have to look down to meet his eyes.

"Got you. What do you want me to do?"

"The earth will close in over the top of us. Dragging air out of the earth for us to breathe would be exceptional. Otherwise, we'll probably suffocate."

"Cheerful thought."

"I've done this once before, but I was right near the surface. So I could pop up and refresh the air. This time I'll be going straight down."

"Don't worry, *amiga*. I'll keep us breathing."

"Good. Here we go." I close my eyes and focus on that gritty, sour taste. I will the ground to open up and swallow us. The pain increases to a point where it feels like Paul Bunyan split my head open with his axe.

In the past, I've always formed a partnership with the earth. We each gave of each other to make mutual goals take place. This time I feel as if I'm having to force my will upon an unruly child.

I need to move down. Please let me pass.

Not only do the clay and rock not cooperate, but they also won't respond to me.

You must let me pass. Lives are at stake.

Time passes as I burrow every foot with my mind and will. Where I once wore a chill from the metal, I'm now dripping with sweat, at least from the waist up. I'm panting, gasping to catch my breath as if I've just run across Boston Commons with a tiger chasing me.

My concentration finally breaks from the continuous ache. I open my eyes. At least I think I opened my eyes. I've forgotten how dark it is beneath the earth. I also didn't count on being thigh-deep in frigid water.

"Stella?" my friend says, his teeth chattering.

"Carlos?"

"Still here. Still wrapped around you, but I'm freezing to death in this water. I think we need to go back up." His body shakes against mine.

"I agree." The heat from my mental exercise has been keeping me warm. *Mi amigo* hasn't had the same benefits.

Despite the pain, I urge the earth to release us upward. This goes much faster and easier. It wants to be rid of us. The ground vomits us forth only moments later. The pool of water around our legs and feet spills all over, melting the snow it touches despite being only a few degrees warmer.

"Stella!" Lucy calls out in surprise. "I was worr—" She stops mid-sentence. Carlos is white as the surrounding snow. I am afraid for him.

"How long were we down?" I ask.

"I expected you back in just a few minutes. It's been over two hours," Lucy replies.

"*Madre Dios.*"

"Ladies, as much as I like to learn from our mistakes, can we please do it somewhere warmer?" Carlos's teeth chatter like a telegraph receiving a message. Only his arms around me are keeping him standing. For that matter, I can't feel my feet either.

"Help me, Lucy," I say.

Together, we get his arms over our shoulders between us and make for the town.

# # #

Carlos has a bearskin robe over his shoulders. His trousers are off and hanging. Thankfully, he is wearing long woolen underwear, but they are soaked and sagging under the water weight. My bloomers are wet all the way up to my waist. My boots are sitting right next to the heat of the cast iron stove. I have several blankets over my shoulders.

Gretchen dumps another pot of hot water into the galvanized washtub around Carlos's and my feet.

"Mommy, why is Auntie Stella showing her feet to that man? Are they going to get married?"

"Not a chance!" Carlos exclaims. I cast him a dirty look.

"No, Gretchen. Remember when the Wilson boy got lost?" Lucy says. "He was so cold when he was found that his mother put him against her bare skin. Sometimes in emergencies, we do things that aren't proper for normal times."

"Auntie Stella, are you really cold?"

"Yes, and so is my friend, Mr. Aldana."

"You want me to take my clothes off and—"

"Gretchen, will you quit bothering them and pump some more water!" her sister Holly snaps. "We need to fix them up."

"Thank you for the offer, Gretchen," I say. "But the heat of the fire and the hot water will warm us right up."

I whisper to Lucy as she bends down to pour another pot of hot water into our tub. "She is a handful, isn't she?"

"Yup. More trouble than my other two and my husband combined," she whispers back. Then she continues in a more conversational tone. "I'm sorry that we only have one tub. There are only a few in our town, and we share them around. I couldn't find another one."

"That's alright, Mrs. Riley," Carlos remarks. "I've seen much more of Stella than a little bit of feet. Hellfighting is a rough profession that often ends with one or more of us partially disrobed."

"That may be, Mr. Aldana, but Gretchen is right that it isn't proper. As soon as you are warmed up, I'll want you to be heading on out."

"That brings up a good point," he replies. "Where am I sleeping tonight? Not that I need much more than some warmth and a place to put my head."

"Old Frank Harbin lost his wife last year. He agreed to let you stay there."

"Excellent. Thank you, Mrs. Riley. We ready to talk about what went wrong, Stella?" Carlos asks, pulling his robe tighter around his shoulders.

"Well, moving through that earth is like trying to write through a sheet of unpulled taffy."

"How far down did you get, Stella?"

"One hundred sixty-four feet."

"In two hours? That means you can get to thirty-one hundred in about twenty hours," Lucy says hopefully. Carlos shakes his head.

I respond with, "Lucy, nearly that entire two hours was going down. Coming out was quick. I don't know that I could have continued without a prolonged rest. I think it's more like fifty feet an hour or something more like sixty hours to just reach the level of the mi—"

The door opens and Adam stumbles in. From the bruises on his face, it looks like he's fought the fishermen on Boston's waterfront—all of them—and lost.

"¡Madre Dios!" Lucy says, going over to help him in. "Are you alright?"

"You should have seen the other guy," he says in a nasal-blocked tone as he plops down onto the couch. Other than the bruises, broken nose, and split lip, he doesn't look bad. I guess that is like when I got shot and didn't look bad if you ignored that hole in my middle.

"Holly, bring the whiskey." Lucy feels up and down his arms and legs.

"Mom, I'm fine," he says, using his own handkerchief to staunch the blood from his bleeding nose. Lucy spills a bit of the whiskey onto her apron and is wiping his lip clean. "Ow! Mom! Really, I'm OK." Lucy doesn't say anything but stops with the cleaning. She looks over his crooked nose.

"Move your hand out of the way. I need to set your nose." Adam gives an exaggerated sigh as he drops his hands. "This will probably hurt."

"It didn't feel great getting—Jesus Christ!" Adam yells. His nose is much straighter.

"There. And don't take the name of the Lord in vain."

"Yes, Mother."

"So do you want to tell me what happened?"

"Well, management didn't like the idea of us going in to try to save our people. They claimed that the miners are already dead and that we should prepare to start in the morning on a new shaft to mine coal tonnage."

"Bastards," I say. "I didn't expect anything else from the damned Jaspersons."

"I didn't either, but they are alive. I can feel them," Lucy says. A warm glow goes over me as she uses her white witch capabilities.

Adam adds to his report. "They even said they were bringing in two armadillos."

"What?" Lucy exclaims.

I jump in with, "You know, I saw that in Jasperson's office. He's expecting them tomorrow. What is an armadillo, anyway? I have to assume you don't mean armor-plated mammals."

"Drilling machines," Lucy says. "A massive drill on either end that grinds through rock like it is butter. The problem is that it is damned dangerous, both for those loading the coal behind it and the drivers. Everywhere else they've been used, they've caused tunnel collapses more than they've produce any significant extractions."

"Yeah," Adam agrees. "I think announcing armadillos was the proverbial straw that broke the camel's back. A brawl broke out. It probably would have amounted to just a few black eyes if some idiot hadn't popped off a few shots with a revolver."

"You weren't shot, were you?" demands his mother with more than a touch of concern. She starts looking him over for a bullet hole.

"No, Mom. I'm fine. I'm not sure anyone was hit. But it sure broke up the party."

"I should say," Carlos interjects.

A silence falls on the group until Gretchen pours more hot water on our feet. The heat has me reaching the boiled stage. "I think that's enough, girls. Save the rest of the water for tea or supper."

"So, sixty hours," Lucy says, trying to get us back on our original topic. "That's doable, isn't it?"

I've categorized Carlos's looks over the years. This one classifies as dubious. "Three days underground with no heat and likely little to no sleep?" he asks.

I toss in, "Carlos, I don't disagree. But I don't know anything else to do about it if they won't let us into the mine."

"Not only that, we have to do something about the water, or it will be a race between drowning or freezing to death," Carlos says.

"Exactly," I add with an exaggerated shiver. Actually, the feeling is returning to my limbs. "I think we need to call in the rest of the team." I turn to Lucy's son. "Adam, do you feel well enough to carry a message to the telegrapher?"

"Certainly, Mrs. Ochoa. But if I may be so bold as to ask, sixty hours for what?"

"Jasperson won't let me into the mine, so I have to burrow down thirty-one hundred feet to get to your father," I tell him.

"You can go right down through the rock?"

"Remember what I did in the church?" I reply as a way of answering.

"Then why burrow through three thousand feet of rock? Why not use the mine tunnels?" Adam asks incredulously.

"Honey, they already told you," Lucy says. "Jasperson won't let them. Those goons who beat you up wouldn't have any qualms about doing the same or worse to Carlos and Stella."

"Mrs. Ochoa, you could burrow down to one of the upper tunnels and bypass the guards. There are tunnels as close to the surface as two hundred feet. There aren't any guards in the mine itself."

I just sit there with my mouth open. I turn around, and Carlos wears an equally gobsmacked expression.

"Out of the mouth of babes," I mutter.

"¡Bravo!" Carlos says to Adam.

"I heartily agree. You are incredible," I add.

"Good job, son," Lucy crows.

I get the impression the young man is just a bit overwhelmed by the praise. He also is grimacing at Carlos's overly enthusiastic handshake.

"That's enough. You are hurting the boy," I whisper into Carlos's ear.

"Oh!" my fellow witch says, letting go with a wry look on his face. Adam shakes his hand as if to get blood back into it.

"Adam, when does the telegraph office shut down?" I ask.

"Four, but she stays 'til six just in case Mr. Jasperson has something he wants to send." Adam pulls out a pocket watch. "It's nearly four now. If you want to send a message, I'd better hotfoot it over there."

"Very good. Ten words, Carlos. What do you think?" It must be short and sweet because, at a cost of a dollar for ten words and a dime for every additional word, it isn't cheap.

"Well, we want everyone to come—"

I interrupt with, "But not Donny. He has to stay on the naval yard work."

"But we need a water witch," my friend says.

"Cora. Cora Leaping Fish from *Los Lobos*." The *Lobos* are another hellfighter team in western Boston living as natives in the Fens.

"And Red Hawk is OK with you poaching one of his team members?"

"I told you that I made arrangements before we left."

"OK, how about 'Need *Dos Campanas* here soonest. Bring Cora. Leave Donny.'"

"Well, we need to tell them where here is just to be clear. And just 'Cora' may not identify her well enough. I'll call her out more specifically. How about, 'Expedite *Campanas* to Centralia. Minus Donny plus Cora Leaping Fish'?"

"That is good."

"Before you send that message, know that everyone in town will know about it, including Jasperson, before the evening is out," Lucy says.

"Huh?" I reply with a large level of brilliance.

"The telegrapher is a gossip of epic proportions."

"That doesn't change the fact that we need the team. And if the sheriff and Jasperson want to tangle with the full complement of *Dos*

Campanas, more power to them. Here, Adam." I hand him two dollars and the message I just wrote out.

"I don't need that much, Mrs. Ochoa," he says, handing me back a dollar.

"Fine, then take four more bits just in case."

"Yes, ma'am."

"Hurry up, Adam," Lucy tells him.

"Yes, Mother." The strapping lad bolts out the door.

"Now, let's look at those maps again," Lucy says, pulling out the sheaf of maps. Both Carlos and I step out of our tub and cross to the table. I'm still in bare feet and Carlos is only in his long johns.

Turning to the second page of the map, Lucy says, "Here it is two hundred forty feet down."

"Wait a minute." I soaked in a good deal of the lay of the land on our outing. I flip back to the front page. "See, it's right near this creek. We'll drown in the excess water."

"How about over here? Two hundred eighty feet down," Lucy says, going down two levels and pointing at an old tunnel area now reserved for equipment storage.

"That looks promising," I agree until we pull back to the main map. "¡*Hijo de la chingada!* Right in the middle of the railroad switching yard."

Lucy whispers to me, "Stella, it is hard enough to keep the kids talking right. Could you please curb your profanity?"

"Sorry, cousin. I'll try to tone it down."

Carlos is looking out one of the few glazed windows. "We are getting too much water when we tunnel down, right?"

"Yes. Your current lack of trousers speaks to that, oh great and mighty boss man," I say.

Carlos walks over and checks the drying status of his pants as they hang over the stove. He pulls them down and starts tugging them on.

"So why did you ask that question?" I ask.

"Oh, sorry. I got distracted. Why not dig up?"

Lucy and I exchange a look that is universal to women who hear something stupid from men.

"It may have escaped your notice, oh great one, but the ground is below us, as are the miners." I could have added more sarcasm to my voice, but I'd have had to work hard at it.

"But isn't the mining entrance on Syndicate Hill?" Carlos asks.

"Couldn't we start at the bottom and burrow slightly upward and intersect the downward shaft?"

Impressed, Lucy and I exchange a look that diametrically opposes the one we gave each other moments ago.

"That's *genial*, Carlos!" Lucy offers.

"Well, I won't go as far as brilliant, but it is a good idea," I say. As a friend, mentor, and teammate, I can't let him get a swelled head. "But I think we should hold it until the rest of the group can go with us, assuming they can get here."

"Definitely," he replies.

The outer door opens to admit Adam Junior. "Message delivered. I actually watched Widow Ramos send it." He hands me back the extra eight bits I'd given him. I push them back to him.

"For a good deed done well," I say.

"I shouldn't," he replies. Adam looks at his mother. The two share some unspoken communication that I can't follow. The youngster hands me back four of the coins. "This is fair, cousin," he says to me.

"Fair enough," I say, admitting defeat. I don't want to puncture the boy's pride, nor that of his family.

Adam thrusts the coins into his breeches. "By the way, is there any reason why the Gargoyle would be watching our house?"

"What?" Lucy snaps. She goes over to the front window, which is about the size of a postage stamp and made of circularly rippled glass. She looks out.

"Oh!" Gretchen exclaims. Her eyes light up. "Can I go play with him, Mommy?"

"No! Under no circumstances."

"Awwww. He's fun."

"You heard me, Gretchen."

All of the buildings are wooden. I don't understand how there could be a gargoyle. I look at Lucy as she comes back to the table. "I'm confused," I say.

"Me too," Carlos chimes in. "There is a statue watching us?"

"Gargoyle ain't no statue," Gretchen offers with a certain amount of derision that children reserve for adults who don't understand. Holly cuffs her sister across the back of the head.

"Don't talk to grownups that way," Holly offers in her own tone of scorn.

This prompts the four Rileys to all try to talk at once before Lucy barks, "Quiet! What would your father think of this?" Her interjection takes over the house. "That's better. First of all, Gretchen, your sister is right. You listen to your elders, not correct them."

"Sorry, Mama."

"You don't owe *me* an apology, little girl." The diminutive takes the starch out of the youngster.

"I'm sorry I spoke that way to you, Mrs. Ochoa."

I have to keep myself from laughing at her dejected, embarrassed little girl face. "I forgive you, Gretchen. Always remember that God says to forgive those who wrong us."

"Yes, ma'am."

"That's better," Lucy says. "Now, all three of you, I think I can keep discipline in this house until your father returns without your inexperienced aid."

"Yes, Mama," they say in unison.

Lucy lets out a heavy sigh. "Stella, the Gargoyle is a young boy, about the same age as my Adam over there. He seems to be an orphan, but no one seems to know whose. Also, no one seems to know where he lives, sleeps, or eats. He does make a few coins doing errands for folks around, especially the mine foreman."

"Mama?"

"Yes, Adam?"

"There has been a rumor that the Gargoyle is a bast— By-blow of Mr. Jasperson by one of the wh— Dance hall ladies."

"I would believe that. I think he spends more of his time entertaining those women than doing his damned job."

"Regardless of his ignoble lineage, he is probably spying on us for the Jaspersons," I posit.

"Yes," Lucy says.

"That's no problem. We expected that, anyway. Carlos, we probably should know who it is. Shall we introduce ourselves?"

"I think we definitely should, Stella."

Behind us, I hear, "Mama?"

"Yes, Gretchen."

"What does ig-no-bell mean?"

"You know where the dictionary is. Go look it up and give me three sentences using it."

The tone Gretchen uses to reply, "Yes, Mama," makes me chuckle.

Carlos opens the door to find dusk sitting heavy in the street. It is empty except for a dog chasing a cat through the mud. "Adam? Where did you see this Gargoyle?" he asks.

Adam says, "Look up." Sure enough, a youth perches on the roof of the opposing house staring at us. The boy sits back on his heels with his arms resting on his knees. His inky-black hair is long and wild, as if it had been caught in the main gearing of a locomotive.

"Hello there," I say. He remains still like a pond on a windless summer day. The boy doesn't blink. He doesn't move. He doesn't even seem to breathe. I see how he got his nickname. "My name is Stella Ochoa. This here is Carlos de Aldana."

"You be the one that done made them ground snakes," he says in a voice that might well have been a rusty hinge. He manages to speak without moving anything but his mouth.

"Yes, that was me."

"Show me." As toneless as he says it, I can't decide if it is a command, a request, or a plea.

"Excuse me?

"I wanna saw it."

Carlos whispers to me, "*Loco en la cabeza.*" I ignore him.

"Maybe later. What's your name?"

"Gargoyle."

"You don't have another name? Like one your mother and father gave you?" For the first time, I see him move. His jaw tightens and his lips form a thin line. He clenches both fists, making his prominent forearms bulge. It emphasizes that he is almost skeletal except for what looks like masses of twisted hemp under weathered skin.

"Gargoyle."

"OK, Gargoyle. Can you tell me why you are watching this house?"

"Get coins from boss and star man. Wanna to see ground snakes."

"Why don't you come down here?" Carlos asks with a shake of his head. I think he feels this boy poses a threat to us. Yet he hasn't even shifted his position.

"No. Hurts," Gargoyle says.

"We won't hurt you. We don't bite or hit," I say.

"Not you."

Looking toward Carlos, I say, "He won't hurt you either."

Gargoyle just shakes his head.

"Well then, we'll leave you—"

"Show snakes!" the youngster barks as he stands. He is taller than I expected—a flagpole, tall and narrow. He wears only a torn pair of breeches that doesn't quite cover his ass or anything else between his legs. The clothing obviously was discarded as unrepairable, and I see why.

Carlos tenses beside me.

"Gargoyle, I don't do witchcraft for the fun of it or just to be a show."

"How many coins?" he asks, holding out a handful of coinage that actually total quite a sum.

"I'm not a performer, Gargoyle. We'll bid you a good evening."

The youth crouches down on his haunches again.

I turn around and go back into the house. Carlos backs through the doorway after me.

"He's not a threat, Carlos."

"Stella, you are too trusting," he says, closing the door.

"I haven't ever heard of Gargoyle ever hurting anyone," Lucy says from the kitchen portion of the living area.

"He is a very strange boy," I muse. "There is something about him that seems familiar. At least we now know who will be spying on us."

"Carlos, you are welcome to stay and sup with us," Lucy says. "It's just beans and ham, but I fancy it is much better than what Old Frank would rustle up."

"I'll stay, Mrs. Riley. Thank you."

"Girls, set the table."

A knock at the door prompts Lucy to say, "Adam, will you see who that is?"

"Yes, Mother."

"Hello, Mrs. Ramos," Adam says as he opens the door.

"Telegram for Mrs. Stella Ochoa," says a querulous voice. I turn around to see a plump Spanish woman in her later years holding a folded piece of paper.

"That would be me." I hand the woman the four bits I'd taken from Adam. "Thank you, Mrs. Ramos."

"You are welcome." She stands there in the doorway as if planted there.

"I hope you have a pleasant evening, Sara," Lucy says from the other side of the room. She motions for Adam to close the door. The widow nods but with a sour look on her face as she backs out. "Damned woman would watch the birth of a child just to know what color its skin and hair are to make insinuations on who the father is," Lucy says, scooping beans onto the china plates. Holly follows along behind her, putting a piece of cornbread on top.

I open the note and read it aloud. "Coming. Next dirigible. Arrive 22nd with Leaping Fish. *Dos Campanas.*"

"Great. Let's eat," Lucy proclaims.

5—Wednesday, November 21, 1888

There is a downside to staying with family. I don't mind sleeping with someone, but doing so in such cramped quarters with someone you aren't intimate with is blessed difficult. Luciana's bed can't be even half the size of mine. It is more like the size of the one I had when I lived in Chapman's Boardinghouse. For two people, that makes *snuggly* seem like an understatement. I can't even shift around without waking my cousin. Lucy snores gently with her back to me.

I don't think I ever really fall asleep. I just drift in and out of consciousness. During one of my more wakeful moments, my bladder asserts its presence and demands action. I slip out from under the heavy blankets. The chill hurries me to the outhouse, puffing clouds out of my mouth along the way.

Out back, a sow snorts at the interruption as I hustle to do my business. In her pen, she snuffles my way as if I might feed her. A dog gives a single bark three houses over. The moonlight shows me the path to the necessary. Even with the cold, the smell wrinkles my nose. With the door closed, I crouch above the frigid wood. I miss my powder room.

The thought makes me wonder if I have lost all of those things that made me a tough, independent woman. But it is a topic for another time, not the middle of the night in a dirty outhouse. I reassemble myself in the near darkness before unlatching the wooden planks used as a door.

The full moon over the roof ridge almost blinds me until something crosses between us. I freeze. A person perches up there, almost as if they want me to know they are there. I can't see more than the silhouette. It must be Gargoyle.

The wild child remains still on the gable as I jog back into the warmth of the house and throw the latch. While something familiar about him gnaws at me, his presence makes me shiver—and not just with the cold that the stove is driving away.

Safe in the house, my fatigue won't let me dwell on it long. I climb back into bed.

# # #

Crying wakes me some unknown time later. Normally, it takes a cannon under my bed to wake me, but a few things will cut through my sleep. The tinny bells of Mission Church that would call me to a demon escape are one of them. Someone weeping is the other. I don't know why, but they will me from the delicious depths of sleep every time.

Sunlight prises its way between the dark curtains over the tiny window. The bed shakes gently with the wracking sobs next to me.

"Lucy? Honey, what's wrong?"

I can hear her snuffle and try to turn off the waterworks. Her attempts fail as she dissolves completely. She says something, but it comes out as incoherent bullfrog croaking. Lucy turns over and buries herself into my chest. She wails against my skin, but the sound barely reaches my ears. Without knowing more, I just stroke her hair and hold her tight. She responds by cuddling closer. Her emotional jag continues for long enough that my arm her head is on starts filling with pins and needles.

Over time her raw emotions drift to mere crying. I can hear someone, presumably Adam Junior, stoking the stove with wood. My cousin pulls away from me. We are both covered in her tears. She wipes her eyes and blows her nose.

"Lucy, can you tell me what is wrong?"

"Adam is sick. He is having trouble breathing." I'm not dense enough to think that she is talking about her son. "We also lost two more of the trapped miners." It is added as an afterthought. I know where her loyalties lie.

"Is it because they are running out of air? What about the others?"

"I can't tell more than whether the other miners are alive or dead. Adam and I are so close that ..." She trails off. She shakes her head and sets her jaw. It doesn't stop a tear from leaking down her cheek. She wipes it away with a snuffle. "It feels more like the chest sickness than a loss of air."

Most people die of pneumonia—the chest sickness. I'm not about to mention that. Even if we get Adam out, he may not live through it. I'm not about to say that to my cousin, although she likely knows it. She needs hope. She needs direction.

"Well then, I think we will need to go in now and not wait for the rest of my team. You start breakfast and I'll get Carlos."

"Yes." Together we get up and somehow manage to get dressed in the tiny space. I put back on my rugged denim dress with an undershirt and my steel corset.

"Good morning, Mother. Good morning, Mrs. Ochoa," Adam says as I follow Lucy into the kitchen.

"Morning, son." Lucy goes right to the stove and starts frying rashers of bacon and slicing potatoes. She doesn't share her news. "Could you make sure the girls are up?"

"Yes, Mom."

"Morning, Adam. When you are done, could you show me the way to where Carlos is bunking?" I ask.

"I'd be happy to do so."

Gretchen and Holly come out of their room dressed before Adam even knocks on their door. I'm sure they'd been ready and were waiting to hear voices.

"Girls, go see if Mrs. Grandy has any eggs," Lucy tells them. The children don't catch the flatness in her tone. She hands the girls four dimes and a nickel. The two skip off.

"Mrs. Ochoa?" Adam Junior asks, offering me his arm gallantly.

"By all means," I say, taking his arm.

The town of Centralia is up and bustling. But it seems like the aimless activity of a beehive that has been accidentally jostled. With no jobs to go to, the men look listless, walking one way and then the other or absently doing chores that normally would have been done on Sunday. The children are running in packs, playing games that only they fathom. Only the women seem intent on specific tasks that take place whether their men are at work or not.

"You are going to be a heartbreaker when you get older," I say out of the blue.

"Excuse me?"

"Girls like men who treat them well. Offering me your arm was cultured and makes a woman feel appreciated."

"Uhhh," he responds, his cheeks going red, emphasizing the light freckling on his face.

"You don't have to say anything, Adam. Just remember my words."

"Yes, ma'am."

"It isn't an order, Adam. It's a strong suggestion if you want to keep the ladies interested."

"Thank you, cousin," he says, turning to avoid my eyes.

"That's more like it. Now, have you noticed that Gargoyle has been following us?" Adam's head turns on a swivel. The wild boy has been moving from housetop to housetop like a raccoon, using branches to jump from tree to tree. That he does it so gently and quietly surprises me. He is more like a cat.

"No, not until just now, Mrs. Ochoa."

"Yes, I seem to be of specific interest. He was on the roof of your house last night when I went to the privy."

"That's odd. No one has ever been able to find out where he sleeps at night, but he rarely comes down from the roofs."

"Doesn't he damage the shingles?"

"Nah. In fact, sometimes people have found repairs on their roof that they didn't do."

"Curiouser and curiouser,'" I say.

"*Alice's Adventures in Wonderland*. One of dad's favorites. Mom used to read it for us in front of the fire at night."

"So no one knows much about Gargoyle?" I ask, trying to keep the conversation away from his father.

"He will play with the kids sometimes. They throw stuff up on the roof, and he tosses it back. Other times he plays hide-and-go-seek."

"He doesn't talk very well. He couldn't have been very old when he was abandoned. But he couldn't have survived if he'd been turned out too young," I muse.

"Well, three years ago, some people caught him eating from pig troughs. Since then we take turns leaving a bit of food out on the edge of the roof for him."

"Very Christian of you," I say.

"If you say so. I think it would be more Christian for someone to take him in," Adam says.

I chuckle. "Might not be as easy as you think," I offer. "I've been dealing with stray children in Boston for most of a year now. You find that few of them really want to be tamed."

Adam harrumphed.

"Onto a new topic," I say. "You are about to learn this anyway, but your father is ill. Your mother's gift discovered that he has pneumonia." Adam doesn't say anything right away, but I feel the arm I'm wrapped around tense.

"I've avoided asking this because of what you might answer," he says, "but can you really save my father?"

"My answer hasn't changed, Adam. I'll try. I think with all of the help I've received, I have better than an even chance. I know that isn't much consolation, but I'm much more optimistic than when I first got here."

"A flip of the coin is better than I would have given him even with rescue efforts. Not too many men are saved after any cave-in."

"That assessment is quite stoic."

Adam blushes. "I'm ashamed to say that I cried myself to sleep the first night. After that, I've been too busy."

"There is no shame in crying. I think more men should. It releases poisons that would otherwise cloud our judgment and tear at our sanity."

"Perhaps, but it isn't very manly."

"My familiarity with being manly is limited to the actions of my dead husband. I didn't know him long enough to see him cry."

"How did he die?"

"In the Irish War of Independence."

"I'm sorry."

"Thank you, but it was many years ago. I'm mostly reconciled with it."

"So, you don't have a sweetheart?"

What a loaded question, I think. "That's a long story, Adam." I change subjects to get him off my checkered past. "I know I told you it is OK to cry, but for the short term, you need to be strong for your mother. We are fetching Carlos so we can have a run at getting to the trapped people today. If we fail, I'm afraid of what might happen to your mother."

"I understand." We walk along in silence for another minute before Adam says, "Here we are."

He knocks on the door, and Old Frank, a thin man about six years older than God, opens the door. His skin is white except where the coal dust has impregnated his pores and the area around each hair.

"Ya lookin' fer yer friend?" Old Frank says after spitting a red bit of goo onto the ground.

"Yes, sir, Mr. Harbin," Adam replies.

"I never done knowed a feller to sleep late as him."

I come to the defense of my partner. "Mr. Harbin, we normally work at night. We are used to catching up during the day."

"Sounds good as any," he replies with a scowl. "Him on the couch. Good luck budging him. I done made breakfast, ate it, and cleaned up, and he ain't moved."

"I think I can get him going," I say with a smile. I steal over right next to the barrel-shaped form of the leader of the *Dos Campanas*, which is under half a dozen blankets. I bend down and whisper into his ear, "Demon escape in the financial district."

Carlos springs up. "What? Where? Demon?"

I toss him his trousers. "We have to get moving."

"A demon? Here?"

"Not a demon. It's time to do what we came here for. We'll wait outside for you to get dressed."

"Gonna try to rescue thems miners?" Frank asks.

"That's the plan," I say, giving more cheer to the statement than I really feel.

"Then you be watchin' out fer Grondr."

"Excuse me?" I ask. "What's Grondr?"

As Old Frank opens his mouth to speak, Adam takes me by the arm and leads me to the door. "They'll be careful, Mr. Harbin." I know when someone is trying to end a conversation. I let myself be taken outside.

"Jesus Christ, that was close," Adam says with a heavy sigh.

"What? Adam, you've confused me."

"Old Frank will go on for days about Grondr if you let him. He seems to have collected and concocted more tales than anyone else I know."

"What is Grondr?"

"There is a myth about a miner who intentionally collapsed a tunnel on some of the others because they teased him. But the cave-in caught him as well. It's said that the devil was so impressed that he didn't let him die, but rather turned him into a hulking stone beast. It is cursed to wander the dark tunnels to prey on other cruel miners for all eternity. There have been sightings by one person or the other over the years. It's like our version of the snipe, or the Michigan Dogman."

"OK, I guess I didn't need to hear about that after all. Thank you for sparing me the harangue."

"You're welcome."

The door opens and Carlos comes out holding his hand up to block the sun. "Why do you have me up so early?"

"Saddle up, *jefe*. It's time to get to work."

#

If anyone had said two weeks ago that I'd be out in the snow, surrounded by blackberry bushes, waiting to burrow into a mine, I'd have called them cracked in the head. But here we are.

Between Adam and Lucy, they manage to find what seems to be the best approach. The north side of the hill is steeper and closer to the main shaft. Time and erosion have exposed the sedimentary rock here, leaving only patches of vegetation. Right now the upper edges of each of the layers wear a dusting of white.

Both Carlos and I are in our coats, augmented with woolen underclothing and sweaters provided by my cousin. At the moment, I'm uncomfortably warm, but I expect that to change. And it is always easier to shed a layer than to find clothing underground.

"Here, I brought these for you," Adam Junior says, offering us mining helmets.

"I'm not terribly worried about something falling on my head," I rebut.

"I am. You're sloppy," Carlos teases.

"When I said I wanted you to bring wind with us, I didn't mean to break it," I saltily offer back. With great maturity, Carlos sticks his tongue out at me. We really are more like a family than coworkers.

"No, Mrs. Ochoa, I brought these so you could see." Adam strikes a match and lights the wick sticking out of the concave metal surface on the front of the helmets. The light they produce should see us through our journey. "The flames are fed by the tiny oil reservoirs behind them. And because they are on your head, they leave your hands free."

I am thrilled and praise him with, "*Magnífico*, Adam. Thank you!" Both Carlos and I put on our helmets. Mine isn't a great fit until Adam adjusts a strap on the inside.

"Alright. Just so we are clear," Carlos says, "we travel slightly upward due south until we hit the shaft."

"Make sure you get the main shaft and not the ventilation shaft," Adam says. "You'll know because of the rising wind in the ventilation one. The main shaft has cables for the elevator machinery and lanterns that are never extinguished. In fact, the entire tunnel complex has at least one burning every few hundred feet."

"Adam, if you aren't allowed in the mine, how do you know so much?" I probe.

Lucy speaks up with her mouth drawn tight. "Sometimes his father sneaks him in."

"Mom! You aren't supposed—"

"Adam, I know and I don't approve. But as it is your father who does it, I bite my tongue and pretend that the stories you make up are reasonable." Adam Junior looks at his mother aghast. "I don't want you to be another rock digger, with me just waiting for the message that you're dead or trapped—just like your father!" Tears are streaming down her face.

"But—"

"Stella and Carlos, please go," my cousin says, wiping the tears from her cheeks. "Please save my husband so that I can round on him about making a miner out of my son."

There isn't anything good to say to that. "Yes, Lucy," I reply. "We'll see you back at the house. Carlos, cuddle up tight."

# # #

The mining lamps may have been a mistake. The first time we went down, we couldn't see how claustrophobic the hollow we were in was. This time we are extremely aware of the coffin-like space. As much as I empathize with and love the earth, I can't imagine working beneath it every day for hours and hours. The press of the rock above makes me feel like we'll be entombed forever. But it is only an emotion. I press on, feeling Carlos's warm breath on my neck.

This earth is different. The sediment is very firmly set in its layers. I press through and break each stratum as if it were peanut brittle. It doesn't allow me to pass smoothly but makes all of those sharp edges and smashed corners stick out toward us. I'm forced to make our burrow that much wider to compensate.

"*Cacafuego* but this ground doesn't want me to control it. It's fighting against me."

"Keep pushing, Stella. Think of the miners."

"I am, Boss."

That being said, we have to deal with only an inch or so of water, whatever leaks in as I press mostly laterally. Our travel is a pitch up of maybe a foot's rise for every twenty forward. The water drains away beneath us through the soil before my bubble moves onward. Our boots are good enough to keep the freezing water away from us.

We've gone no more than a hundred feet when I sense an opening in the rock ahead. I can't see through rock and dirt, but I can feel when the earth stops, though rarely the shape or size of that void. I can sometimes feel what is beyond. This time all I get is emptiness. It seems to be too early for the shaft, but what do I know about mining?

A few minutes later, as we are traveling at the speed of a crawl, the opening into a cavern ahead isn't a surprise. There is a two-foot drop down to something that looks like a floor and six feet of space above it. "Watch your footing, Carlos," I say as I step down.

I pan my light around to see a straight tunnel some twenty feet wide running in our direction.

"Are we in the mine?" Carlos asks, dropping down to my level.

"Looks like it to me, but where are the lanterns?" I ask with only our feeble light to pierce the gloom.

"This wasn't on the mine map," Carlos shares, showing once again his long memory.

"True. Well, no matter what, this saves me fighting our way through and will speed our trip. Let's go."

Carlos nods in my lamplight.

The floor is level for another hundred feet until it starts to get rough and turn uphill. But the ceiling doesn't match it. I crouch down and continue forward, only to have my boots crunch into the earth like it's the hard top layer of snow frozen overnight.

I step back and pan my light down. I see white shards poking up out of gray powder. I bend down and brush away some of the gray detritus to reveal a human leg bone all the way to the pelvis. I don't need to remove any more of the rock dust to see that the pile in front of us is nothing more than a mass of the dead.

"That's gruesome," Carlos observes. "An earlier cave-in?"

"Probably. There must be two hundred skeletons here."

"We can't stop for this. We can report it later," my teammate says, urging us forward.

"I agree." I stand up, and my light shines directly onto a man on the other side of the pile. The shape disappears down behind the mound. "Hello?" If it hadn't moved, I would have just assumed my mind was playing tricks on me.

"What is it?" Carlos asks. He obviously didn't see what I had.

"I saw someone."

"Down here?"

"Carlos, when have I ever led you astray?"

"Never, when it counted, Stella."

"Then watch our back. There is someone in here with us."

"Got it."

I start picking my way around the edges of the mass grave, keeping my eyes peeled for any movement. I pan my light around. At the edges of my vision, Carlos's light scans around. I reach the far end of the pile, only to find the way blocked thirty feet farther on by a rockslide and a vaguely humanoid figure.

"Carlos," I whisper, pointing ahead.

"What in all that is holy is that?"

"You've got me."

With both of our lights on it, we can see it better. Humanoid is an accurate description. Take the most muscled dockworker you've ever seen and double him in muscles, but all of it made out of blocks of stone held together by clay. Its arms hang all the way to the ground almost like a gorilla's. There doesn't seem to be any neck, but it sports a headlike bulge. There are depressions where we have eyes, but nothing looks out of them, and an opening about where the mouth should sit.

"If you don't know about something made out of stone, then we likely have a problem," Carlos whispers.

"Don't borrow trouble."

"Maybe the mythical Grondr?"

"Shhh. Let me see if it will talk to us." I turn toward it and say, "Hello?"

[More defilers.] The reply isn't in words. I feel it in the stones around us creaking and shifting. Carlos looks around with some concern as dust drifts down from the ceiling.

"We don't mean to defile anything. We are only trying to save our friends."

[Defilers die. You join them.] I hear the anger in the grinding of the earth of its reply.

"We didn't come to fight. We only want to get more of those like us out of the mine."

[So they tear apart more? More pain? More loss? No. They die. You die.] It shakes with each word, causing the whole cavern to reverberate in the shaking of its fundament.

"I don't know what it's saying, but quit pissing it off," Carlos says.

"You don't hear it?"

"Only the walls, floors, and ceiling threatening to collapse."

"Let me try a different tack," I whisper back. Before I can say anything to the creature, I can feel wind in the room swirling. Carlos shows his initiative as he begins exercising his own witchcraft. He always told me to be prepared. "My name is Stella. What is yours?"

[Protector.]

"If you protect, then you have to know that I do the same for those of my kind."

[You serve thieves. Your kind must die.]

"We don't mean to steal or defile. My friend Carlos and I aren't here to steal anything."

[You help them rip and tear. You join those.] It points at the bones behind us with its massive arm.

"I can't let you stop us as we protect our own."

[Then die.] It rushes us with a fleetness that belies its bulk.

"Incoming, Carlos!" I already feel a cyclone of wind forming around us, but it won't be up in time. With ten times the normal effort, I form a wall of earth between us and the creature. The knuckle-walking beast flows right through it as if it were nothing more than air. "Uh-oh!" I yell.

[Die. Die. Die,] it chants as it swings one enormous arm in a roundhouse punch with the speed of a viper. It doesn't seem to have a hand, but the end of its arm forms a massive spear point that hits me full in the gut. I fly backward, scraping my head on the ceiling as I go. As I land, Protector swings again at Carlos, but my partner isn't there. In our fights against demons, I've seen him use this trick of pushing himself to one side with a gust of wind.

"Stella?"

"I'm still in one piece," I say, spitting something warm and bitter from my mouth. *Thanks to my metal corset*, I say only in my mind. It blunted a good deal of the force and spread it out. I'm having trouble pulling in a full breath, but otherwise, I seem in decent shape. With some pain in my chest, I stand up, leaning heavily on the wall to do so. Now, having felt the creature's touch, I'm convinced it really is completely made of earth and stone.

I see a cat-and-mouse game taking place as I regain my footing. Protector swings again at Carlos. My friend continues to be the fruit fly that annoys you but can't be squashed. The leader of the *Dos Campanas* darts back and forth, evading the earthen creature time and again.

I reach out with my mind to control the beast's body. As odd as it sounds, I try to force it back to solid rock. The movement of the elemental slows to a crawl. Now it appears more like a slow-motion statue rather than the swing of an axe.

It turns its head toward me. Something lights in the sockets where there might have been an eye on a human. I feel the tingle that accompanies earthen magic. The metal around my waist and chest, which had just recently prevented me from being skewered, now tightens like a lady's maid who isn't happy with her mistress and is pulling on the corset laces for all she is worth. I feel a biting pain in my abdomen and another in my chest as my former protection becomes my attacker.

I guess turnabout is fair play. The creature didn't know about my armor. Now, while I hold it still, it crushes the life out of me like a python. It's a losing battle for me. "Carlos," I wheeze out, "I can't breathe."

My friend buffets the creature with gusts of wind, managing to knock it over. It loses sight of me as it falls away. The constriction eases a bit. I work fast to command the metal to flow off my body like water. My chest is no longer held, but I still am having difficulty breathing.

By the same token, taking my attention away from the creature allows it to move. It refocuses on the iron that is now running down my legs. The metal solidifies and begins to constrict again.

"Are you alright?" my friend asks.

"Until it crushes my legs."

"Lean on me to the center of the hall." Carlos drags me, as I can't move my lower half. The magical war between the creature and me continues. It suddenly releases the metal and rushes us. Carlos's air responds by forming a tornado of debris inches from us. I strip the last metal from my body. Blood from a head wound I didn't realize I had drips down my forehead, deflecting off my eyebrows to run off the side of my face

[Aaarrghh!] the earth around us bellows from the blowing barrier.

"Keep it up, Carlos. It can't get to us."

I try to stand back up, but the pain in my chest is too much even for me, the queen of suffering demon damage. My breaths are increasingly shallow no matter how much I try to inhale. I am so focused on my own inability to perform normal bodily functions that I'm not of any use against this earthen creature.

"I ... can't ... breathe ..." I must have a punctured lung. I'm likely to die unless I manage to linger long enough for Maxwell to get here.

"Can you get us out if I carry you?" Carlos asks.

I nod as he scoops me up. To make it as easy as possible, I take us nearly straight up.

[Come back to die! Die! Defiler!] the creature screams as we leave the cavern.

Splitting my attention between breaking a path through the earth and trying to get enough air to survive is taxing me. My vision goes pink. I shake the blood away from my eyes.

"Just a few seconds more, Stella," Carlos says.

"Breathe ..." is all I manage to choke out. I feel a hard gust of wind against my face.

"Open your mouth, Stella." The air is channeled down my throat, expanding my chest. The expansion stabs more pains beneath my breast but gives me enough wind to put an extra push on our exit.

We vomit from the earth into the air like lava from a volcano, reaching forty feet high.

"Bring her down here. I can save her," Lucy says.

My air witch friend floats us down to a soft landing in the midst of Lucy, Adam, and Gargoyle.

I'm bubbling red at my mouth, and I can't manage even a simple breath. Lucy unbuttons my dress straps and pulls open my bloodstained blouse.

Looks like those boys are going to get a show with my chest bared, I think, somehow forgetting that I can't possibly live any longer without air.

"'Jesus went through all the towns and villages, teaching in their synagogues, proclaiming the good news of the kingdom and healing every disease and sickness,'" my cousin says as she massages my chest. The white magic she calls down like a thunderbolt has the subtlety of a locomotive hitting a buffalo on the high plains. It tears away the rest of my energy to heal the mortal wound, and with it my consciousness.

#

"Mama, she's awake," Gretchen says, her face out of focus and about four inches away from mine.

"Are you alright, Stella?"

I haven't gone to meet my maker yet, but I feel like a train ran over me, followed by a herd of wild stallions, and three times with the poderabile, just for good measure. "*Joder.*" I want there to be more vehemence coming from it, but I can't summon up the energy.

"Mama, she said—"

"I heard what she said. Just you never say it. Understand?"

"Yes, Mama."

"Stella, are you alright?"

"No, definitely not alright," I say, filling my lungs. I wince at a small amount of tenderness still deep inside. But I took the breath. My chest did go in and out. "But, I'm definitely much better than dead. Thank you, Lucy. Remind me to have Maxwell teach you some tricks of healing when he gets here. I thought you hit me with a stagecoach."

"I had to hurry. I thought you were going to die on me before I could heal you. I've never physicked anyone as badly damaged as you were—three broken ribs, with one puncturing your lung and another your bowels." With this knowledge, I use my own white witch powers to take stock of my condition. The ribs are back in place, and both organs have scar tissue. Not unusual. Little more than a deep scratch, my scalp wound oozes a bit around the bandage over it. I've been in worse shape—often.

"Well, I'll live with just a little bit of willow bark tincture if you have it," I say, trying to stand up. I don't get past sitting before the world spins like I am poised on a child's top. "Oh, I know better than that," I say, remembering that healing, especially from someone who isn't trained, zaps the strength.

"Mrs. Ochoa looks like Old Frank on Saturday night." Gretchen's precocity will either do her well or get her killed. I think it is a coin flip.

"Yes, honey. Bring your cousin a bowl of soup. Holly, bring the tincture of willow bark." A swig of the pain-dulling elixir will help shortly.

"Thank you, Holly. Thank you, Gretchen. And thank you, Lucy, for saving my life."

Luciana tears up in another random outburst of emotion. "I've already lost my husband. I'm not about to lose my cousin too." She runs to her bedroom. The two youngsters look at me with long faces.

"Don't worry, girls. Your mom is just sad."

"What about my dad?" Holly asks.

"We try again, honey. We try again and again until there is no hope. Miners have been trapped for months and been rescued."

The girls throw themselves into my arms. I get mild pain in the chest. Apparently, my ribs aren't fully healed. I'm not sure my hugs make a dent in their emotions, but one can hope.

"Now go give your mom a hug. She needs it."

# # #

After the waterworks stop, a red-eyed Lucy returns to throw herself into making lunch. I concentrate on just staying upright. The front door opens, and Adam comes in with Carlos and Old Frank.

"It seems you have survived again," Carlos teases. "You really need to stop taking so much damage."

I start to reply, and then look at the children. "I'm inhibited in expressing my contempt of your comment by the presence of children and at least one lady. But you may fold it until it is sharp corners and insert it into your lower sphincter."

"Mama, what's a sphincter?"

"Later, Gretchen," Lucy says with a voice that sounds like one step out of the grave.

"So, ya met Grondr," Frank says, breaking the tension he doesn't seem to notice.

"I thought you might want to pick the brain of the local Grondr expert," Carlos adds.

"You sure take a lot on yourself," I snarl. I'm not mad. I'm actually happy he brought Old Frank. It's a game between Carlos and me. Neither of us intends any real harm despite the jibes.

"Who runs this outfit?" Carlos teases back.

"At the moment, Grondr."

"So, ya was seein' him?" Frank asks.

"I'm not sure if it was Grondr, but it seemed to bear many of the attributes of your mythical, or not so mythical, beast."

"Carlos says it done talked to ya. What done it say?"

"I'll make you a deal, Frank. I'll tell you everything that happened if you share everything you know about the beast."

Adam groans. I can see the lust in Frank's eyes. Whether it is to get new stories or to tell all his tales is immaterial.

"I'll be guessin' that be a bargain."

Adam rolls his eyes.

# # #

Four hours later, Adam's head lolls over in the chair. His snores don't cut through Frank's stories.

"... the warrior crawled home without one of him foots. 'Fore he died, he told of the great earthen beast Grondr—"

I interrupt, setting down Holly's chalkboard with all of my notes. "I think we got it all, Frank. You are starting to repeat yourself."

"Sorry. I be gettin' excited when someone wanna hear 'bout the stories."

"Frank, would you like to stay for supper?" Lucy asks, with some of her normal perk returned to her voice.

"Ain't had a good meal in more weeks 'n I kin remember. I'd be more than pleased to be eatin' yer grub, Miss Lucy."

"Gretchen, set another place for Mr. Harbin."

"Yes, Mama."

"Shall I sum up what Frank has given us?" I ask.

"That sounds good," Carlos says. "This would be better at the pub. I could use a beer. But you know what they say about wishes and horses—"

Luciana turns around and interrupts with, "Holly, get Mr. Aldana a beer from Papa's keg. Does anyone else want one?"

Everyone but the two girls end up with wooden tankards of brew. "Ah, that is so much better," Carlos celebrates. "Thank you, Mrs. Riley. And thank you, Miss Holly, for bringing it to me."

"This is a good brew," I remark.

"Centralia Subterranean," Frank says with a bit of pride. "Marcus Fernandez brews it in his spare time. Couple of folks grows the barley and hops on the north slopes. Careful, 'cause it be packin' a wallop."

"Thanks for the warning," I reply, already feeling the alcohol after just a couple of sips. "So, let's make some assumptions," I say, setting my drink on the end table. "Let's say everything Frank says is the gospel."

"Every word, I swears," Mr. Harbin says after wiping beer foam from his upper lip.

"I never doubted you believe it, Frank. Just that sometimes stories come from nothing. So let's assume it's all true."

Carlos nods.

"We have a creature that has been around for hundreds of years as the Shawnee mythos says from their time of digging for the burning rock here. This entire area is taboo as a result. All of the native tribes avoid this entire valley.

"Also, the native legends say the creature can hide in plain sight. This ties in with some of the later stories from the older miners who say that Grondr can take any shape or size.

"It can cause tunnel collapses to punish those who are cruel or hateful. I'd say we are better off assuming that it can do it anytime."

"Don't forget that arrows and spears bounce off it," Carlos adds.

"I'd say that is a given," I tell him. "In fact, I'd add bullets and fire. Neither has any effect on stone."

Carlos goes on. "Wind, water, plants, animals, and impacts can damage stone, but all of them take time. Nothing that moves that fast will stay around long enough for that."

I nod in agreement.

"Explosives," Adam Junior offers.

"Good Lord, no," Lucy says, crossing herself.

"I agree, cousin. That would be a last resort in my book. I don't know how much it will damage Grondr. And even more so, how will the concussion affect the trapped miners?"

"No way it gonna help 'em," Frank adds.

"What do you think, Carlos?" I inquire to his superior experience. "You've been fighting demons longer than me by a long shot."

He looks thoughtful before taking a pull of his beer. "I say this isn't a demon. Our normal tactics aren't going to get us anywhere. Where would we put it? Besides, as I see it, it's just protecting its home."

"What?" Frank asks. I can see where he is going as clearly as a bull charging a matador.

"Do we hang a man for protecting his land or his home? The earth is Grondr's home. And every time he's killed someone, it has been in protection against miners," I pontificate.

"Damned but I never be looking at it that way," Frank says with a wrinkled-up face. "That do put a different twist on thangs."

"It sees the miners, all of the miners, as intruders damaging and destroying its home," Carlos says.

"And maybe even itself," I add. "Grondr is a being of rock and may be the personification of the earth itself. If we mine the ground around here, Grondr may be hurt as much as if someone ran it through with a sword."

"Why would the ground be attackin' us'ns if it don't at any mines otherwhere?"

"Good question, Frank," I say. "As an earth witch, I do know various grounds act differently when I'm working with them. It may be as simple as that. This one is different."

Frank nods thoughtfully.

"Dinner everyone," our hostess calls.

"So what do you think are our chances with the whole team, Stella?" Carlos asks professionally.

"Fair," I say, shading the truth more than a bit. Carlos gives me a flat look that indicates he isn't quite as sure as my pronouncement makes me sound. I understand his misgivings. Grondr isn't what we've become experts at. I wish my mother were here for me to ask her about this. She has more experience with recalcitrant earth.

I continue. "We have four advantages. We outnumber Grondr six to one. We are a team that works together. Grondr doesn't know about the capabilities of our whole team. And we are flexible." In my mind, I go back to what I told Adam earlier today—a coin flip.

With a stern look from our hostess, an unspoken agreement falls over the dining table to talk about anything but the trapped miners, Grondr, or anything related to our recent adventures. I pipe up with discussions of the *Majesty*. Lucy joins in, sharing her experiences. The children, definitely seen and heard in this household, are all over us with questions. Carlos, who didn't experience any of it, even throws a few our way.

Old Frank tosses in, "Harrumph. Just 'nother new-fangled geegaw. Me, I's be stickin' ta horses and mules. They don't be leavin' ya hangin' in t'air when if'n they break down."

"But it is so magnificent to fly in the air like a bird," Lucy offers, her eyes by this time having lost most of their redness.

"Yes. Did you read about the explosive glider? Not only do you fly in the air but you do it so fast!" Adam adds. Carlos is looking a bit green.

"What about trains, Mr. Harbin?" I ask, steering the conversation clear of airborne contrivances.

"Solid. Earthbound. I can't be liking all of the noise and soot they be makin', but I rode on 'em when I was young as you folk. Used to lay track too."

The conversation grinds on, and the plates empty.

Gretchen and Holly begin clearing the table. I help. This draws concerned looks from both Lucy and Carlos.

"Mrs. Ochoa, this is our chore," Gretchen insists.

"Yes, you are a guest," Holly says. "Besides, you were hurt and need to get well."

"I like to help, girls. How about, since I don't know where things go, I wash, and you dry and put away."

It doesn't take a crowbar to get them to let me help.

The conversation continues and morphs to coal versus demon power. Lucy, Adam, and Old Frank seem to be carrying the entire discussion. They keep trying to wrangle Carlos into the discussion, but he replies only enough to be polite. He sits back and drinks a beer. It doesn't surprise me that the three of them come up with nothing novel to add to an argument I've heard most of my life. I smile as I scrub.

By the time the dishes are done, I'm feeling dizzy. Carlos pushes out a chair for me. A simple nod of his head commands me to sit. I follow it willingly. Closing my eyes, I remain still. It helps. I'm feeling almost human when the Rileys gets Carlos telling tales about hellfighting.

Unlike many, Carlos tells it straight. He doesn't embellish. He doesn't need to, as some of our exploits are rather gruesome and horrific. I'm pleased for the children's sake that he avoids the worst tales—the times when we've found bodies ground up like sausage.

"... when the building corner collapsed, bouncing a bed off her shoulder. She never has learned to duck." The audience hangs on his every word. Hellfighters are considered by many to be romantic figures. I'd beg to disagree. It is hard, dirty, and dangerous work.

"It wasn't an entire bed. Only the headboard," I object.

"I stand corrected," Carlos says. "But be that as it may, it ended up breaking her shoulder. Our white witch, Maxwell, showed up and healed it—"

His comment sparks a thought in me enough to interrupt my partner's diatribe. "Luciana? How did you happen to be Johnny-on-the-spot when we came out of the mines this morning? I thought you were going home. For that matter, how did you know where we were coming out?"

"Gargoyle. We'd started going home when he came up and begged me to come with him because you were in trouble. I thought he was mad, but he promised me anything if I just would come with him. He took me right to the spot where you came out of the ground. I don't know how."

"Earth witch?" Carlos says, looking at me. It isn't really a question so much as looking for confirmation.

I nod. "I don't see any other way it could be. So many things make sense. With the damage to the earth here, I can understand why he wouldn't want to be near it. It would also make sense why he's a bit peculiar. Imagine if you had to live your whole life with someone stabbing a knife in your gut and head every few minutes.

"Carlos, we really need to find a way to help him," I implore.

"One thing at a time, Stella. He's lived here this long with it. He can wait a few more days."

"I really hate it when you are right all the time," I say.

"Part of my charm."

Fatigue rolls over me like a thick morning fog off the bay. "I think I'm done in for the day. I'm going to take my leave. Please don't let me break up the conversation."

6—Thursday, November 22, 1888

The warmth of my cousin spooning behind me drags me back down to sleep, but the pressure of my bladder and the excitement of what the new day promises overrides this.

The noise of Adam stoking the fire in the other room reaches me. My breath turns to white puffs in the air. I slide out of bed, my teeth chattering before my feet even hit the floor. This is reminiscent of winter mornings at Chapman's. I've gotten soft having central heating in my Brick Factory. I dress in haste, lusting for the heat of the stove.

Adam hasn't fully dressed yet. I wait until he buttons his shirt before easing into the room. "Good morning, Adam," I whisper.

"Good morning, cousin. How are you feeling this morning?"

I snuggle up to the stove to feel its comforting heat. "Definitely better. I don't feel as if I'm going to topple over."

"That's an improvement. There's a train in this morning."

"A train? How do you know?"

"Didn't you hear the whistle? Came in about five this morning," he says, tying his boots.

"I thought the trains only ran when there was coal to deliver."

"It was an engine pulling only two cars, each carrying an armadillo."

"I don't suppose that they might be planning to use those to dig out your dad and the others?"

Adam scoffs. For only fourteen, he seems to have more than his share of sarcasm. "I used to be eager to follow my dad into the mines until I saw the danger and abuses. The Jaspersons wouldn't spend a nickel on any of us. There are always hundreds of immigrants willing to work for just about any wages at any job. And that just makes it even more dangerous, with all of the people who don't know what they are doing down there."

"So the machines are here for what?"

"To dig a new shaft into a new vein. With those *pinche* digging machines, they can do it without even hiring anyone else," Adam says, confirming my suspicions about how low the Jaspersons are.

"Well, I think we should warn them of the danger they are running. Grondr is likely to take exception to those things."

"As a good Christian, I should," Adam admits. "But deep inside me, I say let them learn the hard way."

A knock on the door stops me before I can reproach him. "Are you expecting anyone this early in the morning?" I ask instead.

"No. With the mine shut down, everyone has been getting extra sleep, and the kids know better. But then, I think I might have heard the dirigible coming in early a few minutes ago. Maybe it is your team?"

"I guess it is possible." We look at the door, and then at each other. "It's your home. You are the man of the house, at least at the moment."

Adam walks to the door and opens it. Had I guessed for a month, the short, tubby *idiota* standing there wouldn't have been among the candidates I'd pick. He is accompanied by a man wearing a lawman's badge.

"Adam," the sheriff greets my cousin.

"Mr. Riley, is Mrs. Ochoa here?" asks tubby.

Adam steps aside and invites the men in. I might have suggested that Adam be careful about inviting snakes into one's home, but I'm just a guest.

I begin my calculated rudeness by not bothering to stand. "Mr. Bruce Jasperson, what brings you way out here to the Duchy of Pennsylvania? You come to save this poor boy's father and the other miners?" I inquire, proverbially driving a wooden splinter under his fingernail. We've hissed and snarled at one another over clearly defined lines for most of a year. I believe he has been the source of many of the demon releases in the northeast duchies. With his money and connections, he is nearly untouchable without overwhelming proof against him.

My statement puts him off his stride as he blushes and clears his throat loudly. "I'm here because you have once again interfered with my business."

"Because I want to save your workers? I thought you might be grateful, Mr. Jasperson."

"For giving the families false hopes at finding people who already sit at the right hand of God himself? For keeping them from earning honest pay for moving forward with the business at hand? No. You are a pestilence to these people, my family, and my business."

I can't help but needle him. "Pestilence? Three syllables. I'm impressed, Brucie."

He clouds up and replies, "Insult me if you like, Mrs. Ochoa. I've broken people bigger than you. I will enjoy reducing you and your family to nothing more than trash-digging wastrels."

All interest in teasing this man evaporates in a fit of boiling anger. "You can come after me all you want, Mr. Jasperson. But you interfere with my family, by lineage or those I've adopted, and I'll make sure that you suffer for an eternity before sending you to hell."

"You heard her threaten me, Sheriff Billings. Arrest this ... this thug."

The sheriff has a deep voice that matches the breadth of his chest. "I did hear a threat. However, it was phrased in a conditional." The man is smart and believes in his job. I think I like this lawman with his long jaw. "That isn't an offense in the Duchy of Pennsylvania, nor under the laws of the king." The scowl he receives from Jasperson is a threat in and of itself.

"Fine. Then arrest her and her cohort, Carlos de Aldana, for trespassing, claim jumping, and corporate espionage," the shorter man barks with the authority of a small dog. I toss a dirty look at the snarling little man in the fifty-dollar suit.

"You think there is a jail here that will hold us?" I ask with a smirk.

He smiles with his nearly perfect teeth. "Please resist, Mrs. Ochoa. Then I can telegraph for the witch police."

I turn to the middle-aged lawman and hold out my wrists to be shackled. "Take me in, Sheriff. I won't resist."

"One moment, Mrs. Ochoa. At the moment, all I have is the word of a person who hasn't been here that you are trespassing. Of the other two, I have no data."

"Of course she is trespassing. I own this town," Bruce rails.

"Not exactly, Mr. Jasperson," the sheriff contradicts. "The streets, the homes, railroad, and airship port are not within your control. Right now she is a guest in a home."

"She went into the mine. Darrin Jasperson reported it to me."

"Did you do that, Mrs. Ochoa?"

"I'm not sure, Sheriff Billings. Carlos and I went down into the earth to try to rescue the miners. We did find a tunnel that had been caved in. It isn't on any of the mining charts. I will be honest that we were targeting the trapped men and women."

"See, she admits it. Now arrest this lawless wench."

The sheriff gives a deep sigh. "Mrs. Ochoa, would you object to coming with me until we get this straightened out?"

"Not at all, Sheriff Billings," I say, offering my wrists again.

"That won't be necessary, Mrs. Ochoa. If you are half the witch the townsfolks' gossip says you are, then metal cuffs wouldn't hold you five minutes."

I don't disabuse him, though it would be less than five seconds.

Luciana bursts out of her room, still in her shift. "Don't you dare, Zack Billings! Stella is the only one who can possibly get my husband and your daughter out of the mine alive."

"I have to do it, Mrs. Riley. The law is the law."

I follow the lawman's instructions out the door.

"Suck on that lemon, Mrs. Ochoa," Jasperson crows as he follows us out.

Behind me, I hear Adam curse, "*Tu eres más feo que el culo de un mono.*" I'm not sure who it is aimed at, but the Rileys' door slams.

"Adam!" Luciana exclaims through the now-closed door.

#

Imagine the stub of a pencil sharpened on each end, made of metal, and twenty feet tall and fifty long. The pointed ends are actually massive screws with grinding wheels at the leading edge of each thread. Each of the two of them sits on a railroad flatcar. Men swarm all over one of them, opening panels and performing all manner of tasks. Darrin Jasperson oversees the beehive of activity. He waves his arms energetically and bellows orders.

"Sheriff Billings, what is that?" I ask, pointing at the metal monster.

"Those are the armadillos. They are getting the first one ready to go down into the mines."

Right into the jaws of death, I think. I can't not give them a warning.

"Sheriff, can we stop over there?" I ask. "I have to give Darrin Jasperson a message." He gives me a stare. "I assure you that I'm not going to cause trouble or even try to delay you taking me to jail."

"As you will, Mrs. Ochoa."

I pace the lawman.

"C'mon, you maggots. This machine has to be digging by noon, or we'll dock your pay," Darrin barks.

"Mr. Jasperson," the sheriff says.

"What is it, Billings?" the tubby man asks, not taking his attention from the activity on the armadillo.

"Sir, I have someone here who wants to speak to you."

The foreman turns his head back to glance at who it is. He does a double take. "What the hell are you doing here?"

"Mr. Jasperson, I'm not here to do anything but give you a warning," I say.

"Warning? By the jumping Jesus, what is she doing here, Sheriff? I thought my brother had her in your jail?"

"We are on our way, sir. She felt she needed to speak to you. I didn't see any harm."

"I really don't want to cause any trouble, Mr. Jasperson," I tell him. "I want to tell you that there is a creature, a powerful creature, down in the earth."

"Grondr, I've heard the tall tales. It is nothing more."

"Sir, he wants to kill anyone going down into the mines. You send any more men in, you will condemn them to death."

Darrin unsnaps the flap on a holster I hadn't noticed. He draws a revolver and fires at the unmanned armadillo. After the bark of the pistol, the bullet ricochets off the skin with a *tweee*. Most men, many veterans of the Irish War of Independence, have ducked and now look for the shooter. "Nothing is getting through that armor, Mrs. Ochoa. Now, if you will please take your fables and malarkey out of here, we have a job to do." He turns his back on me as he reholsters his gun.

"Don't say I didn't warn you, Mr. Jasperson. On your head be it."

# # #

The sheriff's office is a simple clapboard pine building with no internal walls. I'm in the center of the three wrought iron barred cells. A pair of drunks, who sport more bruises on their faces than an entire novice hellfighter team, have the one to my right. Neither of them is much company other than the stink of their body odors and residual liquor.

Sheriff Billings has been nothing but a gentleman. Unfortunately, he left me in the charge of his two deputies. On the other hand, they spend their time playing cards and making disparaging comments in my direction. They both would be a credit to a gang of highwaymen. I lie on the cot resting, facing away from their vileness. My chest still aches, and my body feels drained from Lucy's healing.

"I wonder what *puta barata* is in fer?" one of the deputies says.

"Probably couldn't get Darrin off with her loose *culo* after he done paid for it."

"Maybe she asked him if it was in yet?"

The two jokesters laugh wickedly. "Course, she don't look so cheap. I'd do a piece of that. How about it, honey? How much?"

"And me too?"

I figure the best course is not to reply to any such prompting.

"Marco, I don't think she is a very cooperative prisoner."

"I think yer right. Should we teach her a lesson?" The pair get up with squeaks from their chair legs being pushed back. I can hear their footfalls moving toward my cell. I don't turn around even as my heart beats faster.

The sheriff has obviously failed to inform them of my talents. I'm trying to decide whether to incapacitate them, hurt them, or kill them outright. I sit up and turn to stare at them, keeping eye contact with one as he eases his revolver out of his holster.

"*Furcia*, ya better be getting ready to entertain a couple of real men," one says.

They get as far as reaching the key toward the lock when the front door opens. Carlos enters, followed closely by Sheriff Billings. The pair of deputies turn away and walk casually back to their card game.

"You're still here?" Carlos asks me with a smile.

"Thought I'd see this through. Can't be running away from a simple trespassing complaint."

The sheriff shows Carlos into the remaining cell. "Well said, Mrs. Ochoa."

"I try to be articulate, Sheriff Billings. But you might inform your would-be-rapist deputies that I'm a witch. I nearly had to teach the pair of them a lesson to save my virtue."

The sheriff looks at the pair with narrowed eyes.

"We ain't done nothing, Sheriff," one says.

"God's honest truth, Sheriff."

"On the Virgin Mary," the first one says, crossing himself.

I am sure God is paying attention to the hypocrisy. He will extract the correct amount of penance at the right time.

"I'll talk to the pair of you later," the sheriff says. "In the meantime, both of these prisoners are witches, and either could kill you as easy as look at you."

They both look my way, and I wink at them. They become much more somber, realizing how deadly their mistake would have been. From their faces, it doesn't make them respectful—only wary.

A knock at the door startles everyone.

"Come in," Sheriff Billings calls out. My entire team flows into the room. "The *Dos Campanas*, I presume?"

"Sheriff Billings?" Menaj, who leads the procession, asks.

"That's me. Let me see if I can get this right. You are Raquel Ruiz. The man seemingly intrigued by the mud on his pant legs is Maxwell Parker. The pretty Hispanic *señorita* is Bea Media. And I'm afraid I don't know the name of your other colleague."

"I'm Cora Leaping Fish of the Powhatan tribe."

Deputy Marco Moreno opens his mouth and spews forth more hate. "I didn't know they have niggers in their tribe."

I credit Cora for not even losing the smile on her face. As a water witch, she could drown him right here in front of everyone from water condensed from the air.

"Deputy!" Billings barks. "I'm sorry, Miss Leaping Fish. I'll have a few choice words with him about this. I assume you were born in Cuba?"

"Yes, sir, the island of San Juan."

"Well, you are all welcome here," he says, glaring at Marco. "I'm assuming you are here to talk to your friends."

"Yes," Menaj says with the bluntness of her nature.

"Be my guest. Here is the key." He holds out a set of keys to Cora. "You are more than welcome to open the cells and huddle together for your conference."

"That seems odd," Maxwell opines.

"Under normal circumstances, I'd agree. But Mrs. Ochoa and Mr. Aldana are not normal prisoners. I also have reason to believe there is no evidence against them. If the accuser doesn't provide something by tomorrow, I'll be releasing them."

"We appreciate your courtesy, Sheriff. We won't abuse it," Cora says. She opens our cells. I find myself crushed in a series of hugs. I wince more with each one.

"Stella, are you alright?" Maxwell asks after he squeezes a squeak out of me. "Mrs. Riley mentioned you had been injured."

"I was, probably the worst I've ever been since being burned as a teen. Lucy kept me alive, but my ribs still ache. She doesn't have your touch."

He reaches for the side I'd been favoring, then stops. "With your leave?"

"Oh, hell yes, Max. You've handled me more than my husband ever did." Maxwell's youth shows as he blushes at the comment. "'And the rib that the Lord God had taken from the man he made into a woman and brought her to the man,'" he says, putting his hand against my side. My ribs grate against one another, feeling nothing less than like the tip of a knife drawn across them. Then, the pressure, pain, and even ache fade to nothingness. "There."

I press my middle and feel nary a twinge. "Thank you, Maxwell. We better get into the scrum, or we'll be left out."

We all huddle into Carlos's microscopic corner stall.

"So what do you all know?" the boss asks the newcomers.

"All we know is you met up with something named Grondr and got dusted off like a pair of *neófitas* trying to handle a demon on their own," Bea says.

"Yeah, what were you thinking?" Raquel adds. Cora maintains her quiet serenity.

"Lucy has determined that her husband, Adam Senior, has pneumonia. We decided to take a shot ourselves," I say in defense.

"Empathetic but turnip-headed," Maxwell says.

"In hindsight, yes," Carlos says. "However, our previous trip only encountered an issue with excessive water. We solved that problem but instead ran into Grondr."

I add, "I'm not sure I know exactly what Grondr is. For once I wish my mother was around to ask her. It is no demon. It is more like an elemental force of the earth defending itself. According to Shawnee lore, it has been around for three hundred years or s—"

"Longer than that," Cora Leaping Fish interrupts. "When I was a girl fresh on these shores, the elders of the Powhatan tribe told stories of Grondr as a handmaiden to Okeus, the god of war and vengeance. Our vocal traditions go back over five hundred years."

"I'll buy that," Carlos says. "No matter how you slice the cake, this creature has been around for a long time, and it's *muy enojado* ... Like someone in one of the waterfront bars after they've been punched in the nose."

"Other than it being angry, what do we know about it?" Bea asks.

Carlos says, "Looks like a prizefighter who ate not only all of his vegetables but yours too. For dessert, he noshed on a bull without waiting to kill it first. It's faster than a hiccup, and just one of its punches threw Stella a good twenty feet and broke her armor and ribs."

"Wow," Donny remarks.

"I don't want to think what that would have done to me. While my air powers don't seem to damage it, they can keep it at bay."

"As it is of earth," I put in, "I was able to slow it down to a crawl by putting all of my concentration on it."

"Good lord, that's all?" Maxwell exclaims. I realize he is talking about my ability, not the lack of information. "I would think you would shut it down hard."

"No such luck," I offer with a wry look.

"Oh, and Stella can understand it," Carlos adds.

"It speaks?" Menaj asks.

"Yes, it calls itself Protector," I reply. "But it mostly just insisted that it would kill all men defiling the earth. Oddly, seeing what is being done here, I can empathize." This causes a pause in the conversation. "So how do we get the miners out when we have a murderous earth creature in our way?" I ask, switching gears to the practical.

"Prayer," both Cora and Maxwell say.

"As much as I respect the power of prayer, I think it would hold as much weight with Grondr as it would with a hungry grizzly bear."

"All-out attack," Carlos suggests. "Six of us against one of him/her/ it. Beat it down until it's dead or can't interfere."

"Direct and rather brutal," Maxwell grumbles. "What happened to turn the other cheek?"

"That went out the door as soon it nearly killed Stella," Carlos growls.

"Carlos, I'm not angry at Protector. Just wary," I offer with a wry smile.

"How about misdirection," Raquel proposes.

"How does that work?" Bea asks Raquel, who is petting a vole that peeks out of her unruly hair.

"How about we go in like we are in it for a donnybrook, but Stella goes off and gets the miners while the rest of us keep it busy?" Raquel suggests.

I start to talk, but Carlos interrupts me. "Folks, I know you are used to danger and being adaptable, but Grondr isn't like a demon. It's smart and fast ... Really fast. You can't taunt it like we are used to. It takes a different mindset. Without me there, I worry that as good as you all are, you would be putting your lives at serious risk."

I add, "And what if Protector comes after me instead? If it incapacitates me, you five would be trapped with no hope of rescue."

"The lady has a good point," Maxwell says.

"Is there any way we can lure it out into the open or at least a tunnel we can escape from if necessary?" Bea asks.

"That's not half bad," Carlos says. "Stella, you keep burrowing us to the main tunnel even as it is attacking us. Once we have it there, you head off and rescue the miners."

Something bothers me about this plan, but exactly what won't come to me. "I still think you guys are at risk, but I don't see any way around it."

"Our backup is to go full-out attack," Carlos says. "Objections?"

We all look at each other, shaking our heads.

"When?" Cora asks. "We have you two in jail, and our primary goal has pneumonia."

"And Stella is as weak as a kitten," Maxwell offers

"What? I'm not weak."

"You of all people know how healing saps your strength," Max admonishes.

"True, but at the moment, I feel fine."

"I wouldn't want to risk it until she's had a night's rest and a couple of good meals," Carlos says.

Looking up to see that the sheriff and his deputies are not paying us the slightest bit of attention, I whisper, "How about tomorrow morning?"

"You won't have any trouble getting out? Wait, what am I saying?" Raquel says, flicking one of the metal bars with her fingernail.

"Say five?" I ask them.

"We'll be here," Maxwell says eagerly. "We better go settle in. Mrs. Riley was having a dickens of a time finding places for all of us."

The more cynical Bea asks, "Aren't we wanted here? I would think there would be any number of folk willing to put us up."

"Yes and no," Carlos temporizes.

"I think what Carlos is trying to say is that the Jaspersons have terrified the public, making them fear for their jobs and livelihoods," I say. "Only those with family members unaccounted for are helping, and even they are giving us aid sporadically."

"Then why are we here?" Bea asks.

"Because it is the right thing to do," Cora answers.

"But the right thing doesn't pay the bills," Bea counters.

I knew this moment was coming. I shouldn't have waited this long to bring this up. "I dragged you into this because it's my family. Not to worry, folks. I will make sure that all the bills are paid on top of the normal fees we collect, even if I have to pay for it out of my own pocket," I say to end this potentially corrosive conversation. My offer surprises the rest of my compatriots. I can see the indecision on their faces.

I take the problem out of their hands by saying, "So, on another note, you might be followed by a boy, maybe age ten, who likes to walk on the roofs. He wears ripped clothing, and little of that. His name is Gargoyle. Carlos and I believe he is an earth witch. He has already managed to save my life even though he is spying for the Jaspersons."

"Interesting dichotomy," Maxwell notes.

"Just letting you know if you happen to see him," I say.

"OK. We'll keep an eye out. See you tomorrow," Maxwell says.

"Oh, Stella, this ought to keep you busy through some of the day," Raquel says, handing me a pair of newspapers. "You might find the headlines interesting."

The four members of our team walk to the door. Cora hands back the keys to Sheriff Billings. "Thank you, sir."

"You are quite welcome, m'lady. You have a nice day."

I get back into my cell as the officer strolls over to us. "Would you like to check the newspapers to make sure they haven't given us a file?" I offer.

"Mrs. Ochoa, I'm not naïve enough to think that these bars would hold you if you wanted out."

"Oh?" I offer as sweet as a piece of sugar cane.

"Your sarcasm is wasted on me, Mrs. Ochoa. I may have a couple of less-than-intelligent deputies, but I read. I listen. These bars are for show only."

I give him my best smile. "Thank you for understanding, Sheriff."

"And thank you for honoring my authority, Mrs. Ochoa and Mr. Aldana."

Carlos nods with respect. After Billings has turned his back on me, I sit down on the cot and open the first paper. The headline does indeed grab me.

"Wonder Witch Performs Death-Defying Midair Repair of *Majesty*."

"*¡Joder!*" I curse under my breath. Susan swore that she would be truthful about the account. Instead, it seems to have found its way to the front page in lurid ink. The headline alone takes up most of the space above the fold.

> On Monday, November 19, 1888, the airship *Majesty* of the Boston and Seattle Airline suffered an engineering casualty. Her rudder became damaged in the launch. The bent steering mechanism of the *Majesty* didn't threaten the lives of the passengers and crew. The manufacturing error did, however, promise to add weeks to our cross-country trip. Many of the perishable goods in the *Majesty's* hold would have been ruined, and critical business meetings would have been missed. Tens of thousands of dollars were at risk, not to mention the reputation of the Boston and Seattle Airline.
>
> Instead of remaining a passenger, Mrs. Ochoa volunteered to perform a difficult repair while being hung like a piñata high over the earth, where any gust of wind might have dashed her to her death.
>
> Suspended by wires three thousand feet in the air, Mistress Witch and Heroine of Boston Stella Ochoa performed a feat of magic worthy of a concert violinist playing a solo on the back of a galloping horse.

So much for restrained journalism, I think. *This woman is making me out to be the next Molly Pitcher.*

"Stella, can I read the other one or at least get the sports?" Carlos asks. "I want to see who won a soccer game. I bet twenty dollars on the Beacons over the Philadelphia Royals."

I just shake my head and hand him the second paper. My mind can't get off the lurid prose of Miss Queensbury. I go back to it.

> There, hanging over potential doom, she performed her magic behind her back and unable to see what she was doing.

In the middle of her Herculean task, Mrs. Ochoa was struck by a massive goose that ripped away a number of her safety wires.

She survived the impact but dangled a hair's breadth away from a grizzly, horrific end. Instead, she finished her self-imposed chore and returned unscathed.

The impromptu fix by Mrs. Ochoa was so successful that the *Majesty's* chief engineer, Robert D'Oro, claims, "It is unlikely that the Boston and Seattle Airline will replace the fin. Mrs. Ochoa has repaired it better than new."

The article gives more details, including comments from senior officials at the Boston and Seattle Airline company mentioning an award and generous reward for my valor. *Bother.*

The end of the article is what really infuriates me.

Once again Stella Ochoa has put herself in harm's way to help those around her. Can the monarchy have a better champion and role model than Wonder Witch Ochoa?

"*¡Gracias por nada!*" I hiss at the written word. "Like I need any more publicity."

"Then you picked the wrong profession," Carlos says, showing me the headline of the Wednesday paper I gave him.

It announces, "Trapped Miners Abandoned," with a subheading, "Wonder Witch Thwarted by Coal Syndicate."

"What the hell?" I whisper. The byline on the piece is Susan Queensbury. That is why she stayed in town.

I absently hand Carlos my paper in exchange for his.

November 10 saw the collapse of a significant portion of the Centralia Mine in the Duchy of Pennsylvania. One hundred ninety-seven miners were trapped in this disastrous cave-in. Now, according to the mine's foreman, Darrin Jasperson, those souls are lost.

Per Mr. Jasperson, "It is clear to those of us in the industry that there never has been any hope in rescuing those valiant workers. They perished before even the final rumble of falling stone finished. We grieve for those who have lost loved ones, but we must move on."

What the Coal Syndicate didn't bother to mention is that the Heroine of Boston and Wonder Witch Stella Ochoa traveled to the Duchy of Pennsylvania in order to free the trapped workers. By the white witch powers of others, Wonder Witch believes the men and women still live. But upon arrival, she has been denied the right to enter the mine to save them by the same said Coal Syndicate's Foreman Darrin Jasperson. Mrs. Stella Ochoa, our bold, valiant protector, is willing to risk her own life to bring home, dead or alive, so many men and women who have toiled in these mines for decades, only to be rebuffed by the economically greedy and shortsighted corporate dictatorship.

The wife of one victim said, "Even if our loved ones are dead, recovering the bodies would give us some peace and allow us to give them a Christian burial."

When asked to comment, the representatives of the Coal Syndicate chose silence and refused our request for additional interviews.

There is more, plenty more, but once again, Miss Queensbury ends her article on a high note.

Based on her history, this writer doubts that Stella Ochoa will allow the denial of access by the Coal Syndicate to keep her from her task. What form her courageous disobedience will take I leave to the reader's imagination until we have more information.

I'm boiling in fury. "The bloody woman is trying to turn me into the next Calamity Jane or Annie Oakley. This is—"

"Exactly what you've become, Stella," Carlos interjects. "Think about it. You've accomplished more than any hundred other witches do in their entire lifetimes, and you accomplished it in just the last year."

"But I didn't do those things for the fame or notoriety. I didn't do them to make a name for myself."

"*Amiga*, I know that, and it only makes it that much more impressive."

My anger turns to concern. "How do I stop it?" I plead.

"I don't think you can. Even before this, I saw people back in Boston devouring stories about you. You've become a popular folk heroine, and these articles are just going to add fuel to that fire."

"I should say so!" I say shrilly. I must sound like a pedantic teen. I lay down on the bed and turn away from Carlos.

"Uh-oh. Did you see this?" Carlos hands me the newspaper, pointing at a quarter-page advertisement in the Help Wanted section.

The Coal Syndicate seeks strong miners for Centralia, Pennsylvania. Good Pay. Good working conditions. NO EXPERIENCE REQUIRED. Multiple positions open.

Apply in person to the East Gate of the coal yards.

"Bloody hell! They really are abandoning those miners, aren't they?"

"You ever had any doubt?"

"No, not really, but ... *¡Joder!*"

"That about sums it up," Carlos says as he settles down in his bed.

Other than ignoring the looks Deputy Moreno gives me through the bars, I pass the rest of the morning quietly. I spend emotional solitude trying to come up with a way around being some kind of folk hero and figuring out how I can save the workers buried deep in the earth. Everything is so peaceful, I figure I must have fallen asleep.

"Wake up in there. It's lunch for you," Deputy Moreno says, banging against the bars. He puts a bowl of mostly liquid down on the floor. I look at the cabbage soup with a twisted face and the wrinkled nose of disgust its smell elicits. "More than you deserve."

This man is going to be a problem, I think. "Thank you, Deputy. I know how hard this is for you."

"The witch police are going to have a field day with you, whore."

Yup, going to have a lot of problems from this one.

If it weren't for the cravings my body screams at me for nourishment following my healing, I wouldn't touch the soup. It tastes as sour as it smells. What I wouldn't give for some of Lucy's beans and ham hocks with a piece of cornbread on the side.

"Hello? Sheriff Billings?" I hear a girl's voice say from the door.

"What you want, Janet?" Deputy Moreno asks with his nose buried in my newspaper and his feet up on the desk.

"I gots a telegram for Stella Ochoa. Adam Riley said she were here."

The *pendejo* doesn't even look up. He just motions in my direction.

The Hispanic girl, maybe nine years old, comes over to my cell. "Stella Ochoa?"

"Yes, *señorita*."

"I have a telegram for you. Would you please sign here?" She hands me a clipboard. I sign on the appropriate line, wondering who the sender is. "Thank you, *Bruja Maravilla*," she says. I grit my teeth at the appellation. I'm NOT anything special. "A response has been prepaid," she tells me. "I can wait or you can come to the—"

"I think you had better wait, Miss Janet. I seem to be stuck where I am at the moment."

"*Sí, bruja.*"

I unfold the form. It reads, "We found solution to problem. Required who is your father?"

Problem? What problem? Getting around an angry earth creature ... and element of nature?

I read the sender box—Viscountess Adrianna Helms. My heart skips more than one beat. It seems to stop functioning entirely. Here I am, hundreds of miles away, and she can still sunder my emotions just like the days I see her on the streets of Boston or sitting in a restaurant.

I've loved two people in my life: my husband and Viscountess Helms. Both have been torn from my life. My husband died in the war to liberate Ireland. The Church has forbidden me to love the viscountess, as she is already wed—in a marriage of power to my good friend and benefactor.

So is the problem she has a solution for our mutual love? I guess if I was given someone else's heart, that might be a solution. Did she decide to divorce? Each of them seems equally likely.

Then there is the request embedded in the telegraph. Does she want my biological father or my father confessor? As they are the same person, I guess it doesn't matter much, does it?

I get ten words to respond. I write, "Father Juan Dubois y Cantonio. What is solution? Respond soonest." I hand the clipboard back with a quarter on top.

"That's way too much, ma'am!"

"So how much do you usually get tipped?"

"Me? I's lucky if'n I get a penny. People here is poor."

"Well then, this might make you a little less poor, Janet," I say, pointing at the quarter. "Enjoy."

"Thanks, *señorita*." Janet skips away and out the door.

As I settle back to the cot, my mind muddles over all the new questions I have. My emotions, on the other hand, dart like birds racing up and then diving back down. I have nothing more to do but wallow in the emotional conflict.

"Howdy, Sheriff," Marco says as Billings enters the front door.

"Any trouble?"

"Nah, Sheriff. Even them drunks made up."

"Great. Now go get some shut-eye. Relieve me at midnight."

"Yes, Sheriff."

The leader of the small police force brings around supper, a rather meaty venison stew. My mouth waters as he passes the bowl to me. Included is a sourdough roll so large that it barely fits between the bars.

"I know it isn't the Parker House," Sheriff Billings says as he gives us each a cup of mild beer to wash it down.

I take a big spoonful of the stew. The warmth and meaty taste work their way into those voids left by the spiritual healing I've received. A flush of well-being rushes through me. In response, I say, "This is wonderful, Sheriff. Your wife make this?"

"Only in spirit. I learned from her before she died." I stop just before stuffing the roll into my mouth for a big bite. The bread has too much flour but still has a chewy texture and sustenance that my body craves.

"I'm sorry, Mr. Billings."

"Me, too," Carlos adds.

"Nah. It was a long time ago. I lost her in childbirth of our daughter, Genevieve. It was hard at first, but I tried to put it behind us."

The sheriff goes back to his desk and cracks open the Bible to read. I can't make out where in the book he is. The curiosity lasts about as long as the contents of my bowl—that is, almost no time at all. With my stomach full, my mind drifts to darkness.

#

My eyes snap open when I hear the sound of the front door closing. This isn't like me. There are those people who would say that I'd sleep through the Second Coming.

"Ready to be relieved, Sheriff?"

"Yup, Marco." I hear the chair creak as Sheriff Billings stands. "I definitely can use some shut-eye."

"Did you hear that they sent down one of the armadillos?"

"Figures. I just hope it doesn't hurt anyone." There is some sadness in his tone.

"Getting the mine open is most important," Marco declares. I don't hear any response from the sheriff. "Anything I need to know about?"

"Nope. Everything is quiet. Everyone is asleep. Keep it that way until I get back."

"You got it, Sheriff."

I'm lying on the cot, facing away from the cell door. Silence returns as the head lawman leaves. I can feel Deputy Moreno's eyes on me. It makes my skin feel like a hive of wasps under my skin. This isn't a witch thing. This is a woman thing. He blames me. He wants to hurt me.

I lie there waiting for Marco to succumb to his own idiocy and prejudice. It is like those ha'penny rags that have two gunfighters standing down the street from one another, waiting for some imaginary signal to draw their weapons and blast away at one another. I don't need to see him. I can feel the mass of refined metal in his gun. I remain still, wondering when the scum will make his move.

My mind drifts over the telegram I still have clutched in my hand. "We found solution to problem. Required who is your father?"

What problem? Joder, *woman. Couldn't you have spent another dollar to let me know more?* Before that puzzling bit of paper, I was in the dark and separated from Adrianna across the chasm of faith, religion, and miles. Over the last six months, I've managed to patch the fatal wounds to my heart so that only a constant, dull ache remains. This tears apart my scars to hurt just as bad as before, if not worse.

"Stella," I hear across a gentle wind. One of Carlos's abilities is to talk without sound.

Marco's pistol moves, not from being drawn but rather from its owner standing.

"Mm-hmm," I offer back in an appropriately titled prison yard whisper. The same breeze that brought his warning to me takes my response back. Apart from slowly sliding one hand from under my blanket to touch the bars nearest me, I hold still as a corpse. I don't react to the key clattering softly in the lock of my cell door. *One more step,* pendejo.

The only one who thinks he has the upper hand is Marco. Behind him, the bars become the hair of Medusa, lashing out and wrapping around the deputy. He gives out one brief squeak before another bar goes across his mouth and jams it shut.

I roll over to find the worthless idiot with his billy club above his head poised to strike. A net of metal fills the doorway of my cell, shackling each of Deputy Moreno's limbs in the exact pose he had moments ago, like a photograph frozen in time. This tintype is writhing by fractions of an inch but not getting loose. Marco's eyes are wide, and he is grunting excitedly.

"Shush," I order. "If you don't, I'll send a rod right up your *ano*. And if that doesn't do it, I'll have one of these bars start swinging at your *cajones*." The grunts stop. "Now, continue to behave, and I'll let you out when the sheriff arrives."

Applause erupts from the two men in the drunk cell. I nod toward them in recognition of their praise.

"Well done, Stella," Carlos says groggily. "Doesn't even look like you hurt him."

"That was the point. Now, shall we get some sleep?"

7—Friday, November 23, 1888

Sleep has been rough, and even the slightest noise wakes me. This is why I sit upright when the door to the sheriff's office opens before I hear the five bell chimes. Sheriff Billings stands in the still-darkened doorway, examining my weaving skills around his deputy. He closes the door behind him to limit the early-morning chill.

"Very impressive, Mrs. Ochoa. Is he hurt?"

I shake my head. "Only his pride, Sheriff."

"May I ask what happened?" The prisoner, Marco, grunts with excitement. "I was asking Mrs. Ochoa," the sheriff says. "Shut up."

"I think the tableau speaks for itself, Mr. Billings. Your deputy was about to club me when I stopped him."

"That were what 'appened, Sheriff," one of the former drunks says. "He sneaked up and were gonna bash 'er when them bars started waving around like a nest o' snakes."

"Wrapped 'im up right like a hog waitin' t' be slaughtered," the other one says.

Billings walks over to their cell. "You boys slept it off and made up?"

"Yassir, we done."

"Yup, Sheriff."

"I don't mind you tying one on, but you have to behave yourself. Remember that in the future. Get out of here, boys," he says unlocking their cell door.

"Kin we watch what she's gonna do with 'im?"

"Want to stay in that cell for a week?" the lawman growls. The two skedaddle out the front door so fast it couldn't possibly hit them in the buttocks on the way out.

Sheriff Billings comes over. "Do you mind, Mrs. Ochoa?" he asks as he indicates that he wants to get in to face his imprisoned subordinate. I move to the back of the cell and sit down on the cot.

"Now, Marco, I've given you any number of chances. I don't know what you planned to do after you clubbed her senseless. I probably don't want to. So I give you a choice. I can fire you and let you go, if you never, ever talk bad about our two guests again. I'm not worried about you hurting them. I think you've learned enough to know that action against a witch is about as useful as whispering in a tornado.

"Option two, I fire you and arrest you for attempted murder. With four witnesses, plus what I see, should put you in Eastern Pennsylvania Duchy Penitentiary for several years.

"Either way, you're finished as a lawman." Zack leans forward and plucks the deputy badge from the man's shirt. He then draws the ex-lawman's revolver out of its holder. He empties each of the chambers before putting it back. As an afterthought, he takes the truncheon from Marco's hand. "So, what's it going to be?"

The wrapped-up man grunts once.

"Very nice. Mrs. Ochoa, would you please free this citizen?"

"My pleasure, Sheriff."

I mentally untie the knots in the bars, releasing Marco to freedom. I even go so far as to return the bars to their original shape and placement.

The look the former deputy gives the sheriff could sear flesh at fifty paces. The look he gives me while rubbing muscles sore from holding one position for three hours somehow crosses fiery anger with wary apprehension.

"Get out of my office, Mr. Moreno. And walk a very straight line in this town or get out completely."

Marco Moreno doesn't turn or say a word as he walks out the front door.

"That took a lot of guts, Sheriff Billings," Carlos says. I nod in agreement.

"Marco has been riding the ragged edge of disaster for some time. This isn't the only thing I've got on him. This was just the last, and most egregious, of them all."

Not that I'm not grateful for the sheriff's intervention, but now I'm concerned about how we are going to get out at five, with Sheriff Billings here.

"Still, it takes a good man to stand up," I say.

"Thank you, Mrs. Ochoa. I have to say that I would have given a week's pay to watch that snot get wrapped up. But seeing the aftermath is almost as good."

I chuckle. While I do, the lawman unlocks my cell door and that of Carlos as well. He motions us out.

"Ah ... I'm confused, Sheriff," I say.

"As am I," Carlos adds.

"I'd rather let you out myself than have you break out. That's why I'm here so early this morning. I have to be here to swear that you stayed in your cell the entire time."

"That doesn't clear it up much, Sheriff Billings," I admit.

The sheriff turns and walks back to his desk. He sits down with his head hung down low before answering. "Mrs. Ochoa, I don't have much in my life except for my job and my daughter. The Coal Syndicate has turned its back on the workers buried in the mine. Mrs. Ochoa and Mr. Aldana, my daughter is one of those trapped."

"Your daughter?" Carlos and I say almost in unison.

"Yes. Unfortunately, Genevieve took after my barrel-chested physique. She is quite strong and doesn't go in for the feminine ways most women do. Two years ago, she hired on as a miner. Now she is buried deep in the earth. And if you and your friends can't get her out, I will have lost the most important thing in my life, again. I'll give you any help I can.

"That's why I was so early this morning. I had to get rid of anyone who might be a witness to me letting you 'escape.'"

I look at Carlos for some wordless communication before I answer. "Sheriff, we can't guarantee anything. We aren't even sure that we can ... Or that even if your daughter is still ..."

"Dead or alive, at least I have a chance of getting her back. A good chance, if your display here is any gauge."

# # #

I'm sweating as I push an even larger bubble through the earth with all six hellfighters inside. My chest aches from the exertion, but we need to go now.

The artificial, globular cavern is well lit by five miner's yellow-tinted lamps and the soft white light glowing from Maxwell's hands.

"We're getting close," I whisper. Familiarity has made me more attuned to this volume of earth, like someone who can walk to the privy without even opening their eyes. "Everyone ready?" With affirmatives from my team, I inch us forward through the rock and dirt until we emerge into the abandoned mining tunnel. Our multiple lights play out around the area to get a lay of the land. Grondr isn't obviously present.

We edge forward, on our guard for anything that might leap out at us. I swear that if any one of us breaks wind, we would snap.

"This is where we found it. Or it found us," Carlos says as he toes the edge of the ossuary. One of Carlos's breezes swirls through this stagnant place. It edges out the dead air.

I start when I hear [Defilers never learn] from the rocks around us.

"That's the sound Grondr makes," Carlos says to the groaning and crackling of the earth around us. Everyone's head is jerking around to identify the threat. They can't understand the vibrations as words.

"Yeah, it knows we are here and isn't happy about it," I say to my team. Then I turn to the dark tunnel. "Grondr, we mean no harm. We beg to pass so that we might return our friends and loved ones back out of your earth."

[So they can rape more? No! Die!]

"Incoming!"

The apelike shape of Grondr shoots up in front of us from the very floor of the cavern.

Menaj sprouts a thorny blackberry briar that twines itself up one leg of our opponent. Bea lashes out with a frosty blast that strikes its opposite shoulder, forming several inches of ice around the joint. Cora jets water at its unbound knee. Around all of this, Carlos swirls a miniature tornado.

[No!]

Grondr appears hemmed in. This is my cue. I run at the wall, parting it with a much smaller bubble than the one that has brought the six of us this far. The reduced size is a good thing, as the force I need in this recalcitrant earth is taxing. I just need to get to the main mine shaft.

[I will destroy all of you,] the creature says with a scream, followed by a grunt. I look back to see its earthen body crumble to dust and get caught up in Carlos's wind.

Just as quickly I see a new mound of earth forming behind my team. "Behind!" I shout. As one, everyone shifts like a perfect clockwork mechanism. Maxwell slips between Bea and Carlos to remain behind the defensive line to heal as necessary.

The rest do such a perfect about-face that I want to clap. The new earthen gorilla receives a new volley of spells. I'm intent on my team and don't notice that the ground has risen up and wrapped around my leg. I can't move forward. I concentrate on the specific tendril of the gripping stone. I wish it away. But it doesn't go. It squeezes tighter. However, I do get its rock-hard consistency to soften to something more like taffy. With effort, I pull my boot out of its grip, like I'm getting it out of some terribly thick knee-high mud.

"Everybody switch right!" Carlos shouts. The beast has once again shed the body the team had been attacking. It reforms. Worse, this time it forms with eight long tentacles instead of two arms and two legs, like some enormous land octopus.

I once again try to sneak away, but one of the limbs wraps around my waist.

[Die usurpers!]

Appendages lash out to take each of the rest of my team, with limited success. Maxwell and Bea grimace in the beast's crushing grip. An enormous mole that Menaj must have called is also being wrapped up. One tentacle strikes at Bea, only to be solidified in a coating of ice.

One of Cora's water jets severs a limb closing in on her. The detached piece wriggles back toward the main body. In the space of seconds, a blackberry bush erupts from the earth to clamp the errant bit down and grow all through it. In response, Menaj gets a clout across the face by one of Grondr's arms she didn't see. And another tentacle pushes its way out of the main body, leaving the amputated limb to crumble to dust.

Carlos darts to one side, missing an attempt to wrap him up, only to get another one of Grondr's limbs as a spear through his thigh.

"Stella!" Carlos shouts through the pain. I don't need a guide to tell me this is going badly. Me sneaking away isn't an option. I start to focus on Grondr. I can slow and soften it, allowing me to extricate my comrades.

"Bea, now," Cora says. I don't know what they are talking about, but I have a job to do. I envision forming Grondr into solid granite, which slows but doesn't stop its movements. Cora fires another knife of water, cutting the appendage that held Bea. In the dim light, I see Bea hold something up to her headlamp—a stick of dynamite. The fuse lights with a sizzle.

How in God's good graces can I keep the team safe if she throws the red stick at the beast? The dynamite goes flying, but not where I expect. It soars out beyond the pile of bones.

[No! Don't!] Grondr screams, with the earth crackling and quivering ominously.

Time seems to stretch out. The explosive tumbles through the air. When it lands, embers from the burning nub of a fuse spray outward. I'm too far away to protect my friends from the inevitable cave-in.

I race forward, but my actions slow like I'm moving through a vat of molasses. My concentration on Grondr slips. Max cries out as the creature's arm lifts him off the ground and constricts his waist to a dimension that no corset ever should manage, even on a woman. Carlos screams as the spear through his leg becomes a sharp blade and draws out through the flesh. Blood spurts like a broken valve on a cistern.

The dynamite bounces up.

A blackberry vine stretches up and wraps around Carlos's leg, right around the groin, and cinches tight, digging its own thorns into his leg. The arterial gushes drop to a gentle flow, but I can't imagine the pain Carlos suffers. Cora launches more severing water, forcing the creature to drop Maxwell. Grondr rushes through everyone toward the explosives. Its mass pushes everyone apart, flipping our white witch in midair.

Even the blast stretches out in time. Instead of a shattering boom, it lights up, pushing a wave of air ahead of it. The solid impact throws us all away. The earsplitting crack of the detonation lasts forever.

I find myself thrown against the same wall Grondr had made me familiar with just two days ago. As the blast echoes and the ceiling begins to collapse, I see the most remarkable thing.

Grondr's fluid form halts and spikes out like a porcupine with a very bad haircut. All of the edges look sharp enough to cut glass. Its scream is swallowed up by the rumble of the falling ceiling. I urge the mass to divert around my team and me. Concentrating against the collapse feels like a spike through my head.

# # #

Dust hangs in the air like a curtain in my lamplight. The world spins gently around me for some time before I can focus.

"'For I will restore your health, and I will heal your wounds,' declares the Lord," Maxwell intones. His hands glow even brighter as he lays them on Carlos's thigh. Even though I've seen it a million times, the flesh folding over, sealing shut, and puckering to scar, as if it's had weeks of rest, holds my attention. The blackberry vine drops off during this evolution.

Menaj is digging herself and Bea out from under some loose debris. Cora whimpers off to my right. Her arm is trapped beneath a large boulder.

"Max, grab her legs, and I'll move the rock off her." Without moving from my prone position, I mentally reshape the stone so that her arm will be released. Cora screams and faints.

Maxwell doesn't hesitate, and a good thing, too. Her right hand looks like someone hit a block of modeling clay with a sledgehammer. "'Fear not, for I am with you; Be not Dismayed, for I am your God. I will strengthen you, yes, I will help you, I will uphold you with my righteous right hand.'"

Isaiah 41:10, I think. *Maxwell always knows the right quotation.*

I wish I had been a better daughter of God. I've let down my team. Raquel has a broken ankle. Carlos is recovering from a mortal wound. And Cora may never use her hand again. Some earth witch I am.

Carlos grimaces through the after-ache of healing. "Stella, can you get us out of here? It may come back at any time."

"How long has it been?"

"You and Max were both out for the better part of five minutes."

"If it's been that long, I doubt it is coming back soon, but caution is called for. I will say I'm dizzy and weak. To do this, I need everyone close to me." I wince when I sit up. Damned shoulder again. Dislocate it once, and it pops out every chance it gets. That being said, it is one of the least of our wounds. The ceiling in my little area allows me only the ability to crawl. I move closer to Cora.

"Sorry," I whisper to her.

"Not your fault," she offers through gritted teeth.

After a great deal of cursing and trying to move, Carlos lets Max drag him to me on his bum. Both Bea and Menaj scooch over near us.

Fortunately for all of us, the fallen rock and loose earth prove easier for me to move through. I run out of energy and strength to both move us and burrow through the ground just about the time I see the predawn sky.

#

"From your appearance and the speed of your return, I'm guessing you weren't any more successful than before," Sheriff Billings says. Battered and bruised, we limped, tails between legs, back to the jailhouse. It isn't even six thirty yet, and the town has barely begun to stir. So our fruitless adventure isn't known.

Looking at the ground, I shake my head. Maxwell can now make more permanent repairs to our bodies, but not necessarily to our souls and spirits.

"I don't think there is any way to defeat that thing," Carlos offers. He is usually one of the more upbeat members of our troop. To see him throw in the towel tears away any morale we had left.

"I cut off pieces," Cora says as Max's white powers work to envelop the remains of her hand.

"But when it can just discard its body like that and inhabit any other bit of rock and earth?" Bea moans. "Or even pull that bit back to itself and reattach it? My Lord."

"So, Grondr is real," the sheriff says with as little heart in his voice as the rest of us have.

By way of a response, Raquel turns the left side of her face toward the sheriff. The bruises forming there are epic. They even have the round sucker marks of the earthen octopus's tentacles. "My team didn't do this."

"Not only that, but he has some tricks that even the wildest of Old Frank Harbin's tall tales didn't hint at," Carlos adds.

The sheriff sinks into his chair, hanging his head. "Then my Genevieve is lost forever."

"Maybe not," I toss in with a rare show of my own optimism. I'm usually the damp blanket at any party, but I see a glimmer of hope. The eyes that look at me have nothing but beaten puppy written in them.

"When that explosive was tossed, why did Grondr care?" I ask. "If it could reform at will, why not let us pull the ceiling down on ourselves?"

"What does it matter, Stella? We've lost this one. I don't like it any more than anyone else," Maxwell adds to the general misery.

"No!" I bark. "I saw and heard something that it seems none of you did. When that explosion hit, it screamed. It was hurt. Even more, it seemed to freeze in place."

"I saw it," Cora offers.

"I heard something. Not sure it was a scream," Maxwell says.

Carlos jumps in with, "That's all fine and good, Stella, but we can't go lobbing dynamite around. Just one stick nearly killed us all."

"True. But what if any explosion on the earth nearby freezes it? Hurts it? Makes it charge off to try to stop it?"

Carlos goes from pessimism to cautious optimism in the space of a dozen words. "What are you thinking, Stella?"

Why be coy? "Why not place explosives all over the surface, or buried just below the surface? Grondr will either run after them or be frozen in place by their explosions. Either way, it won't impact the main mine shaft all that much."

"That won't be easy," the sheriff says. "You'll have to get a bunch of people helping."

"And buy a load of explosives," Maxwell adds helpfully.

"I never said it would be easy, but if we enlist the families of the miners, that might be enough."

Cora's hand is looking more like it has some thickness and at least marginal mobility. "So why are we still sitting around? I feel the Phoenix within me," she says, evoking the name of one of the native gods. "And I want to share it with that devil."

"Despite a very generous jailer, we still are nominally under arrest," Carlos offers in defense.

"Well, I can fix that," Sheriff Billings says. "No evidence has been brought forward to accuse you. You are free to go as of right now. And despite anyone's demands, I'll require you to stay in town just to make certain," he adds with some solemnity and a twinkle in his eye.

"We wouldn't dream of leaving, Zack," I add with a wink of my own. "We will stay at your disposal."

#

Holly lugs a pot and tops up the china coffee cups around the table.

"I am so happy the sheriff let you out," Luciana says, heaping up any plate that dares to be half empty. I beam at her as I tuck into my second—or is it third?—plate of her scrambled eggs and fried onions. I hadn't realized how much my body needed the food until I smelled it. Then, like a drunk after his whiskey, I couldn't be kept away from it.

"Ma'am, if you ever want a job, we'd hire you as a cook in a heartbeat," Maxwell says, his mouth still half stuffed.

"Sorry, Max. I have my hands full with three kids and a husband. Speaking of which, you say you need help from all the families?"

Carlos picks up the question. "Yes, we have a theory that Grondr becomes incapacitated at explosions in or on the ground."

I don't feel short shrift. He isn't touting the theory as his, only driving it to completion. We are a team. Sometimes he has ideas, sometimes it's Bea, and other times it's Max. We work together.

"I can gather everyone together at the church by ten," Lucy says. "Will that work?"

"Sounds good. Adam, how much dynamite does the store have?" I ask.

Lucy's son wrinkles his mouth. "I'm not really sure, Stella."

"How much does it cost?"

"'Bout thirty cents a stick."

"About," Lucy the ex-teacher corrects her son.

"Yes, Mama."

"Well, could I get you to head off to the store and find out how much they have?" I hand him a twenty-dollar gold piece.

He holds it in his palm like he might a sugar-tit and stares at it in awe. "Jesus. I haven't ever seen that much money."

"Don't blaspheme," his mother admonishes.

"Take it down there and tell them to deliver every bit of dynamite they have to the church this morning. If this isn't enough, tell them I'll pay for the rest," I say.

"Yes, ma'am." Adam bolts out the front door like someone lit his pants on fire.

"I'm sorry, Lucy. I didn't ask you if I could borrow your son."

"Not an issue. If any of us can help maybe bring those trapped miners out and my husband back to me, you don't need to even ask. We are at your beck and call. I'd walk through a pit of lime to make it happen."

# # #

A few hours later, my team leans up against the inside wall of the church as townsfolk come in. The locals move to the other side of the aisle from us in nervous apprehension. I'm not sure if it's because of my demonstration a few days ago, the mine owners having declared us persona non grata, or our representing a boondoggle in trying to bring their loved ones back. In the end, it probably is a combination of all three.

"Friends," Lucy begins, "we told you we would need you to help bring our loved ones up from the bottom of the mine—the tomb that currently imprisons them. That time has come.

"I will turn over the floor to Carlos de Aldana of the *Dos Campanas* to explain exactly what we need."

Carlos, despite his craggy face, can lead a virgin to a sacrificial altar. He has one of those personalities that make you want to believe in him. He takes the one step up to the podium before speaking. "Folks, the rumor mill in this town is as strong as anywhere. I can confirm that we have run into a creature you call Grondr, or Protector, as it calls itself. As strong and capable as we are, it has prevented us from going in to save your friends and loved ones." A murmur goes through the crowd. "It seems to want them to die for destroying its home."

A woman wails, and more than one weeps. They say time heals all wounds, but these are still fresh and raw.

Carlos continues. "All this being said, we think we have found a weakness—a way we can debilitate the beast long enough to get your loved ones out.

"I won't lie. There is no guarantee. What we are asking you to do is dangerous and likely will draw the ire of the Jaspersons."

Carlos waits, but no one says anything. "Talk amongst yourselves. Those who want to participate, come over here, where we are gathering, and we will give you specifics."

"What about the Jaspersons and the mine management?" one woman asks. "If you say it will anger them, won't they fire us?"

"What of it?" Lucy retorts. "Eloise, do you want a job for your son or a live husband? No matter what we do, the Coal Syndicate will object. But these are the same *pendejos* who won't try to save our people because it costs too much. They can import more Germans or use machines to mine coal instead of saving the ones who have given their lives to dig black rock for them."

Lucy's admonitions cause a hush to fall over the crowd. Several moments pass before the locals begin to mill around, talking to one another. Every once in a while, a parishioner shakes her head, then inevitably rounds up her children and walks out the door. Meanwhile, others point at us and argue.

"Nice being a sideshow attraction, isn't it?" I say to Carlos, who has joined me in leaning against the wall.

"I'd much rather be back in the Bell in Hand with a pint in front of me," he replies.

"And a wench in your lap?"

"I wouldn't say nay."

"My friend, it won't be long, either way. I'd call this a last-ditch effort."

"Not quite," Carlos offers. "I thought of another one."

"Really? Please tell me."

"How about we take that other armadillo? It may not be fast, but it is armored."

"That won't work, Carlos. Think of what Grondr did with my armored corset. Even if it didn't crush that machine around us, it could break it open like we tear through the peel of an orange."

"Damn," Carlos curses. "You're right."

"I do have another plan, but no one will like it."

"Oh? Do tell," my friend says.

"I'm not going to even bring it up unless this fails."

"Keep your own counsel, then."

I look as the number of people arguing has dwindled. The final naysayer turns her back on us and walks from the nave. A knot of people has formed around my cousin. As one, they move over to us. Lucy announces, "This is what we have, Stella. They are committed."

I do a quick count and, eliminating children, come up with thirty-nine. And that is counting Lucy.

"You didn't tell them exactly what we were doing?" I ask.

"Per your instructions, I didn't. Only that it is dangerous."

"Adam, go and close the church doors. The rest of this needs to be private, else the Jaspersons or their lackeys will find a way to stop it."

When the room is as soundproof as possible, Carlos breaks out a map. He starts explaining. "Thank you for staying. We are being stopped from reaching your trapped loved ones because of a powerful creature that even we can't defeat."

A brief scuffle interrupts when two burly men come in through the vicar's private entrance toting wooden crates labeled "Danger." You can't live in a mining town without knowing what they contain.

"Dynamite?" someone in the crowd asks.

While Carlos sells our plan, I lean close to Adam Junior and whisper, "So, how many sticks of dynamite did we end up with?"

"They had forty-nine. They charged fourteen dollars for the lot," he whispers back. He hands me some coins and a single bill. "Here's your change, Stella."

"Thank you, Adam. Let's just hope this works."

"It's got to, ma'am."

"I don't disagree, Adam. I don't disagree."

Our attention returns to Carlos as he says, "That's right. We've learned that an explosive will incapacitate the creature for a time. If we set off an explosion, it seems unable to act. We want you all to take a single stick of dynamite and bury it six inches down in a specific place on the mine grounds here." He points at the handwritten locations on the mine's upper-surface map. "Then we will coordinate having you detonate them in sequence. If we do it right, the beast should be so debilitated that we ought to be able to save the miners."

On the whole, the volunteers look eager. Only a couple look skeptical.

Carlos continues. "Remember, this really is our last chance," he pontificates, looking directly at those few who are wavering. "It may be a long shot, but it is the only thing that is likely to work. You know that the next dirigible will be stuffed with new immigrants eager to replace everyone down in the bottom of that mine. We've shown you the newspapers. The syndicate is abandoning your kin."

Even the couple of people who looked questionable before are now nodding. Carlos has a way of speaking that pulls people in. I think he could convince a mama bear to give up her cubs. "I'll give each of you a number. It corresponds to a place on the map." In front of him is a numbered grid across the surface of the paper, centering on the town. Each intersection is labeled with a number. "By two o'clock in the afternoon, you will go out and dig a hole at the spot associated with your number and put the dynamite in. Luciana will have the number one. She will light the fuse of the first explosive exactly at two. As soon as the detonation of the person who has the number before yours goes off, you will count fifteen Mississippis, and then light your own fuse. Then make sure you back off at least a hundred paces before hunkering down.

"We have spaced these out so you will each be safe from one another's explosions.

"The timing is very important. If you all do this correctly, we can have a bit more than twelve minutes to get the miners out."

"How ya gonna do that? It takes 'em almost an hour to get down there and back to do their job," says one woman.

"Well, getting out should be much easier than getting in," I interject. "And for getting in, we're going to fall."

"Wha'?"

"We're all going to join hands and jump into the elevator shaft and fall the four thousand or so feet down. Our air witch will stop our fall and land us at the bottom." This prompts some murmuring among our helpers. I look over at Carlos, who seems a bit green around the gills.

"Any questions?" I ask when he doesn't. Everyone is shaking their heads. "Then come up for your assigned number and to find your location."

Carlos mingles with the crowd, coordinating the effort in front of us this afternoon. I sit down next to Bea.

"You think this is going to work?" she asks.

Maxwell hands out a single stick of dynamite to each person as they get their assignment. I catch him fumbling, as his eyes are elsewhere. I follow where he looks to find at the other end of his gaze a young, just-husband-high girl casting doe eyes back at him.

"Just a second."

I stroll over to Max and tap him on the shoulder. He hasn't noticed me, so he jumps. I lean over and whisper, "That's dangerous stuff you aren't handling very well. While I know you want to go to God when your time here is over, don't speed it along. Keep your mind on what you're doing, and I'll find out who she is."

I see the back of his neck go red in a blush that probably covers his whole body. He hides his embarrassment with a cough. "Yes, right. Of course."

I wander over to the young lady. She has shiny brown hair, a slender physique, and a smooth, poxless face that would launch a thousand ships.

"Hello there. I'm Stella."

Softly, with a little shyness, she replies in a light German accent, "Yes, Mrs. Ochoa. I know." She turns her best feature toward me, her large, blue eyes. It is then that I notice the cross around her neck. Anyone who would catch Max's eye would have to be a good Catholic girl.

"What's your name, miss?"

She gives a curtsy. "Bernice Schmidt, Mrs. Ochoa."

"Bernice, that blushing young man over there. His name is Maxwell Parker. He is a hellfighter and a colleague of mine."

"Yes, ma'am, I know."

I wonder if her voice would be loud enough to be heard even in a confessional. "Well, I've known Max for years. He would like to be introduced to you after this is all over." Bernice tosses a shy smile over at my friend. "Yes, I can see you also are interested in such a meeting.

"Bernice?" I say, getting her attention back. "Can I get you to do something for me?"

"Yes, Mrs. Ochoa?"

"Would you please stop flirting with Maxwell at least until the day is over? It may have passed your notice, but he is handling explosives. I wouldn't want his inattention to cause another disaster here in Centralia."

Miss Schmidt puts her hand to her mouth. "Oh! I'm sorry."

"Normally it wouldn't be a problem, Bernice. But explosives and courting just don't mix."

"I understand, Mrs. Ochoa."

"Thank you. By the way, Max is a great man. Be good to him, because I know he will be to you."

I saunter back to sit next to our ice witch, Bea. "It may work."

"You think she will keep her eyes on her work rather than Max?"

"No. I mean yes. But I was answering your earlier question. Will this work? I just say that it has to work. I want those people out of the mine."

# # #

"Are we ready?" I ask, checking the time on my husband's pocket watch. It shows me the time as ten 'til two.

Carlos, Bea, and Max all nod.

"I'm good to go," Menaj says.

"I'm ready to go set the first fuse," Lucy says.

"Yes, Bird Chaser," Cora Leaping Fish replies.

"Huh?" I ask, wrinkling my brow.

Cora smiles and explains. "I think it is time for you to have a name in my tribe. After reading about your adventures in the dirigible, I think this is appropriate."

"I'm honored, Cora. But right now we have a schedule to keep. You can explain it to me later. Although, I have an idea where it came from. Any word on what the Jaspersons are doing?"

Sheriff Billings, who somehow insinuated himself into our little troupe, says, "I heard they are barricading and guarding the main mine entrance for fear that you will use the dynamite against it. The company store employees told him about the explosives you bought."

Carlos interjects, "Good. That will keep them busy and out of our way. Alright. Lucy, let us get underground and count thirty chimpanzees before lighting yours off. And pray."

"Yes, Mr. Aldana."

"Fire up your miner's lights." Carlos checks that everyone but Max, who provides a glow with holy light, does so. "All you, Stella," Carlos directs.

"Group hug and down we go," I say.

I hear "One chimpan—" as we transition from the world of light to the embrace of darkness. The earth we're traveling through—the same area we have used twice before—has loosened up and lets me pass without the same fight as before. I file away the fact for future evaluation. We break into the tomb of the poor, long-dead miners.

"Let's move forward slowly until we hear the first explosion," Carlos orders. We form a skirmish line, with our hands able to touch one another. I take one end, and Carlos takes the other. Max's hands glow white among the yellow lights from our lamps. A stiff breeze whips around us as Carlos maintains preparedness.

[Once again you enter to defile.] I hear the voice all around us.

"That's the sound," Carlos announces. "Everyone be on alert."

"Please, Protector. We mean only to get our friends out of this grave," I offer to the unseen creature.

[You are worthy opponents, but this is my domain. I reign here.]

The floor, walls, and ceiling shake with a single pulse. The echo of the event reverberates and makes dust drift down from the rock roof.

[AAAaaaaa!]

"Forward! FAST!" I yell. The six of us run forward, losing speed over the difficult and shifting pile of bones.

As we reach the far end of the chamber, we bunch together again. If these were normal circumstances, I could open a space so we could run full speed into the earth. "Slow down. Everyone pull up tight," I say.

I reach out with my mind and will the earth to let us pass. It resists, and I have to put more and more force into getting us into the wall. Our movement slows to the rate that a toddler just learning to walk might manage. Each foot costs me energy from my very core. Maybe even from my soul.

A second dull boom thunders through the rock. And a third. And a fourth. And a ninth.

I'm weakening, yet I push harder against the intractable earth. Ten. Thirteen. Twenty. We are running out of time. "I don't know if we are going to make it. I feel empty like I have nothing left," I say.

The pure white light off Max brightens as he intones, "'Come to me, all you who are weary and burdened, and I will give you rest.'" I feel a warmth course through me. My energy is renewed like when I get new air bottles for the poderabile. I never knew he could do anything like that.

"Thanks." I redouble my effort and can feel the yards slide by. "Anyone keeping count?"

"Twenty-nine," Bea offers.

"Wait a minute. I can feel an empty space up ahead. That's probably the shaft." I can feel Carlos's heart beating faster. He is breathing almost like a racehorse. He and I both knew this was going to be the hard part for him. I lean over and whisper into his ear. "Just concentrate on the walls and keep us in the center of them. The chute probably won't be straight down."

In the gloom, he nods.

I ease us forward, my bubble of space piercing the wall of a vertical tunnel maybe twenty feet across. There are raw, regular chisel marks on walls, as if the tunnel has just recently been carved rather than having been here for decades. My headlamp can't pierce the darkness to the roof above or the bottom below. A stiff wind blows down the seemingly bottomless pit. I swallow hard, but I trust my team—especially the leader.

"Here we go," I say. Everyone hold tight." As almost a single entity, we go over the ledge. As we do, I can't help but think of those idiots who think they can go over Niagara Falls. Here, we are not even bothering with the barrel.

Someone, a female, yells out. With the rushing of the wind, I'm not sure who it is, or if it is in fright or excitement. Personally, with my stomach falling out of the bottom of my corset, I'd definitely say fright. But the sound cuts off as soon as it starts. Hellfighters aren't known for being afraid of much, especially after the fact. The wind extinguishes the helmet lights as we plummet. Only Max's white illumination remains as we race down. If it wasn't for this, I think I'd piddle myself.

I yelp as the wall rushing by scrapes the back of my denim dress and, I'm sure, leaves more than a few bruises on my backside. I hope the fabric holds out. Moments later, I hear Max grunt as we lurch against another side.

"Look out!" Cora screams. I look down, and we are about to be dashed onto a giant metal screw that fills the passageway. The winds grab me and all the rest of us. Like a violent storm, it pushes harder than any ten men. It slows us.

It feels like I'm in the poderabile, pulling full back to avoid some idiot who has driven his team of horses out in front of me. I'm heavy. I hope the rubber in my bloomers will take this abuse and stay put.

It is odd to be so scared and worried about something as inconsequential as your wardrobe. It isn't as if, through the years, my team hasn't seen most of my bare skin because of ripped clothing from the maelstrom of fighting a demon. Still, deep inside me, there is a lady who feels that having my underpinnings exposed isn't proper.

Our landing on the angled surface reminds me of jumping out of a tree when I was about seven. It won't leave any marks, but it sure hurts. More than one person grunts.

As we check to make sure everyone remains in the land of the living, Menaj says, "Hey, it's the drilling machine. We are on the end of the armadillo." Sure as anything, she's right. The dad-blasted thing is wedged in the passage straight up and down. Now it dawns on me that the fresh chisel marks on the shaft are from the cutting screws of this monstrosity. The passage down must be not quite large enough for it, causing it to continue downward.

"How are we going to get past this abomina—" Cora starts. Her voice cuts off when she sees the same thing I do. The armadillo is no longer cylindrical. There is a massive dent, the size of a hogshead, smashed in one side.

"Everyone relight your lamps," Carlos orders. "Max, go down there and take a look." Matches work just as well as a fire witch to get our thin yellow lights back.

"Jesus!" Max hisses below us. I can't remember ever hearing my young friend blaspheme before. "Be careful coming down. It's messy and slippery."

Carlos, barely bigger than the hole, slides down feet first. "Good God!" he exclaims. I hear, "Keep going, Max. Nothing we can do for these poor bastards anyway."

I'm not sure I want to see the carnage they are describing. Several of our previous adventures featured the gruesome remains of someone caught by a rampaging demon. Even so, I never have inured myself to the copper smell of blood, the bitter smell of urine, or the rank shit smell of a corpse that has been disemboweled.

One by one, we climb down, and at least my fellow teammates refrain from further commentary. I am last. As I pass through what once was a marvel of engineering, I learn what everyone has been talking about. The entire side of the armadillo has been smashed in. It looks like a housewife kneaded a particularly soft bread dough. Two fists, each larger than a prize pig, would be required to fill those rents. Everything—man, metal, and machine—has been flattened against the far wall. The red remains of what were once God's children cover everything. The mess is so horrific that I can't even tell how many men there had been. I can't move without getting it on my hands, dress, and everywhere. I'm going to have to scrub the life out of me when I get the chance.

"We have to keep going," Carlos says. "We only have a few more minutes."

The smashed machine is wedged, but there is a path for us to get out one side, and even a small ledge to stand on while we gather together.

"Once more into the breach?" I ask in bad humor.

Carlos scowls at me. I notice he isn't nearly as nervous as before when he says, "Everyone together. In three ... two ... one ..." As a joined group, we once again fall into the abyss. But it isn't the same fright as before. We've been through it once and can do it again.

The fall seems interminable, but just as I start to count chimpanzees, Menaj calls out, "Floor!"

The wind buffets us to a much calmer landing in a puddle of crimson mud. I choose to believe that the material is purely red clay as I take stock of my surroundings. About eighty feet off to my right is a large fire burning cheerfully. The wind from our tunnel crosses over to feed the fire. I've heard that they sometimes use fires to circulate air. To my left is a tunnel that traverses maybe thirty feet before being choked with rocks, boulders, and earth. Pickaxes, jackhammers, shovels, carts, and all manner of other tools lie where rescuers had been digging. A pile of shoring timbers lie beside them.

In the near silence, I can hear a faint, muffled tapping sound. I first think it is dripping water. There is no lack of liquid here. However, the more I focus, the more it seems like metal tapping against rock.

I pick up a hand sledge and pound a stone in the walls three times.

"Wha—" Cora starts

"Shhh!" I bark for silence.

The tapping becomes louder and faster. Then more beating happens at the same time. "They are still alive," I say.

"We already knew that," Carlos replies.

"An untrained white witch? I will say I had my doubts," I say, with Menaj nodding with me.

"Then let's get on with this," Carlos commands, checking his watch. His has a second hand on it, whereas my Aaron's doesn't. "We are out of time."

"It will be easiest through the rubble. Everyone cuddle up again," I say.

[You are difficult prey.]

"¡Dios mío!" Bea says.

"Everyone, back-to-back," Carlos orders. Our circle turns upon itself like a snake shedding its skin. From trying to hold each other tightly, we face outwardly to protect one another. We now form a porcupine with much sharper quills. Menaj would appreciate the comparison.

[It must end here.]

There is a screech of metal. From far above us I feel the armadillo being ripped. "Run!"

It doesn't matter who says it. As successful hellfighters, orders from a teammate trump nearly everything in our lives. All of us scatter. I head toward the fire. Four agonizing seconds pass before the cacophony of metal striking stone and the shaking jar of the floor overtake us. The metal shatters like glass. I hear a scream outside my circle of light. Three times objects fall before only the echoes remain. "Come back," Carlos says.

The bottom of the shaft is awash with debris in a pile as high as a man, but we can move around it to meet up again. Carlos limps into sight with a shard of metal the shape of a dinner knife protruding from his right thigh. A quick head count shows we are all in place. I reach out and cause the metal to flow away and out of his wound.

Max steps up with, "'You restored me to health and let me live. Surely it was for my benefit that I suffered such anguish. In your love you kept me from the pit of destruction; you have put all my sins behind your back.'" Carlos's wound closes over. I've seen it so many times that it no longer holds fascination.

"Where is the thing?" Bea asks.

[Right here, defiler.]

A massive stone arm moves out from the wall, knocking the slight witch down the hallway and right into the fire as if she were a bullet fired from a gun. She screams as the firelight from that direction wavers. The illumination dims suddenly.

No time to waste on something Bea can handle herself. So I deal with the immediate. I use my powers to order Grondr's arm held. While I'm holding that one, another earthen appendage reaches out and clubs Maxwell, knocking him to the floor. He doesn't get up. I have to split my attention to mentally grab both granite limbs. The pair of arms now move slowly and are easy to avoid. But yet another one extrudes from the wall and just misses Cora's head. It doesn't, however, miss her arm. I hear the snap as her forearm breaks. She stoically backs away and sends a jet of water at the limb, severing it. It clatters noisily to the ground.

Both walls grow roots at the speed a frightened snake might travel across the flat ground. This traps two other limbs behind their growing network. *God bless, Menaj.*

The collapsed pile that was once a massive machine is moving and taking a humanoid shape. I switch my attention to the metal, forcing Grondr to form slowly, if at all.

A wind moving toward the fire changes to swirl around, forming a vortex around us. Bea, her clothes smoldering and harboring ice crystals, floats toward us in the air as Carlos stretches his magic. The transportee isn't idle, firing twin beams of ice at the developing creature.

"Stella, get us out of here!" our leader barks.

"But the miners are just over there! We won't get another chance," I implore them.

"We can't stop that thing, and Maxwell is down."

He's right. Maxwell's head is seeping blood, and he is still, not having moved since the creature clobbered him.

"It's too far," I say. "It will catch us. Fly us out, Carlos. I'll slow him down."

The vortex around us changes shape, and I find myself being lifted off the earthen floor. I keep my concentration on the pile of metal, not letting it change.

I can feel Grondr's spirit leaving the metal to reform inside the shaft walls. I change my focus and slow the creature down.

[Aah! Come back to join the other defilers!] it screams.

"FASTER," I urge over the volume of the gale-force wind.

Carlos does us all proud. We zoom along at a speed that would outrace a fast horse.

Every time Grondr bounces from place to place using its ability to translocate its spirit, I localize the new location and stop it. What saves us is that several seconds pass between it changing places. It also can't travel but a few dozen feet.

I don't give up on my task, though I know we are safe. While it takes considerably longer to reach the surface than to get down, we find the mine's main entrance. I turn the chain holding the door bound to liquid. Menaj and Bea carry Max between them. Cora and I push open the big wooden doors to find ourselves in the bright afternoon sunlight. Carlos just stands there shaking. Looks like we pushed his fears too far on flying.

"Hey!" claims one of the four guards. The group of toughs turns on us. Menaj grows a hedge of kudzu over the first one to say something. What's more, Darrin and Bruce Jasperson are sitting in chairs to one side.

I look at the other five and say, "I wouldn't if I were you. She was very kind to that guy."

"You!" Bruce shouts, jumping up and pointing at me. "You are behind all of this!"

A sickness shrouds my soul. We were so close—only a couple hundred feet away from the trapped miners. We failed. They will die. The depression comes with teeth and a bark. "Shut up, *pendejo*! Get Luciana Riley here, as soon as possible. We have an injured man."

"No! You've gone too far. You set off dangerous explosives. You trespassed. You violated—"

Everything in my body and turbulent mind tears into the earth. The ground shakes and boils around the elder Jasperson. Like some prophet of old, I lift my hands up to the sky. The earth complies with my unspoken commands and emotions. A tube of stone erupts around Bruce from below. It closes at the top in the length of time it takes to hiccup. The scum is entombed.

"BRING LUCIANA!" I yell. As if by an earthquake, the ground shakes with my words. From the startled looks around me, I've gotten everyone's attention.

"I'm coming, Stella!" I hear from the coal road. The sheriff has her in a buckboard and has the horses in a gallop up the slope.

"Lucy, treat Max! He's hurt," I say.

With my body full of anger and adrenaline, I look at the dichotomy of asking my cousin to save my friend when I haven't saved her husband. My mind crashes in despair. Tears roll down my face. I feel someone walk up beside me, but I don't have the emotional energy to turn to even see who it is. I stand there as a cold breeze rolls over me.

"You better let him out," Cora says softly beside me. She cradles her broken arm but doesn't cry out against the pain she must be feeling.

"Huh?"

"*El jefe.* You better let him go before he throws a fit," she says, pointing at the man-sized egg of red rock. Several people are trying to break it open with a pickax. Absently, I link with the stone and cause it to open like the bud of a flower. The president of the Coal Syndicate stands in the center like the stamen. Bruce scampers out, gasping and panting like a dog.

"You ... You!" he stammers, pointing his finger at me. "That's it. Sheriff, arrest her. Arrest her now."

Sheriff Billings spits out a long stream of chewing tobacco before pushing out his jaw and saying, "No."

"What did you say to me?" Bruce Jasperson snaps as Darrin tries to dust the red clay dust off his brother's expensive suit.

"Excuse me. No, sir. I will not arrest these heroes."

"Heroes? They are villains. They've trespassed, damaged syndicate property, and imprisoned me. Now, do your job or I'll fire you right now!"

"No, sir. You can't fire me. I was elected by the people."

"Because I told them to do so. I fucking own this town."

"That may be effectively true, but not legally. Until the people vote me out, I am the law here. I tell you, Mr. Jasperson, that these people have only been doing what *you* should have been doing. And they're doing it despite your interference."

"Fine then, *Sheriff* Billings. I can't force you to do your job. But you can count on this town removing you from it in short order. And you," Jasperson says, pointing at me again. "Your day of reckoning is only delayed. I'm contacting the witch police. They will know what to do with you!"

Bruce clouts Darrin upside the head. "This is your fault. I want this mine drawing tonnage tomorrow, or brother or not, I'll ruin you."

"But we haven't heard from the armadillo."

"Oh, about that. Your invincible machine is a heap of scrap at the bottom of the mine," I taunt.

"And you won't arrest this ..." Jasperson's head swells up and turns the color of a radish. "This ... This bitch for damaging property? Do you have any idea how much an armadillo miner costs?"

"I had nothing to do with it, Brucie," I offer with a bit of gravel in my tone. "Had I known it would get you this worked up, I might have done it out of spite. But I can't take credit for this work. The mythical creature, as you called it, crushed your technological marvel easier than you can smash a can of beans with a sledgehammer. Better luck next time."

"Y- Y- YOU DID IT, *PUTA!*"

I just shake my head.

Bruce stalks off down the road with Darrin following like a puppy. "You will get the second armadillo operational and in the mine by five in the morning," he almost yells at his brother. "And while you are at it, get the damned workers ready. The new batch of miners will be here at nine. I want them all in and loading no later than ten."

"Yes, Bruce."

"They don't learn, do they?" Cora asks.

"No. And never will," Menaj agrees.

"And every miner who goes down that shaft will die," she says.

I nod.

"Is there anything we can do about it?" Carlos asks from beside me.

"Not a damned thing. To be so close and not bring them home seems like a bigger failure than what little we accomplished on day one." The tears leak down my cheeks.

"Don't kick yourself, Stella. We did all we could," Cora says.

"J- J- Jesus H. Christ!" I hear with a heavy squeak on the last word. "What hit me?"

I don't turn but know that Max is still in the land of the living. My inner turmoil grows, knowing that we've left those miners down there to die, and more on the morrow. We weren't strong enough. *Is it the sin of pride that we might thwart your will to get them out, God?*

"No, don't try to stand," Lucy says to Max.

"Whoa!"

"I told you not to stand," my cousin remonstrates.

8—Saturday, November 24, 1888

While I'm certain it is past three, I'm not sure what time it is. The darkness outside is lit up only by a quarter waning moon.

I'm sitting on a pew in the Centralia church, watching my breath come out in silver puffs in the candlelight. There are so many candles around the room. Many of the families have lit them and left them to extend their prayers for the safety of the trapped miners. I feel like more than just a little bit of a Judas bringing my troubles here.

My team and I sat up to past midnight discussing alternatives. Maxwell's inputs were weak as he drifted in and out of sleep. He was constantly dizzy and sometimes complained of double vision. Lucy assured me that he will live to squeak again.

As the mighty hellfighters evaluated the situation, every suggestion fell like a lead balloon. No more explosives. A powerful, homicidal creature blocked our path. There was no method to keep it at bay while we collected the trapped men and women. The weight of responsibility crushed me. After five hours and more than a few beers, we reluctantly agreed as a group that it was impossible.

I just couldn't stand to listen to my cousin crying in bed tonight, so I snuck out of the Riley house to the church to salve my soul, ask God for his help, and maybe ask for forgiveness. My team has no more ideas, but I have one—one more plan that almost certainly is madness and yet another reason to be here. I pray to the Lord and ask him not only for forgiveness but guidance. I pray that what I have in mind is not the penultimate sin of suicide. It may be the ultimate risk for a tiny chance—an infinitesimal chance.

For once, I can't feel God's love. I can't tap into the wellspring of my faith. I'm empty when I feel I need it most. Tears that have been rolling down my cheeks off and on since this afternoon are back on.

I write, "I'm sorry" on a piece of paper. I sign and seal it in an envelope. On the outside, I address it to Luciana and the *Dos Campanas*. I walk up to the altar and place it next to the Bible. I look up at the carved image of Jesus and make one more silent prayer that I might save at least one. I cross myself and walk with determination out the door.

# # #

Even in the waning moonlight, I can see the scars on the ground where I've parted the earth, multiple times.

I look at Aaron's pocket watch in the wan light of the moon. Four fifteen. I kiss the face of it, wishing it were his lips. "Soon, my love. Soon." I'm sure he met his end bravely. I, on the other hand, am afraid to my core. I won't need the watch ever again, so I put it on a tuft of grass so that if everything goes wrong, they will know what happened.

I light my miner's helmet. I put it on and look up into the sky for one last look. The earth has always been my bedrock. I chuckle at my own graveyard humor. "Earth to earth …" For the umpteenth, and last, time, I part the terrain and head in.

I've passed this way many times, so this earth doesn't fight my presence or movement nearly as it had. The passage is but the blink of an eye, but with the terror in my soul, every inch is like the slow, steady pace toward the hangman.

I slide out into the sealed tunnel we first discovered and fought in. This time, I alone won't be able to put up much of a fight.

"Protector!" I call out. I try to move the earth the way it does when it speaks. [Protector!]

There are no words. I sense the presence behind me. "Protector, please let me speak!"

The swinging of a massive fist shouts that it is in no mood for parlay. I do nothing to dodge but throw enough of my magic at the blow to slow it to something less lethal. The slam hits me in my shoulder, rolling me pell-mell over a small pile of rocks. I end up on my side with my legs splayed and my petticoats up around my neck. Embarrassment at showing my undergarments doesn't even register, but the familiar pain of my shoulder out of alignment does.

"Grondr. I do not beg for my life! But please hear me out!"

Fast as a striking cobra, a tentacle lashes out like a whip, wrapping itself around one leg. I let it grab me without even an attempt to escape. It yanks.

I scream as my leg is turned the wrong way at the hip. Panting and wincing between each word, I manage to get out, "Protector, please. I can spare you pain!"

The tentacle lifts me off the floor, exacerbating the pain in my hip. "Ahhh," I grunt.

[Speak before I kill you.]

"Yes, Protector. My life is forfeit to you. But some defilers will be coming in tomorrow morning. They bring another digging machine filled with explosives. In about one eight of an earth rotation."

There is a pause. Hanging there, I rotate around to see the broad humanoid form Grondr is wearing now. [Don't you claim these beings as your brothers?]

"I do, but—"

The spaces where its glowing eye pits are narrow, like a person squinting. [Why do you condemn them?]

"They are doing wrong to you. I can't allow that."

[You have wronged me before. They have wronged me before. Why change?]

"We're wrong. I wish to right it before you take my life."

[You do not fight to save yourself?]

I swallow hard. "No, Protector."

[That is strange.]

"Call it penance for wrongs. In addition to my sacrifice, I do have a proposal that may keep you from ever being defiled again."

[If your words are true, I will consider more words. I must stop the pain.]

Like a piece of hail on a hot summer day, Protector disappears into the earth. Now having felt its essence, I can sense it moving rapidly off toward the main shaft. If the armadillo doesn't start down until seven, then Protector won't be returning soon.

I grab hold of my upper arm and pull with a hard jerk. Relocating my shoulder is becoming a regular event. It hurts less each time, but that doesn't help me when it is out of joint. I look down at my left leg. The foot should be pointing straight up. Instead, it and the knee point off to the outside of my body. Dislocations are even worse than broken bones. *Maxwell can always* ... I stop my train of thought.

There won't be any more Max, Carlos, Bea, Danny, Menaj, or anyone else. Well, in that case, using my own white powers won't matter one whit. I empty the fear in my heart and reach out. "'Heal me, O

Lord, and I shall be healed; save me, and I shall be saved: for thou art my praise.'" My hand flashes brilliant white, and my leg realigns, somewhat. The pain abates. I stand up and walk across the floor. My limb still isn't pointing perfectly straight. I hobble a bit because of it. Shrugging at the mild limp, I make my way back to where I'd been sitting. I'd at least partially warmed up that spot.

I choose to spend the time praying. *I'll be with you soon, Lord. I pray that my Aaron is there to greet me.*

# # #

The resignation when you know your fate calms the soul. That I've confessed my sins and will meet my maker as a good woman is enough. If I'm successful, the trade of my life for theirs will be a worthy one.

While I have no sun to warm me from the sky, I don't feel Grondr makes me wait any longer than necessary. I feel it swimming through the earth until it comes up in front of me.

[You didn't save yourself. You could have left.]

"I gave my word, Protector. And were my other words as true?"

[Yes. The digger machine is no more.]

Please, Lord God, forgive me for my part in the death of those men, but their sacrifice and mine may save many more. Amen. "Then may I make my offer to make it so the earth hurts no more?"

[Speak.]

I've rehearsed this multiple times in my mind. "If a badger digs in the earth, do you blame its claws?" With the pause, I get the impression that Grondr didn't expect a question.

[The claws are part of the badger.]

"But do the claws decide where to dig? How long to dig? How deep to dig?"

[But it is part of the whole.]

"What makes the decision? The claws just carry out the will of—"

[You ask odd questions. The claws have no anima. It must be the brain of the badger.]

"That's right. The brain holds the responsibility. And if a bear bites a hand, do we blame the teeth?"

[They are the ones that do damage, but the bear did the biting. The bear's brain.]

"So the miners you have deep in the earth are nothing more than the claws of a much bigger creature. They dig because its brain tells them to do so. They have no more culpability than the bear's teeth. They don't care to dig, but they must because the brain tells them to." Grondr won't understand money, economics, employees, immigration, poverty, or any pot to piss in. This is the only way the situation will make sense to it.

[What does this have to do with no more pain?]

"If you were to show mercy to the claws, I think I have a plan that will keep you from pain."

[Without pain, I would sleep. I've been fighting for so long. I want sleep. I want to be no more.]

"Let me help you. But you need to help me. Let the teeth and claws go."

[Tell me how to have no pain.]

I can't tell if the pact has been made or not. "Collapse all of the tunnels. The brain will realize that digging this space is too difficult to dig the tunnels once again. But first, you must let the claws free."

[I no longer have the strength to fill all the emptiness.]

"What if I help you?"

[I agree if you tell me where the brain is.]

I ponder the implications. It wants to know about the Jaspersons. What will it do with the information? *You know what it'll do, Stella. Don't be naïve.* I'm not committing an act. I'm only pointing the weapon. Grondr has the same free will as any other creature. It isn't a sin on my head.

"There is this hill ... Do you understand *hill*?"

[Earth that sticks up into the not earth.]

"Good. There is a hill south of here about a mile."

[What is a mile? What is south?]

¡*Cacafuego!* How do I describe a mile? Or south? *Think, Stella.* "If you face the rising sun and put out your right hand, yes, that one, that direction is south."

[Good. I call that *arhastplo*.]

"Sure. So go sou— arhastplo. If you lay me foot to head one thousand times in that direction, you'd be there."

[I know that place. The brain is there?]

"On that hill is a house, like an above-ground animal burrow. The brain moves, but it is always in the burrow when the sun has set for two-thirds the rotation of the earth." If I've done my math correctly, that should be about two in the morning.

[Good. Do we work together to collapse tunnels?]

"Yes. First, let's get the claws and take them to the top of this hill and set them free. Then we collapse the upper tunnel so no more defilers or their claws can enter."

[Agreed.]

# # #

I no longer have an air witch to allow me to throw myself down the main mine shaft. I must go the hard way by forcing my way through the recalcitrant earth along the side of the shaft. I'm forced to take many breaks.

The sphere of my passage intersects the shaft like a small cave moving down the side. This open-sided travel not only gives me air to breathe, it also prevents water from pooling in the bottom more than a couple of inches deep.

Unfortunately, this is exceedingly slow. The earth spirit darts ahead through the rock itself. It circles back from time to time.

A bulbous head-like appendage sticks out during one of my frequent breaks. [Slow.]

"Best I can do. Can you make the ground less hostile? I try to work with it, but it fights me."

[I can carry you.]

Panting from exertion, I say, "That would be acceptable."

I may not have an air witch, but I am working with a creature of the very earth strata. It wraps me up in a cocoon barely an inch around my body. Without waiting, it speeds off through the rock.

I've been in small spaces before, but this is like being buried alive. The tremendous pressure of stone and soil above me presses on my mind. I like being close to the earth, but this is too much. Breathing becomes difficult, and my candle is beginning to sputter.

"Stop."

[What?]

"I need air to breathe." My words come out in pants.

[What is breathe? What is air?]

"I cease to be if I don't get air—not rock."

Grondr eschews words. It just slides over and opens a side of itself into the vertical shaft just like I'd done with my own movement.

I suck in heavy draws of if not fresh air, then much less stale. "Thank you, Protector." It is at this point I realize that the wind that had been steadily downward isn't blowing. The pumps are off. The emergency air circulation fire hasn't been tended. We have to get the miners out before they suffocate. Much faster than I'd hoped, we reach the bottom. Protector spills me onto my own feet next to the scattered wreck of not one but two mining armadillos.

I was right: the air circulation fire has completely gone out. My helmet light is the only thing that illuminates the area. As I scan the area, it dawns on me—no elevator. Worse, with the shattered metal remnants, we couldn't get one down in any case. How will I get the miners out? "Protector, how many of me can you carry?"

[There is only one of you.]

Communicating without a common frame of reference is difficult. "How many of the claws can you carry?"

[All.]

Thank you, Mother Mary. "I'm going to go through the earth here and talk to the claws. When I call, come over and take us up."

[Yes.]

The caved-in earth has less resistance, and I move through it with only a little more trouble than it would normally take. I pop back out into a long tunnel, not unlike the one I just left. However, the air here reeks and is stale.

"Hey," someone says weakly. A man gives a wet cough. The few who can still move put their hands up to block what must be the brightest light they have seen after having been in total darkness for so long.

Miners sit on the floor, leaning against the walls. Their faces, clothes, and every surface are almost black in coal dust. It isn't any surprise I missed them at first. The best of them are lethargic. Most are unconscious in the dead air. There is no time to waste. I can talk after I get them to safety.

"Protector. Help me now."

[Yes,] my companion says, popping out of the solid floor.

"We need some not-rock from the other side of this area," I say, pointing at the collapsed area. "This not-rock is bad."

[Yes.]

Grondr presses against the rock pile, moving the entire hundred feet or more of it a few yards at a time. I realize we will soon have good air, but I need to find everyone, as they aren't together.

My task likely will take much longer than Grondr's. I find a man and will the earth to slide him over. I struggle so hard that I'm blacking out in the foul atmosphere. I settle for scratching the wall with a rock so I don't forget. I do this dozens of times until a cool rush of breathable air flows in. Greedily, I suck it in. Now I find that I can function almost normally.

Protector shows up at my side. [Not-rock good?]

"Yes, thank you. Can you help bring all the claws into the same place? Even the ones who are no longer alive."

Without a word, the creature starts dragging all the miners into the same place. With the good air, some of them are beginning to rouse. One of them fights and kicks at Grondr's arm but to little avail. When Protector releases the man, he scrambles backward as far as he can from the creature within the confines of the little alcove where all the miners are being stored.

"GRONDR!" the man shouts. "Run!" Fortunately, most of these poor souls haven't recovered.

"Listen to me," I say. "Grondr is helping get you out. We are both working to get you out."

Most of the miners nod weakly. They are in no condition to do more. Two cough in the gloom.

Protector brings in each of the miners, two, three, or seven at a time. Some with broken limbs and other injuries. One man has a bandage over an eye. Several just weep. I don't have time to specifically find Luciana's husband.

[Done.]

One hundred twenty-seven living, thirty-eight dead make up all we can find. I scour the tunnels for anyone else but find no other living or dead souls. If there were more, then they have been crushed under the rocks and are lost to everyone but God.

"Good. Protector, take us up to the sunlight. Don't forget that we all must have not-rocks to live."

[Understood.]

Protector does the same thing going up that it did going down. After engulfing us like a crust over an enormous meat pie, it opens up one side to the shaft as we travel up.

"Adam Riley!" I call out, hoping to get a response. A man raises his hand as he coughs wildly. I rush over to his side as he shivers. "My name is Stella Ochoa. I'm your wife's cousin. She brought me to save you and your friends."

His eyes are white globes in the center of his blackened face. I see a certain amount of confusion there.

"Don't talk. I know you have pneumonia." Even with the chill of the earth, his body sheds heat like the radiators in my home. I can hear the boneyard rasp in his breathing, which is shallow enough to concern me. "Even though we are taking you to the surface, I'm not sure you will live without some help. I have white witch powers. They are crude. What I do will make you somewhat better, but it will hurt. And you can't tell anyone."

Adam nods as tears leak from his eyes. It makes the black run down his face like indigo rain. I tear open his shirt and winter underwear to find his flesh, gray from lack of air.

I close my eyes and reach out to touch the love of God, once more at my disposal. I gather it together as easily as a five-year-old collects all the jacks no matter how many times the ball bounces. I am not trained for this. Maxwell has always been our healer. And few, if any, know about my latent white powers.

"'And the people all tried to touch him, because power was coming from him and healing them all,'" I say, quoting Luke 6:19. My hands glow, more yellow than the pure bleach white that Max always manages. I put them on Adam's chest skin, which is hot enough to fry an egg. My glow disappears as he bucks against the touch. He coughs four times before looking at me with bulging eyes. He opens his mouth and puts his hands up to his throat as he begins to turn purple. Just when I think he is going to pass out, he starts coughing, his chest heaving. Suddenly he leans over and spits up green mucus the size of a bullock's ball. The mass of air that he sucks in whistles. Three deep breaths later he says, "Thank you, Mrs. Ochoa. I don't feel a dagger in my chest any longer."

"Save those thanks and give them to your wife. She is the one who orchestrated all of this."

"Lucy probably did more than that. I'm surprised you don't have footprints over your back."

I smile back at him with a nod. "She is a formidable woman."

Adam tries to struggle to his feet only to slump back onto his fundamentals. "Whoa."

"I didn't cure you, Adam. Only helped. You still need to recover."

I'm barraged by what seems like a million thanks.

"Thank you for rescuing us, Mrs. Ochoa."

"Thank you."

"God bless you."

"You are a godsend, Mrs. O."

"Any good person of the Church would do the same," I reply. "Now everyone hush. We are almost to the surface, and there is something I need to tell you. When you get to the surface, let everyone know that the mines will be collapsed. I mean every tunnel, drift, and drilling. It may take days because there are many of them, but it will happen. Make sure everyone stays away from heavy things that might topple over. Remove pictures from walls. In fact, if you can stay outside away from buildings, it would be better."

"Why don't you tell them?" one of the miners calls out.

I'm elated to save these one hundred twenty-seven souls, but I know the cost. I will pay it happily. "I can't go with you. I made a bargain."

I use my earth powers to speak to Grondr without the others knowing. [Protector, leave me in the cavern where we met when you put these claws into the light.]

[Yes. Get off here,] it says, opening a passage for me to exit.

"Why not? What bargain?" Adam asks gruffly.

"Give everyone my love," I say, stepping out. Grondr's earthen bulk whisks the rest of the miners to their salvation—at least to their physical safety. I watch with a smile on my face. Adam Junior, Holly, and Gretchen will have a father. Lucy will have a husband. And so will many other children, wives, husbands, and families have their loved ones because of my sacrifice. My life for theirs, and the happiness of their families is a bargain I wish I hadn't had to make. But it is more than fair.

And why isn't this good for me anyway? I can't have my dearest in this world. So why shouldn't I go to heaven, sit at the right hand of God, and receive his love and that of my husband? I will get to spend eternity with Aaron. Is that such a bad thing?

Grondr returns before I can finish mulling over my mortality.

"Shall we heal?" I ask.

[Yes, Ochoa creature.]

"First we need to go to the top and seal it so no more claws come in."

[I will take you.]

Grondr knows its way around. Before I can barely blink, we are at the very beginning of the mine. Only the great wooden doors stand between us and the outside.

"Protector, can you pull down the supporting beams?"

[Yes.]

"Those will have to come down. I'll analyze the earth's structure to decide how to bring it down."

I put my hand against the cold wall and send out my senses. If I analyze earth anywhere else, it is like a dinner party of three couples who are all talking together about the same subject. Here, the response more closely resembles a three-thousand-person food riot, or maybe two warships boarding one another. The angry growls, bellows, and yelling are insane. It takes much longer than expected to get an image of how the earth is layered and where weak points are. The upper structure of the mine is rather fragile, being held together with pitch, tar, and baling wire—and the odd metal or wooden beam.

Finishing my analysis, I hear the angry voice of Bruce Jasperson outside the main wooden mine doors. "That *puta* will probably bring it down herself, and there are no magical creatures of the earth, no matter what those damned miners said."

"But, Bruce," Darrin says. "When she gets out of there, she is going to be more popular than ever."

"Then we have to make sure she doesn't."

"Doesn't what?"

"Get out of the mine, at least alive."

"Damn it all, Bruce. Every time you tangle with Mrs. Ochoa, she gets the better of you."

"She's got the pope's own luck, Darrin. This time we'll finish her for good. You got the key to the explosive shack?"

"Of course."

"Let's get it. All of it. That should finish off Miss Busybody. I can read it now, 'Heroine Saves Miners But Dies in a Tragic Accident.' We'll even give her a medal, posthumously."

"That sounds about right," Darrin replies.

I've never had proof that the Jaspersons have tried to end my life. I guess I still don't, but I no longer have any doubts. It does put some urgency on getting the upper mine sealed off.

[Supports removed.]

"Let's move back to the room where you found me. This is going to be rather spectacular."

Grondr transports us there in a flash. Once safe—which is laughable, as I will be dying soon—I take hold of the rock and feel my way back to the crux I analyzed. There I find the moral equivalent of a keystone and turn it into mud.

We can feel the vibrations of the collapse through the floor and even in the air. A bass rumble accompanies it. The roar goes on seemingly forever. Once it subsides, I send feelers out like before and find the top two hundred feet of the mine collapsed and effectively sealed. It would take a steam shovel weeks to clear it enough to get back down into the remaining navigable tunnels. Not only that, but the pumping and ventilation systems are crushed beyond salvation.

[Good,] Grondr says without me saying anything.

"Does that feel better?"

[Yes, a little.]

"Then we have much more to do."

[Yes, Ochoa creature.]

I think about telling Grondr that calling me Stella is good enough, but should you get friendly with your executioner? Instead, I suggest, "I think we should start at the bottom. That way the collapses may trigger other cave-ins above, and we won't have to do those areas."

[Yes. I will take us.]

"Thank you, Protector."

# # #

Time ceases to mean anything. The only light I have is that from my headlamp, and the outside world no longer exists to me anyway. I'll never see it again.

The creature of stone and I fall into a rhythm. It takes us to a new place and removes the mining support beams as I analyze the best way to bring down the unbraced ceiling and walls. Then Grondr moves us to a safe distance, and I collapse the tunnel.

We implode thirty or so tunnels, working our way up. From the growls in my stomach, it must be about eight hours. But then what does food matter? Without the water-pumping systems, the warrens are slowly being reclaimed by the water table. I do take drinks from the dirty puddles I find nearly everywhere. With my skills, it's easy enough to get the soil and clay to leave so that I have cold, clean water to drink.

Each location is not much different from the last—rough-hewn rock walls and ceiling, wooden braces, and ceiling joists every eight feet of tunnel distance, and a floor so heavily traveled by foot and cart that it is smooth, if uneven.

I put my hand to the rock. There is an unstable segment just twenty feet away. "Protector, no!" I yell as it pulls the brace from under that area. A different, smaller rumble erupts as sixteen tons of rock, sand, and gypsum bury the creature.

"Grondr!" I race to the pile and begin moving the pieces I can.

[What, Stella creature?] I hear from behind me. I turn to find him unscathed.

"I thought you'd been hurt under there."

[Why?]

I can see where it is going with its question. If it dies, I don't have to. Why would I aid in my own death? "Because you are a living creature. I have empathy for all."

[Even the brains?]

"Ahhh." He inadvertently reminds me that I once caused the death of Manuel Gomez y Ruiz, a loathsome, vile human who believed only in hate. I sent him to hell itself, which has no outcome other than his physical death and the torture of his immortal soul. Then I remember the conversation I overheard between the Jasperson brothers.

"I can empathize without agreeing with their actions. It also won't keep me from doing what is needful. One can needfully destroy a rabid dog and feel sad about it afterward."

[Too complex. Brains bad.]

"I can't disagree."

9—Unknown

Sometime later, going through yet another of our rote procedures, my headlamp goes out. The total blackness startles me. This isn't the dark of the bedchamber. Always some illumination from the stars, moon, or even lamplight leaks in through the curtains or cracks around the doors. This is the absence of all light. My stomach starts churning acid in that primitive, primal fear of the dark that we all have.

I think I whimper, knowing what those miners must have felt like—trapped in the dark and waiting to die. I reach out to touch the rock. It lets me mentally map out my space, allowing me to sit down.

[Ochoa creature.] His words startle me in my little optical prison. [Heal more?]

"I can't see, Grondr."

[What is see?]

"It's dark. I don't know where things are."

[No longer heal?]

This gets me thinking. Can I still do it? Why do I need to see for what I'm doing? My job is to scan the strata, find weak points, and exploit them. Grondr takes me from place to place. It is the one that moves me to safety each time. I don't need to measure distance by eye. It will lose out if a collapse kills me before I finish healing the ground.

"Yes," I say, getting back to my feet by touch against the wall alone. "I can heal. Let's get to a safe distance."

# # #

As we move forward with our reclamation plans, I realize that I mostly don't need my sight here anyway. At our next stop, I untie my boots. I strip off my stockings and leave them off. The earth is cold against the soles of my feet, but getting sick is the least of my worries.

Traveling in the darkness of my grave (yes, I've reconciled that this will be the place my mortal remains will rest), my sense for the earth improves. I can see with my mind the lay of the rock and soil. I can see joints of different strata. Even the stress points where beams support the rock are clear. In my mental vision, Grondr positively shines like a network of cracks, especially as it moves. I start walking about with confidence until I bark one shin on a wooden tool handle. It slows me down but doesn't stop me.

I measure time by the number of tunnels we destroy, the number of times I stop to relieve myself, and the number of times I have to fill my stomach with water to keep it from growling. But honestly, I am not keeping count.

I certainly am not sleeping even though I'm certain I've been in this dark hell for at least a pair of days. I'm starting to get woozy with fatigue, but Grondr and I push on. Each cave-in brings the earth in the area closer to something more homogeneous, solid, and healed.

The thing that puzzles me is the lack of coal. I find traces and the trailing end of seams. Everything here seems to be played out for at least a thousand feet in any direction. They must have been exploring for new veins, but they certainly haven't been taking out tonnage.

I'm cold, dizzy, and close to the end of my rope. "Grondr, are we nearly done?"

[One more healing, Ochoa creature.]

"Quickly. I'm fading fast."

[No.]

"Excuse me?" I wonder if I heard it right.

[You are done. I finish the last healing myself.]

I'm too tired to fight or argue. "I understand. Can you do me a favor? Make it quick and don't tell me exactly when."

[Yes.] With my magic, I *see* Grondr ease up behind me. It forms its upper limbs into a massive pair of stone scissors. I'm sure that this will be a swift ending. I get down on my knees for a final prayer.

"'Surely your goodness and love will follow me all the days of my life, and I will dwell in the house of the Lord forever.' I love you, Aaron."

[No, Ochoa creature.]

"No what? I'm ready for my payment of our bargain."

Protector pauses. It then puts a tender touch on my shoulder. I jump, but its voice soothes me with, [I can't end your life.]

"What? I don't understand."

[The Ochoa is a healer, not a defiler. You kept your word. I cannot kill any such as that.]

"But ..." Tears form in my eyes. I'm beginning to wonder if I just might see another sunset. A reprieve from the headsman's axe.

[I ask but one more thing of you before I send you back to the claws.]

"What is it?"

[When I sleep, the land needs a new Protector. Will you be it?]

"I always protect the earth when I can."

[Then it is time for you to rejoin the claws. Save the land, Ochoa creature.] Grondr engulfs me for movement.

"But what about the last healing?"

[That I must do alone. Alone.]

I am pushed through the ground into the light, blinding light that threatens to sear my eyes. I can't even tell where I am. I crawl—

10—Wednesday, November 28, 1888

I wake up at an angle to everything. It's like the bed wants to roll me from it, but something soft and firm holds me in place.

An angel, looking just like my sweet Adrianna, hovers over me. "Eat, Stella. You need to eat." I open my mouth and let her spoon food into it like I'm a baby bird. A glorious dream, remembered from the past, when my lady love nursed me to health. I will cling to that memory. Alive or dead doesn't matter, as long as I have her touch and the caress of her heart.

11—Thursday, November 29, 1888

When I wake, the bed is still uneven. The sun peers in from a different angle through the cracks in some boards. Adrianna, with her blonde hair, slumps over the edge of the bed and snores on my pillow. She would be appalled at her disheveled state. In the meantime, God must have taken pity on me and taken me to heaven. But curvaceous Adrianna shouldn't be here. It should be my brawny husband, Aaron.

What I'd earlier taken for a surrealist's dream is quite genuine. Pictures are hung at an angle. The lean of the chifforobe has its doors and one drawer hanging open. Boards on the outside cover up the broken glass window. A pair of pillows hold me from rolling off the small bed. The room's angle isn't severe, just enough to twist my mind and tug at my body. I recognize the furniture and trappings as Lucy's bedroom.

Come to think of it, there are voices that I can hear through the door—Lucy, Adam Junior, and the precocious Gretchen. I try to move, but I'm dizzy. As if the oddly canted room isn't enough to throw off my equilibrium.

Adrianna wakes up next to me. "Stella! You're awake!"

My heart leaps and then sinks all in the space of five seconds. My beloved is here to nurse me, but she is still forbidden fruit. "Adrianna? By the Virgin Mary herself, what are you doing here?"

"I'm sorry, but that is not for me to say. Henry can answer that question when he gets back."

"Henry? Gets back? I feel like I've stepped into the looking glass."

"Enough of that. How are you feeling?"

"I'm hungry enough to eat one of your prized black Morgans. I'm also woozy. And I may be hallucinating, because the room seems tilted."

Adrianna laughs. The melodic ring alone soothes my soul. "It *is* tilted, Stella. Apparently part of your handiwork."

"Mine?"

"You collapsed the mine, didn't you?" she asks, bringing a bowl to my lips and spooning a thick beef stew into my mouth.

"With help, but yes," I manage after I clear my mouth. I recognize Lucy's delicious cooking right off.

"Well, we—Henry and I—arrived right in the middle of the whole thing. Earthquakes, many earthquakes, sank most of Centralia. Lucy and Adam told me what was going on after we struggled our way through the debris."

"I did that?" I say, mumbling around another spoonful of stew.

"The collapses outright destroyed about a quarter of the buildings in town. Another quarter burned down when stove fires lit off. I don't think there are three buildings that are still level."

"Was anyone hurt?"

"One broken leg taking a step at the wrong time, and a couple dozen bruises."

"Wow, I have a knack for making a mess, don't I? Look at us."

"This town may be a mess, but ... Well, the rest of it can wait until you are better. You know, nursing you is becoming quite repetitive. Maybe I should hire a full-time medical staff for you."

I struggle up into a sitting position. Adrianna automatically stuffs pillows beside me to keep me upright. Once I'm upright and the world stops spinning so fast, my golden-haired goddess spoons another mouthful of the thick, beef-rich soup into my maw.

"Why?"

"Why what, Stella?"

"Why are you here?"

"I really can't say, honey." She delivers it with a broad smile.

Every word this goddess speaks both salves my soul and stabs daggers into my heart. Worse, she is opening up a whole new mystery, one that I'm not sure I want to find the answer to.

The door opens and Luciana pokes her head in. Seeing me half propped up, she lets the door go, which opens further to match the lean of the room. She has a broad smile on her face that I haven't ever seen on her. Her inner contentment shines through. "I see the heroine of the hour is finally awake."

From the other room, I hear, "She is?"

"C'mon, let's see."

Lucy is pushed into the tiny room, and the heads of Adam—looking nearly fit—Adam Junior, Gretchen, Carlos, and half a dozen more peer in. Gretchen somehow sneaks between the legs of the crowd and bounces right up onto the bed. I tousle her hair and give her a broad smile.

"Good Lord almighty," my hostess says. "All of you are going to suck the air out of this room. Off with you! She'll be out to visit soon enough. She just needs feeding up and rest. Get!" She shoos the small army away with her hands. The throng reluctantly sidles off back into the living area of the cottage. Her admonition obviously doesn't include herself. "That means you too, Gretchen."

The young girl pouts but lingers long enough to put a wet kiss on my cheek. "Thank you, Mrs. Ochoa." She jumps down with just as much energy as she'd swarmed up into bed with me.

"So how are you feeling?" Luciana asks as she edges in the minute walking space around the bed.

"Like I just woke up after a two-day bender." Adrianna's musical laugh infuses me with well-being. I wonder if she might be the cure for the common hangover. "Might I inquire what day this is?"

Lucy looks at Adrianna. "So just woke up, then?"

"That's right," Adrianna says.

"Today is Thursday."

"Which Thursday?" I ask in all seriousness. The two women both titter.

"Thursday, November 29, in the year of our Lord 1888."

"The last time I remember, the day was Saturday," I say, grabbing the bowl away from Lady Helms. "I'm quite capable of feeding myself."

"Then eat. You are wasted away."

"Not hardly," I retort. I am hungry, so I relent and shovel the warming food into my mouth.

"Yes, we found you on Tuesday afternoon."

I look at Adrianna. "I've been out for two whole days?" The love of my life nods.

"Jesus, Mary, and Joseph!" I bark. "Well, working three and more days straight has its costs."

"We could see it," Lucy says. "You were unconscious in a field, pale as a ghost. I thought we were going to lose you, but Viscountess Helms knew you'd pull through. I think her words were, 'Stella is one tough bitch.'"

I look at Adrianna, who blushes and nods.

"Oh, and we found you with nothing on your feet. We still don't understand that bit of lasciviousness. We wonder if a pervert is wandering our streets."

I shake my head. "Don't worry. I took them off and left them behind. It's a long story." In a very unladylike manner, I scoop spoonful after spoonful into me until my stomach no longer thinks I've cut my throat.

"Well, for once, we have plenty of time," Lucy says, perching on the edge of the bed.

"If you don't mind, I'd rather have to tell the tale only once." I'm mindful that I'm wearing only some bloomers, an under-blouse, and some blankets. Surprisingly, I feel quite clean. I notice a washcloth and pitcher on the floor next to Adrianna. I wonder if my friend has been peeking at my charms. It gives me a wonderful shiver to think in the affirmative. "If you ladies will be so good as to help me get dressed, I'll be happy to tell it to anyone out there who wants to hear it."

"Actualllllllly," Lucy draws out the word, "the family and friends of those you saved, pretty much the whole town, want to hear what happened."

"The church?" I ask.

My cousin laughs. Adrianna smiles, putting warmth in my heart. "One of the few buildings that you and God chose to spare."

"If you will help me get dressed and let me walk between you so that I don't fall over, I think I can manage that."

# # #

In a new gown of shimmering gold, one of two given to me by Henry and Adrianna, I ease toward the church hall. I protested the gifts, but as my valise was damaged by the earthquakes, it was this or wear the heavily coal-dusted and otherwise dirty work dress. I relented after a few strong words.

The beautiful boots that go with it aren't exactly perfect for the snowy, muddy conditions of the town, but I manage a slow stagger with my badly healed leg. I try my darndest not to lean too much on my two supports.

Adrianna isn't kidding about the mess the town is in. Of the houses still standing, only about half of them are even marginally habitable because of their cant. Burned and crumbled houses pockmark the streets on our way. I try to put it out of my mind and focus on keeping one foot in front of the other, which is much more difficult than it sounds.

When we arrive, people are still streaming in the entrance. Those outside part to let us pass. The moment we broach the threshold of the church, a cheer and thunderous applause start, with everyone leaping to their feet. As I scan the inside, it really does seem the entire town is here. There must be three times the number of people I initially addressed. I catch sight of my team, huddled against the front stage. They are ruefully shaking their heads at the reaction but at the same time adding their own clapping. Sheriff Billings has his arm around a very broad-chested woman, whom I vaguely remember from the trapped miners Grondr saved. The entire Riley family occupies the front row next to Old Frank, all adding their own ovation. In the middle of the crowd, I note Henry, tall and pristine in a suit that looks like it just came from under the iron. Images of people I've only glimpsed here and there through the town flicker across my vision within the mob.

There is just too much to take in. I shut it out and focus on gutting out the fatigue that is already rolling over me. My cousin and my friend walk me forward toward the dais, where Darrin Jasperson's overblown chair perches. It makes me wonder if the Coal Syndicate are off sulking or making their next plans to murder me.

I'm weak by the time my nurses have deposited me in that cushy chair. The three days in the mine took a bigger toll on me than I'd thought. It takes several minutes for me to catch my breath. The town doesn't even slow down the applause. The noise is punctuated with whistles and wordless yells.

I look up at Lucy with a plea in my eyes. She has been a capable leader in the past. She reads my intent. Lucy holds up her hands for attention. The crowd's approval lessens but rumbles on.

"Friends! Please!" The tumult eases off. "Please! Stella is still weak. If you want her story, you have to give her quiet to tell it." As if choreographed, people quiet and take their seats—at least the ones who can. Townsfolk are standing around the edge of the room, and more are trying to push their way into the small house of God.

"Thank you," Lucy says to the gathering. "Cousin Stella, I think we all know what happened up to the point where you disappeared Friday night, or maybe Monday morning." She then sits down on a straight chair somewhat to my left.

I look at all the expectant faces. They overwhelm me. I look over to my right, where Adrianna sits beaming at me. Somehow she does just the right thing. She reaches forward and squeezes my hand. Her touch gives me the fortitude to speak.

"I must say that I didn't expect such a welcome. I did nothing more than anyone else woul—" Applause interrupts me. I'm embarrassed. I'm overwhelmed. I just wanted people to live, not to become some object of worship.

That reminds me. I look around to find Susan Queensbury leaning against the back wall, scribbling for all she is worth. *Damned and double damned!* I hold up my hand, and the ovation dies off.

"I'm going to just tell the tale, because no matter what I say, you are going to think I'm some kind of heroine." I see most of the crowd nodding and whispering to one another.

"More like a *gilipollas*," I hear in Maxwell's squeaky voice. There are a couple of giggles and a couple of angry growls from the audience. I smile down at Max, who holds the hand of young Bernice Schmidt. She is blushing. I am not sure if it is because she is courting openly with Max or because of his comments. Either way, I'm happy for my young friend. I'm also pleased that at least my team will keep my head from swelling up in praise.

"Friday night I came here, to that very pew, to pray to God for forgiveness. I needed absolution for the sin of pride. I thought the *Dos Campanas* could deal with any trouble. Many times the creature known as Protector, or more widely known as Grondr, repulsed us."

Whispering starts in the gallery. I wait a few moments for it to die down.

"Yes, Old Frank was right." Frank beams at the congregation. "Grondr existed, but if I understand it correctly, it is now gone. I don't know what it was, but it was put *in* this earth to protect it. But that is for later.

"I made my peace with the Almighty that early morning. Instead of going into the mines as an avenging angel or our savior Jesus Christ, I knew I had to go in as a penitent. I sought out Grondr and offered my life for those of the miners." I don't let them know that had negotiations gone bad, I'd have given up my life for just Adam's. I let them all think they are special.

The room buzzes. The whispering boils over, taking over from my talk. Shortly it erupts into more applause. Everyone is on their feet clapping, many with tears in their eyes. I squeeze Adrianna's hand and look over at her. Her makeup is running down her cheek in lines from each eye.

"Why are you crying?" I ask.

"I almost lost you," she says with more waterworks and a wry smile.

"I don't know if you've been keeping score, Annie," I say, using my nickname for her, "but we have already lost one another. It hurts. That's why I've kept my distance."

"I mean permanently."

I wrinkle my brow at her in confusion. But the people are settling back to their seats at Lucy's direction.

"When I finally got Grondr to stop beating on me, I made a bargain with it. I would forfeit my life and collapse the mine, healing the earth. In return, it would release all the miners and bring them to safety. That really is about all there is to it. You know more of the rest than I do."

The hall erupts with people shouting questions.

"One at a time. One at a time," Lucy calls out to control the suddenly unruly crowd. "Bart," she says, nodding at a man raising his hand.

"How did you get away? Did you trick it?"

"No. After we finished the demise of the mine, I offered it my life. Protector wouldn't take it. It claimed I was no longer a defiler but a healer." I hear Max snort. "I didn't claim that mantle," I assure him.

"Mark," Lucy says, calling on the next person.

"So you admit that you killed the Jaspersons?"

"What? Bruce and Darrin are dead?"

Lucy fills me in. "The last earthquake swallowed up the Jaspersons' home."

It reminds me that I did in fact tell Grondr where the brains were. It also said it had one more healing to do. Could it have intentionally killed them? Do I care? I do care, in the negative. Putting away my own personal hatred and the fact that they tried to kill me more than once, those men hurt and killed many. So, I do care that they are dead. I'm happy about it.

"What a shame," I offer with more sarcasm than not. "I wish I had, but I was nowhere near their hill and definitely not below it. No, I didn't kill them." I won't even ask for absolution for their deaths, although I might have to do so for being happy they are gone.

"Jerry," Lucy says, pointing to someone else with his hand up.

"What are we supposed to do now?"

This man definitely hadn't been trapped in the mine. "What do you mean?" I ask.

"I mean the mine seems closed. Probably forever. How are we supposed to live?"

The very question infuriates me. While his query doesn't exactly draw cheers, many in the crowd nod. "Jerry, was it? Well, Jerry, I didn't come here to play nursemaid to an entire town. I was brought here to rescue the trapped miners. I risked my life more than once to bring them home. And you have the *cajones* to stand there and ask me about your future? Do you need Mommy to pack you a lunch?"

My ridicule hits its mark. Jerry blushes and sits down to the titters of his fellows in the crowd.

"Seriously, folks. I've experienced two different industries here that could be expanded. Your home-brewed beer is first rate. Also, the hand-painted china some of your womenfolk make would fetch a handsome price in Boston. If you insist on sticking to your trade, there are more mines, many of them more ethically run. But the choice is yours—the life is yours. I'm not your mother or your wife."

While I answer minor questions for the next hour, recounting my adventure underground, there isn't much else to say.

"Thank you all for coming. For those men and women I saved, you needn't thank me directly. Thank me by living a good and godly life. But for now, I'm just tired."

I stand up, and the applause and cheers start anew.

"No, you aren't going to carry her on your shoulders," Lucy barks as she tries to make a path through the exuberant crowd. "Now, get out of the way." I see my cousin kick one persistent well-wisher in the shin. "Mr. Twitcher, I asked nice. Now, move before I match that one with another or maybe go a little higher." The gentleman eases to the side, and at the same time unconsciously covers his crotch with his hand.

With Lucy in front and Adrianna fending off those behind, we make it outside, all to the continuing standing ovation. "Lucy, is there any way I could take a look at the remains of Jaspersons' house?" I ask.

"You are in no shape to walk. I could get a wagon or buckboard to take you out."

I get the feeling that because I saved her husband, my cousin would murder the pope if I asked her.

"Why?" Adrianna asks me.

"Call it morbid curiosity. They have been a thorn in my paw for some time."

"Let me get some of these brawny men to hitch something up," Lucy says.

"We'll do it," Adam says with his son at his shoulder. Lucy smiles at her husband and plants a kiss on him. She gives a little jump and a happy squeal as he squeezes her bottom.

"C'mon, Junior. Let's get a chariot for the lady of the hour," he says.

#

The whole trip turns into a parade. Eight buckboards, two wagons, a sled, and no fewer than a hundred people on foot head to the remnants of a once splendid home. Snow fell last night, coating everything with at least four inches of white powder.

Adam drives a wagon with the rest of the Riley clan in the back. Following closely behind are the Helmses. Somehow they've gotten a buggy so fancy it looks like it is rented out only for weddings and funerals. We all pull up to a crater in the top of the hill.

In the bottom of the hole, I can see what might have at one time been a roof. If so, it has been crushed beyond its normal lines, with roof shakes splintered around huge, gaping rents.

"Has anyone searched for the Jaspersons?" I ask.

"We found the arm of one sticking out of a clay slide," Adam says. "It didn't have a pulse. We found Darrin's shoes on two feet almost underneath a rock slide. Also, no pulse. The structure isn't stable, so we left them where they lay." He gives a stifled cough to end his explanation. So he isn't fully well yet.

I climb down off the wagon.

"Stella!" Lucy and Adrianna both bark almost simultaneously.

"I'm not an invalid," I say, knowing that I really still am.

"Adam, go with her!" Luciana urges as I climb down into the hole. Her husband coughs three or four times. "Someone go with her!"

I may be rash, but I'm not an idiot. I test each step before I put my weight on it. I make my way to a point where it looks as if mud has poured through a horse-sized tear in the layered wood and then solidified. I trust the earth much more than the shredded wood. I find the scarecrow-skinny Henry Helms beside me.

"Stella," he says in greeting.

"Henry. Nice of you to come out here." I don't tell him whether I mean Centralia or down into the hole.

"My pleasure, m'lady. Before we go down in, might I ask if I can call on you tomorrow?"

"Henry, you are calling on me now."

"Well, I want you to have at least one more good night's rest, and it isn't a discussion one should have out among strangers."

Oh my god! He's found out about my affair with Adrianna. I can't duck it. I'll just have to convince him that it is over and can never go anywhere. If he is going to go all formal on me, I can return the favor. "I would always receive you, Lord Helms."

"Would there be a time better than any other?"

"I'll place myself at your disposal all day."

"Mrs. Ochoa, may I bring my wife with me?"

"Of course, the viscountess is always welcome with you." I try to stress the last two words.

"Many thanks, madam."

I've been living in the now so much that future issues seem insignificant. I put that trouble out of my mind.

I reach down and put my finger against the earthen surface. I can feel that the slope of the ground will likely cause me to slide, especially on the clay. It is easy enough to form crude steps going down. Henry follows, but my attention is elsewhere.

Even I don't know what I'm doing. I trust that they are dead. I trust that I didn't have anything to do with it. But it's still something I have to confirm.

I walk down and find the first body. The pale fingers have no more warmth than the ground around them. I speak with the earth, which no longer fights me in any way, and part the ground atop the corpse. The body has taken significant damage. Bruce Jasperson's head has been severed cleanly from the torso. Grondr's handiwork—as if the sinkhole and mud flows didn't already telegraph it.

"Henry, will you call some others down to remove his body? He deserves a Christian burial."

I don't wait for an answer. I keep moving around before I find Darrin under a pile of pea gravel. With one hand I wave a mountain of it to roll to one side. It uncovers the badly mutilated carcass that was once Darrin Jasperson. His body looks like it has been hit repeatedly with a hundred-pound anvil—Grondr's fists.

"There's another one in here," I call out to Henry.

I turn to leave, not looking back. It's over, finally over. There is nothing more here for anyone except maybe historians.

12—Friday, November 30, 1888

The Helmses show up so promptly after breakfast in the Riley home that I fear there is a spy in my midst. Not only that, but after Adam lets the viscount and viscountess in, the whole family has mysterious errands to run in a town effectively destroyed.

I don't think I've ever seen Henry or Adrianna so well dressed. The wool suit he wears has all the hallmarks of a court tailor. Henry also wears the orange sash with the rampant eagle of his house. Adrianna wears a deep-gray dress that matches the color of her husband's suit. She has a gaudy brooch bearing her husband's heraldry. On anyone else, I'd assume it was costume jewelry. Knowing this pair, it probably costs more than my entire house.

I stand up and curtsy. I wear the second dress the Helmses have given me, a silver gown that would belong at any high-society party. With as many petticoats as it requires, it took forty-five minutes to get ready this morning.

"Welcome, Viscount and Viscountess Helms," I say.

"Thank you for seeing us, Mrs. Ochoa. We have a matter of some delicacy to discuss with you," Henry says.

Adrianna stands uncharacteristically demure and subservient beside her husband.

"Would you please sit down?" I offer.

"Yes, thank you," Henry says. "We would have awaited your return to Boston to talk to you, but we had no idea when you would return. We chose to take the dirigible here to expedite matters."

"Then it must be urgent," I say. "By all means, what is it?"

Adrianna looks as if she is about to throw up. Henry's Adam's apple bobs as he swallows hard before he goes to one knee.

"Stella Ochoa, will you marry me?"

I'm not a swooner or a fainter. But I come as close to it as I ever have in my life. My vision goes gray, and you could knock me over with a feather, literally.

"W- W- I don't understand."

Henry holds out to me a box with an engagement ring. The ring has two diamonds straddling a yellow opal, each of them the size of a steel rivet.

"Henry? I don't understand."

"What's to understand? I would be honored if you would be my wife."

"But you are married!" I insist, pointing at Adrianna, the love of my life. Tears are welling up in my eyes. This has to be the most horrific practical joke ever.

"True, but even your Father Juan has admitted that the Church accepts, if not encourages, plural marriage. Father Church says there are too many examples in both the Old and New Testaments to reject it."

"Father Juan?"

"Yes, in fact, I have a letter here from him confirming what I've told you." Henry hands me a letter sealed with my name across the flap. I tear it open.

Daughter,

I'm writing this to let you know that should you accept his suit for your hand, I will endorse your marriage to Viscount Henry Helms with all my heart and all the blessings of Mother Church.

Should you go through with this, I know that I have no right to give you away. That privilege belongs to your mother. But I ask the boon of at least presiding at your wedding.

Come talk to me when you return to town.

With all the love I can give,

Father Juan Dubois y Cantonio

The letter is as alien as is everything running through my brain. "But is it legal?"

"The king's laws state that any marriage accepted by the Church is a legal one," Henry states categorically.

Maybe this is real! I don't know what to do or say. "Do you want this?" I ask of Adrianna.

Speaking for the first time this morning, she manages to choke out, "With all my heart."

Someone puts one of those newfangled mechanical mixers into my brain and connects it to a locomotive engine. Everything in my heart screams to not look a gift horse in the mouth. My conscience won't let me run heedlessly down a path that might put my emotional health or my soul in danger.

"Adrianna, will you allow me to talk to Henry alone?"

The viscountess looks at her husband. They share an unspoken communication.

"As you will," she says. "Shall I go into the other room?"

"Could you at least step outside? Maybe you could wait where you are staying? I have some serious questions for Henry that I'd like to be private."

Adrianna nods and walks to the door. She turns and locks her eyes on mine, pleading, but I have to be alone with Henry to get the truthful answers I need. Instead of inviting her back as she hopes, I say, "Thank you, Lady Helms. I will not keep your husband long."

After the door closes, I wait ten chimpanzees. I know my lady love, and she can be sneaky.

"Why?" I ask Henry bluntly.

"Why what?"

"Why ask me to marry you?"

"Because you are a goodly woman, and I feel warmly toward you."

"So you've just described your sister, not someone you want to take as wife," I retort. "What's the real reason?"

"Do you mean do I know you and my wife are lovers?"

I should be shocked and fearful that Henry knows, but I'm not. He is far from a stupid man. "Were lovers," I say, correcting his tense.

"Pardon me. Yes, I knew my wife and you were enjoying carnal relations and a bond beyond that. But before I go any further, I need to tell you a little more about my wife and me." I give him a curt nod. "Initially, ours was a marriage of convenience; however, over the years, we came to support one another. We backed one another. We became a team to face the world. Through it all, I came to care for her with an intensity that few husbands manage. The viscountess feels much the same way toward me. "

"I know that. I've seen it in action. At the wrong end, if you recall,"

I say, making him remember how I'd come calling with an introduction from his mistress.

"Very much so. Now, I know Adrianna doesn't appreciate the male form. I have never imposed my marital rights upon her, save the legally required consummation after our wedding. She is my life partner.

"With that in mind, I want her to be happy and healthy. This is why I have looked the other way when she entertains her female 'friends.' She does the same the few times I dally with—"

"Daring Karie."

"That's right. You are her friend. Did she tell you about me?"

"I should say no, but you know better," I admit.

"I do. Karie doesn't spread our liaisons to the *Boston Herald*. In fact, you are the only one I've known she has told, and I'm ever so glad she did.

"Getting back to answering your question. Over the last months of your being parted, my wife has been miserable. I find her crying over nothing. Adrianna has been neither happy nor healthy without you." Henry gives a wholehearted smile. "I've known about your relationship, and thus suspected the cause of her grief. But I couldn't break our unwritten agreement of not bringing up our carnal infidelities."

Tears now stream down my cheeks. I knew I hurt but hadn't realized just how bad it had been for her.

"Finally, she came to me and confessed everything. I listened and promised her that if anything could be done, we'd do it. I hired a defrocked priest to look into it for us. It took no time at all for him to suggest that I marry you."

"But making your wife happy is no reason to marry another woman."

"You haven't been listening, Stella. Remember how Adrianna and I started? We were thrown together for nothing more than money. Yet, we meshed. I already know that you mesh with me and my wife.

"You have spent more time over the last year protecting me, my wife, and my business than you have on your own troubles. I respect you as a friend and confidant. I admire your intelligence, your passion, and your goodness. On those alone, I'd be a happy man to have you as my wife. I certainly care for you more than I did my wife when we wed. If that wasn't enough, when it became clear that you could hurt me by intentionally or accidentally disclosing your affair with my wife, you instead chose to deny yourself the love of the person you desired.

Seriously, what more could a man want of a wife?"

I am trying to put everything he has said into perspective. Instead of becoming more ordered, my mind feels as if it is drawing a random card. "So about those marital rights you mentioned before. Where would those stand between us?"

"Other than the consummation required by law, that would be your choice, m'lady. If you want to move in with Adrianna and remain monogamous together, I am accepting of that. Most of my drives are toward my inventions and business.

"That being said, I find you attractive and would be more than happy to be your husband in more than name. But if not, the few needs I have can be satisfied in other ways, with discretion, as you well know."

I'm sobbing, but everything explodes in my head. "Go get Adrianna."

Less than five seconds later, the door opens and she comes in, her face anxious. I knew she was sneaky. She heard everything. "One last time, do you want this too?" I ask her. Adrianna is tearing up as much as I am. She nods emphatically.

"Should I get back down on my knee?" Henry asks.

I shake my head.

"Stella Ochoa, will you marry me?"

"Yes. Yes. YES!"

Author's Note

Welcome to more steampunk love with your favorite witch and mine, Stella Ochoa. When I finished *Courting Witchcraft*, I couldn't wait to write this one. As a professional author, I should be writing to close the gaps in my series—like the final book of the Toy World series. But the calling of Stella's stories is just too strong.

My feelings are just as strong about the next book in this series. I've left a proposal accepted but not consummated, either in the church or the bed. Not quite a cliffhanger, but to all of you who have fallen in love with Stella, I'm sure you HAVE to know. Mean of me, eh?

Now, if I followed only my heart, I'd immediately launch into Monarchy book four and the wedding of the century. But risking a mutiny from my other fans isn't anything to be sneezed at. Rest assured that despite how I left this, there will be more of Stella's tale.

Now onto the regular feature of my author's notes. Where did I get my idea?

This particular novel, I'm sure you will agree, is more than just "the next book." I got a review by a reader that called this "steamasy"—steampunk and fantasy. Not bad, but I wanted more punk. Thus, I needed a bit more STEAM in my steampunk. This is where the dirigible scenes came from.

Next is Grondr. I'd already set the scene that the earth can defend itself even as far back as *Of Demons and Coal*. I wanted to explore an extreme case of this, all the while wrapping up, with some finality (kinda—see the next book) the fate of Bruce Jasperson.

And finally, it just so happened that I've recently been involved in some projects that are much more relationship/love-oriented. It made me realize that the tension between Viscountess Adrianna Helms and Stella had to have a resolution one way or the other. It's moving that way. Maybe the next book we will have a wedding. Maybe. Yes, I am a tease.

I think this was about a four-hanky book. Yes, as an author, I cry when something intense happens to my characters. I even knew what was/is to happen (I outline rather than fly by the seat of my pants), and I still was sobbing at points.

But, I have fans who are waiting for the end of the Toy World series. I have other fans looking for more CorpGov Chronicles. I even have one very loyal fan who would like to see a sequel to Wayward School (although I have no plans in this area). Needless to say, more books are coming.

Thank you for supporting my efforts to bring you the twisted visions from my head.

Translations (and other odd terms)

<Alphabetically>

absolutamente – absolutely
aether – a parallel universe touching but not seen by our world; mythical and theoretical only
amante – lover
amiga – female friend; not girlfriend
amante – lover
amigos – friends
amor – love
ano – anus
arroz – rice
arroz a la marinera – seafood over rice
diablo – devil or demon
bebés – babies
bien – good
borracha (fem.) or borracho (masc.) – drunk or drunkard
bravo – well done, excellent
brujo – warlock
bruja maravilla – wonder witch
buenos – good
buenos dias – good morning or good day
buenos noches – good night or good evening
bufón – buffoon
buque naufragado – shipwreck
cabrón – stubborn goat
cabrones – fuckers
cacafuego – shit fire or also braggart
cajones – testicles, nuts, balls
campana – bell
capullo/capulla – like *gilipollas* but with a certain amount of evil

intentions, aka wanker

cariño – sweetheart

casa – house

cocina – kitchen

concha – literally shell, but sometimes used by high-society woman for vagina

chimpancés – chimpanzees

chocho/chocha – senile person, also cunt

cicatriz – scar

coqueto – flirtatious

cuidada – careful

culo – ass

de – of

de nada – you're welcome; literally 'of nothing'

descongelando el bistec – defrosting the beefsteak, a Spanish euphemism for a woman's menstrual cycle.

dias – days

dios – god

¡Dios mío! – Oh my god!

disculpe – excuse me

dos – two

dubloon – old Spanish currency that equals sixty-four reale, or approximately eight dollars

dulce – sweet

duro – a five-peseta coin where four pesetas equal one dollar

el – the male form of *the*

en sotto voce – in a soft voice meant to be overheard

enojado – angry

flan – a custard dessert, usually with a crust of caramel on the top

follar – to fuck

fopdoodle – dumbass

fuego – fire

furcia – floozy, slut

genial – brilliant

gilipollas – jerk, or stupid in their own right, often through social ineptitude

gracias – thank you

gracias a dios – Thank God

gracias por nada – thanks for nothing
hija – daughter
¡Hijo de la chingada! – son of a bitch
hinchado – inflated, puffery
hostia – literally wafer, specifically communion wafer; when used as an exclamation, "God damn"
idiota – idiot, fool, moron
infierno – hell, inferno, underworld, Hades
jefe – boss or chief
¡Joder! – to fuck, or colloquially just "Fuck!"
jodete – conjugated form of *joder* meaning to "go fuck yourself."
la – the feminine form of *the*
la perra – the bitch
lo siento – I'm sorry
lobos – wolf
loco en la cabeza – crazy in the head, mad, unhinged
madre – mother
Madre Dios / Madre de Dios – Mother of God
magnífico – magnificent, great, superb, beautiful
maldito – cursed, damned, fucking
marinera – sailor
me disculpe – I'm sorry, or I apologize
merienda – snack or afternoon tea
mi – my
mi amor – my love
mierda de toros – bullshit
modista – designer, couturier
mujer – woman
murió – died
muy – very
neófitas – neophytes
niñita – little girl
no les importará – they won't care
no es nada – it's nothing
noches – night
novia – sweetheart
Okeus – Powhatan American Indian god of war
pan – bread

pan dulce – similar to American doughnuts
papas – potatoes
peinetas – Spanish hair comb
pendejo – fool, idiot, asshole
perra – bitch
persona non grata – unwelcome or unacceptable person
peseta – Spanish coin equal to a quarter
pinche – fucking
piñata – hollow paper mâché statues filled with candy used in celebrations; usually hung up and hit at with a stick by someone blindfolded until it breaks
policía – police
por supesto – of course
porras – literally truncheons, but sweet pastries thicker and chewier than a churro
pretendientes – pretenders
professora – female professor
puta – whore
puta barata – cheap whore
¿Qué? – What?
qué demonios – What the heck
qué estafa – what a scam
querida – dearest or mistress
quejumbrosa – complaining
reale – old currency, in which eight reale equal one dollar
salchicha – sausage
scoth – excellent (Irish)
se folla un pez – literally fucks a fish; idiomatically, is screwed up.
secreto del la corona – secrets of the crown
semana – week
Señor – Mr.
Señora – Mrs. without the implication of marriage, a mature woman
Señorita – Miss
serpiente – serpent or snake or demon
sí – yes
sopa de picadillo – minced meat soup; despite the name, stew of mostly tomato puree and minced meat and vegetables
tardes – afternoon/evening

¡Tócate los cojones! – What a surprise!

tortilla – flatbread

trasera – ass, butt, bottom (feminine)

tu eres más feo que el culo de un mono – You are uglier than the butt of a monkey

turmae – troop

viuda – widow, widowed

veinte – twenty

vete a la mierda – literally "to go to shit"; translates as "Go fuck yourself"

xièxiè – thank you

y – and

zorra – literally "fox" but used as the curse words *bitch* or *whore*

zounderkite – idiot

The Alternative History of the Monarchy of America

Like all good alternative histories, there has to be some event or events that have drifted this world away from our own past. In the case of the Monarchy of America series, there are several. If you haven't picked it up from the writing itself, let me share.

Napoleon brings the battle of Waterloo to a draw but is severely wounded, becoming a broken man. France continues to be a thorn in the world's side. Still, without Bonaparte as a driving force, it no longer threatens world domination.

Germanic tribes wrest themselves free of the French grasp but never become a world power.

Spain, with the aid of the Catholic Pope, holds sway throughout a good deal of the world and never leaves her golden age. Charles II has several heirs who continue the line maintaining a strong and united Iberian peninsula. Charles III and IV never seek any world conquest ambitions but rather domination by exploration.

England, with her smaller, more widely diverse empire, is forced to play a much more aggressive and smarter worldview game rather than the massive hammer it was in our world. As a result, there are many clashes with the powerful Spanish. Most of these end with a bloody nose for the English. The Brits choose to bide their time.

In the mid seventeen hundreds, King George decides to honor the troubled American colony's desire for representation. He appoints his son, Fredrick, as hereditary Prince of America.

In 1843, Queen Victoria wants to replace Fredrick with her son Edward as Prince of America. Fredrick and the Americans take exception to this and declare America a Monarchy of its own.

Over the following forty-plus years, tensions between England and America are at the point of war. Spain has declared that it will side with this new country if England intervenes. The Pope himself presided over

Fredrick's coronation as the first King of America, which includes what we know of as Canada as well.

England bides its time but seethes at the humiliations it has had to endure. It continues to find ways to incite incidents with Spain, and America while looking for allies.

Because of the smoother overall political landscape, the industrial revolution kicks off earlier. There is no fight for states' rights (there are no states, only Duchies of similar shape and size), so no Civil War. In an ironic twist to previous policies, the King of America declares slavery to be an abomination, and all African-Americans are forcibly shipped to Cuba.

The "Louisiana Purchase" becomes the "Caledonia Purchase" from Spain. Later, after Lewis and Clarke's fateful trip, America and Spain enter into the "New Cadiz Purchase." It includes modern-day Oregon, Washington, Idaho, Montana, Wyoming, and parts of British Columbia, giving America her ports on the Pacific coast. By that time, the Bonapartes in France have grown powerful again and are threatening to take back the Germanic countries, which are Spanish protectorates. Spain does this transaction not only to be a good ally and to bolster America's ability to withstand the English aggression but also because the New Cadiz sale helps Spain with the finances it needs to blunt French hostility.

By fiat, America annexes Northern Canada and all of Modern Day Alaska.

Native Americans are not kicked off their lands or slaughtered but rather convinced to relocate into the Oklahoma territories. They are given this land "until the sun grows cold." For once, a deal with the natives is kept. Eventually, the Native Americans ask to become colonies of the Crown as the region Ysa, named after the Shoshone creation god.

Catholic Irish are persecuted by the Protestant English. They eventually plead to Spain and the Pope himself for aid. In 1877, the Spanish publicly condemn the English for their meddling in Irish affairs and order them to withdraw from Ireland entirely.

Queen Victoria has the Spanish ambassador beheaded, returning the head in a gilt box as a response.

Spain can ill afford a war on two fronts, so it beseeches King Fredrick II to send his army to Ireland. In America's first flex of her fledgling might, she lands thousands of troops, tons of supplies, weapons, and ammunition in Galway, Ireland, sparking off the War of

Irish Independence, on June 14, 1878. Many more soldiers would cross the Atlantic, and tens of thousands of Americans would be buried in Irish soil.

By November of 1884, the remains of the English army, outnumbered by the Irish Nationalists and their American allies, are forced out of Ireland. The native Irish rejoice for a few short months. But, before Ireland can even get organized as a country, the Potato Famine strikes (forty-one years later than in our world). Many flee to America as their ally in the war and others to Spain.

England eyes the weakened country a mere twelve miles away, but knows to pounce would likely cause a world war. Victoria bides her time and lies about for allies.

In 1888, the date of our first book, there is growing tension between England and America. Spain and France are on the verge of war.

As with most steampunk, petroleum products just never take off. From a scientific point of view, I've made the assumption that it has approximately a quarter of the chemical potential energy of what it has in our world.

Thus coal heated steam is the power of choice. It is relatively cheap and mobile with an existing infrastructure. But coal has a new rival. As the education of magicks has increased, a fusion between technology and magic has led to captive demons coming into their own as a power source. They are summoned to a fixed location where their inhuman bodies heat boilers providing the steam to run homes and industry. No one has been able to hold a demon on a mobile platform.